★ 2 BOOKS IN 1 ★

First Term
at L'Etoile

Second Term
at L'Etoile

School
for
Stars

2 BOOKS IN 1

First Term
at L'Etoile

Second Term
at L'Etoile

School
for
Stars

Holly & Kelly
Willoughby

Orion
Children's Books

This omnibus edition first published in Great Britain in 2014
by Orion Children's Books
Originally published as two separate volumes:
First Term at L'Etoile
First published in Great Britain in 2013
by Orion Children's Books
Second Term at L'Etoile
First published in Great Britain in 2013
by Orion Children's Books
a division of the Orion Publishing Group Ltd
Orion House
5 Upper St Martin's Lane
London WC2H 9EA
An Hachette UK Company

1 3 5 7 9 10 8 6 4 2

A catalogue record for this book is available from the British Library

ISBN 978 1 4440 1540 9

Printed in Great Britain by Clays Ltd, St Ives plc

www.orionbooks.co.uk

Contents

First Term at L'Etoile

School for Stars

Holly & Kelly Willoughby

Orion
Children's Books

For our parents, Lynn and Brian, who gave us the world; our husbands, Daniel and David, who mean the world; and our children, Harry, Belle and Lola, who complete our world.

Contents

Hello Story-seeker,

We are the Willoughby sisters and we have a story to share with you. It's a story about one of the most important things in the whole world – friendship.

Our story begins on the first day of term at L'Etoile, School for Stars, with two of our heroines, twins Molly and Maria Fitzfoster, arriving at their new school, L'Etoile. L'Etoile is an exclusive stage school, and takes girls from age ten through to sixteen. With only twenty pupils in each year group, it is considered the best school in the world for producing superstars and has educated some of the most famous names in the history of music and film. To make sure that every student who attends is determined to achieve their life's dream of becoming a star, the enrolment process is not for the faint-hearted.

So sit tight, get ready for laughter and tears, and enjoy this wonderful journey of friendship. We did!

Love from,
Holly and Kelly Willoughby x

1

New Beginnings

*M*olly and Maria Fitzfoster could barely breathe for nervous excitement as they clutched each other on the back seat of their dad's old Bentley. As the car bounced along the enormous, sweeping drive, they craned their necks out of the window trying to catch a glimpse of their new school. The September sun streaming through the rows of poplar trees completely blinded them.

'Oh, Eddie, are we nearly there yet?' a very exasperated Maria asked their dad's driver. 'We can't see a thing back here!'

'I know, Miss Maria,' Eddie responded. 'The sun is in the wrong spot and making driving a little bit tricky.

I don't think it can be too much further though.'

'Don't worry, Eddie – Maria just hates not being in control. It's not as if we're going to be late or anything. She factored in enough extra journey time to cater for *anything*,' Molly gently mocked her sister.

Maria checked her watch and threw her sister a sarcastic smile.

You see, Maria was extremely well organised. Molly on the other hand was totally the opposite, but more about the twins later . . .

After hitting a few potholes and dodging some wild rabbits, Eddie veered right as the driveway turned sharply, leaving the sun trailing behind and a crystal-clear view ahead. Molly thought to herself that if the sun had been a theatre spotlight, someone had just hollered 'Curtain up!' There stood the school, in all its splendour, nestled against the backdrop of a luscious hillside.

Both girls gasped. The chalk-white building rose majestically out of the green countryside. L'Etoile was everything they had dreamed of – or at least everything *Molly* had dreamed of. Maria, in all honesty, would have preferred to attend a more academic school, but she knew that she would flourish anywhere, and rather than be separated from Molly, with her dreams of stage and screen, she had gone along with her sister's choice.

After all, Story-seeker, you can make more of any situation, when you have a little bit of genius!

'Wow!' exclaimed Molly. 'Mum was right. Quick, Eddie – don't worry about parking, just drop us. We'll work the rest out for ourselves.'

'Now who's *Little Miss Impatient*?' retorted Maria, with a glint in her eye.

The ever-obliging Eddie, as the girls had heard their father call his faithful driver, did as he was instructed and pulled up alongside the grand double-fronted entrance. Fortunately for Eddie and the girls, they had arrived so early that there weren't too many other families around checking their girls in. Almost before the car had come to a stop, Molly and Maria had leapt out and were staring up at the towering black front door. They were transfixed by the enormous gold star door-knocker glistening in the sunlight. It had the words 'Reach for the Stars' inscribed round the edge.

Maria watched that dreamy look she had come to

know and love spread across Molly's face as she read the inscription.

The gold star knocker seemed to be throwing off its own beam of light, warming and mesmerising everything in its path – and the twins were no exception.

'L'E-twa-le . . .' came a frightfully posh and clipped voice through the dark entrance. 'L . . . apostrophe . . . E-T-O-I-L-E.'

As the voice spelled the name of the school, a tall, painfully thin but nonetheless striking figure emerged from the shadows. Suddenly the warmth from the gold star had been eclipsed by a lady with a face caked in make-up, and Molly didn't know whether to laugh or cry.

'Young ladies – or "L'Etoilettes" as you shall now be known. Welcome to L'Etoile, School for the Performing Arts, where only the most gifted of students are accepted. Which of you can tell me what "L'Etoile" means?'

Molly gulped and shot Maria a glance. It was the *as-the-oldest-sister-by-seven-minutes-and-forty-seven-seconds-you're-in-charge* look.

'"L'Etoile" quite simply means "the star" in French,' Maria said, without even the slightest hint of doubt in her voice.

A smile crossed the lady's face. 'Correct, L'Etoilette. And may I have the pleasure of learning your name so I know more about the little star in the making I am addressing?'

'My name is Maria Fitzfoster – and this is my sister, Molly. What's yours?' asked Maria, semi-innocently.

'But of course you are,' the lady replied knowingly, her smile turning into a sickly grin. 'The Fitzfoster Diamond Dynasty twins. How are your dear parents, Brian and Linda? It goes without saying that we know each other well – mixing in the same circles as we do.' She looked both girls up and down, with some approval, it appeared.

'Molly and Maria, I am your new headmistress, Madame Ruby, and you are to think of me as your queen, your mentor and most of all, your inspiration and aspiration. Everything you achieve here at the school, my L'Etoilettes, will set you on the path to superstardom. I, and only I, can make your dreams come true, so let this be the start of something fabulous for us all . . .'

And with that she swooshed round on her stiletto heels and disappeared into the shadows.

'Well!' exclaimed Molly.

'It's OK, Molly,' Maria said, sensing that her sister was still reeling from the make-up.

'My goodness, Maria – did you see her face? How much make-up can one face take?'

'I know – she's a walking blusher brush – but an important one!' said Maria and both girls exploded into a fit of giggles.

Thud . . . thud . . . crash . . . bang . . . wallop!

'What on earth . . .?'

The twins swung round to see the ever-obliging Eddie struggling to drag their matching, designer luggage from the car boot, and immediately ran over to give him a hand. By now more and more cars were beginning to pull up and the chatter and general noise of fearful children and clucking parents swirled about.

Staff members had started to emerge from the main house, equipped with clip-boards stuffed with lists; new student attendance lists; dormitory share lists; dietary requirement lists. In the thirty or so minutes since the Fitzfoster twins had arrived, chaos had engulfed L'Etoile.

Unsure of who they were supposed to register with, Molly decided she'd had enough of headmistresses for one afternoon and opted for the prettiest teacher on the drive – who happened to be the very lovely Miss Helen Hart.

Miss Hart had been teaching at L'Etoile for seven years. She and her family had always had very close links with the school and her father, a man with green fingers, managed its grounds and lovely gardens. Now in her mid-thirties, Helen Hart was a woman of amazing musical talent and had chosen to use her accomplishments to inspire the next generation of potential superstars. When Helen was younger, she'd narrowly missed out on her dream of becoming a world-famous singer/songwriter, having sacrificed her career to look after someone who was ill.

It is from that fact alone, Story-seeker, that you can tell the kind, selfless character of the lovely Miss Hart.

This was her first year as deputy headmistress at L'Etoile – a position she was determined would really make a difference to the students.

'Come on, Maria!' Molly grabbed her sister by the arm and, together, they hurtled towards Miss Hart who was trying to give dorm directions to three chattering girls, who were all asking questions at once.

'One at a time ladies, please . . .' she had a soft lyrical

voice. 'It's important that you take this in as there are two houses at L'Etoile and you need to follow instructions for where to go.'

'Autumn Costello – you are in Monroe House. Follow the yellow flags down past the lake to the West Wing and take this certificate confirming registration to your new housemistress, Mrs Sophie Bell. She'll take it from there.'

'Thank you, Miss Hart,' said Autumn, pretty much courtseying as she backed away towards her parents.

'Actually, Autumn . . .' Miss Hart called after her as she looked down her list. 'Would you mind taking Betsy Harris with you to Monroe – you'll be able to keep each other company. Betsy's majoring in piano too so you'll have plenty to talk about.'

'Absolutely,' said Autumn, trotting back to collect Betsy. 'Hello Betsy – soooo good to meet you. Let's get there early and see if we can share a room, shall we? Come on.' And off they skipped, following the yellow flag road to Monroe.

When Miss Hart had called Autumn back to meet her new companion, the twins had been struck by how young and petrified Betsy had looked. 'She must be quite some pianist!' whispered Maria to Molly, none too quietly. 'She looks about seven!'

'For goodness sake, Maria – when are you going to learn never to judge a book by its cover? Don't you remember that timid little nanny Daddy hired to look after us last summer? You said the same thing about her and look where that got us. She soon found her strength, didn't she?' Molly reminded her sister.

Maria rolled her eyes. Molly always looked for the best in everyone and everything. For twin sisters they really were like chalk and cheese. It's not that Maria was mean, she was just a bit more suspicious of everyone and everything. But that's exactly what balanced the two sisters. Molly's soft, faithful side tempered Maria's cynical outlook – and they loved each other dearly.

The twins hardly noticed the time whizzing by. All around them was a mass of teachers, girls and parents pointing in different directions and talking over each other, not to mention the piles of luggage strewn everywhere. If just one of those bags ended up where it was supposed to be by the end of the day it would be a miracle!

'Now, who's next? asked Miss Hart, looking at the twins.

'Maria and Molly Fitzfoster,' they answered in unison. 'I'm Molly,' said the blonde, 'and I'm Maria,' said the brunette.

Miss Hart stared in earnest at the two faces in front of her, assessing the differences. It was quite amazing. They had the same faces but with completely different colouring. Molly had blue eyes, long blonde wavy hair and an olive hue to her complexion, while Maria had green eyes, long dark wavy hair and a pale, china-doll complexion.

'My goodness, so alike, yet so very different. Would we class you as identical or non-identical twins?' she asked, intrigued.

'That's always been a bit of a conundrum.' Maria took the lead. 'Officially, we're identical twins, but physically now we don't look much alike.'

'Dad calls us Snow White and Rose Red because we remind him of that fairy tale,' Molly piped up. It was so typical of her to get all romantic at a time like this, thought Maria.

'Well, here at L'Etoile, you are all individuals,' continued Miss Hart. 'You've come to this school to be yourselves and find yourselves and you are both very welcome – as starlets in the making. Now let's see which houses you're in . . .' She flipped through the lists on her bulging clipboard.

The twins gulped and shot each other a look of panic. Houses . . . plural . . . not one house together?

Even with all this talk about individuality and finding themselves, neither was ready to be without the other just yet!

'Ah yes, here we are . . . Molly, you're in Garland House.' Molly's eyes started to prickle with tears. 'And Maria, let's see now . . . won't that be nice for you both – you're in Garland House too.'

The relief! Maria flung her arm around her sister's shoulder and grabbed the two registration certificates Miss Hart was holding out for them.

'Garland House is a separate building behind the main school towards the theatre. It's a grand white building with pillars at the entrance. Follow the blue flags along the path. Your new housemistress, Miss Mary Coates, will meet you in the entrance hall and show you to your room. Good luck, girls, and be sure to work hard.'

Molly and Maria nodded, again in unison, and bounded over to the ever-obliging Eddie, twittering about Garland House. 'Come on, Eddie! I'm desperate to see our new room and to meet the other girls!'

Eddie lolloped after them dragging two huge suitcases while the girls pranced in front trailing their coats, certificates and school bags.

'Watch out, Molly!' shrieked Maria, leaping on her

sister just in time, knocking them both backwards over a low hedge onto the lawn.

At that very moment, an enormous, sleek, black car came careering round the turning circle and screeched to a halt halfway across the lavender-lined footpath the twins had been walking along.

There was a stunned silence as everyone who was still on the gravel watched as the car doors were flung open and three rather hideous but extremely famous faces stepped out (and one rather pudgy face who no one recognised). Molly and Maria were still catching their breath and Eddie scrabbling for strewn clothing when they heard an American accent say, 'Oh for heaven's sake, Blue, darling, I told you not to drive yourself any more . . . that's why we have chauffeurs. You never were much good at knowing when to stop.' There was a muffled gasp as the very beautiful Mrs Serafina Marciano stood straightening her very expensive haute-couture suit.

'Lucinda honey, ignore your mommy,' a baritone American voice drawled back. 'Go find out where we need to drop your stuff so I can get outta here. I've got a meeting with Universal Pictures in London Town in an hour and I'm already running crazy late.'

'Pop, Mommy, I already know which house we're

in. Mommy requested Garland House when she spoke with Madame Ruby in the summer. It's where all the big stars graduate from.' Then Lucinda turned to her mother and said in the snobbiest tone she could muster, 'We should sooo have come in the private Garland entrance to avoid the *others*.'

'Darling, remember what I told you. It's all about making an entrance. What you do with that entrance is up to you.' And Mrs Marciano replaced her Hollywood-dark sunglasses back on the immaculately powdered bridge of her cosmetically altered little nose.

And there begins the nightmare, Story-seeker, with the arrival of Lucinda Marciano, daughter to Hollywood's very own royalty, Blue and Serafina Marciano.

Every single person recognised them from numerous Hollywood blockbuster movies and red-carpet events, which Blue directed and Serafina starred in. Most recently they'd filmed a documentary from their home in Los Angeles called *At Home With The Marcianos*, where the whole world had got to know the family – including the young Lucinda in all her horrendous glory.

Even the Fitzfosters had tuned in to watch it. Molly had been shocked to see how unhappy and obnoxious Lucinda Marciano had appeared on the show. It was evident that she had everything she could possibly wish for, just like the Fitzfosters, yet Molly and Maria weren't spoiled and mean like Lucinda. Their mum had explained that it was unfair to blame Lucinda. She said the fault lay with the lack of time and effort that the Marcianos invested in their daughter. She was an only child so had no brothers or sisters to turn to and her parents evidently had little or no time in their busy schedules to guide and discipline her. Mrs Fitzfoster went on to explain how Molly and Maria had always had each other to lean on and that she and their father made sure they knew the value of having everything and nothing in equal measure.

Maria, having dusted herself down, was fuming at the Marcianos' blatant disregard for the rest of the human race and was marching up to Lucinda, one arm gesticulating in anger as she got ready to tell her exactly what she thought about her *big entrance*. But before she had time to even open her mouth, Lucinda promptly threw her coat over Maria's outstretched arm.

'Oh thank goodness. There are staff!' Lucinda snapped. 'Take that to my room, will you?' And she turned her back on Maria, whose jaw had hit the floor in shock.

(And it is not very often that our Maria is speechless, Story-seeker.)

Maria silently counted to ten, threw the coat on the ground and strode back to Molly and Eddie, her eyes wide with fury as she plotted exactly what to do with her anger. She vowed to dedicate herself to upholding the student balance and to never let Lucinda – or Lucifette as she would now be known – tip the scales of the entire school in her favour. Maybe the way she behaved wasn't all her fault but, even so, Maria wasn't going to let her get away with that sort of performance.

'Who's in charge around here?' stormed Blue Marciano, glaring at every single member of staff in turn.

Helen Hart suddenly realised that in her new capacity as Deputy Head, she out-ranked everyone else on the gravel.

'Mr Marciano . . .' she ventured. 'Welcome to L'Etoile, School for . . .' but she was rudely interrupted.

'FOR STARS . . .' There it was again, the clipped voice from the shadows that had greeted the twins when they'd arrived.

'Dearest Mr Marciano, Mrs Marciano . . . I am Madame Ruby, Headmistress – we spoke on the phone in June.' She held out an immaculately manicured hand for Blue to shake (or kiss!). 'Please, do follow me. You are, of course, our most esteemed guests and I would like to escort you and your lovely daughter personally to Garland House. We have held our very best room for Lucinda and her L'Etoile companion.'

With that all eyes swivelled to the fourth person to emerge from the car – the one nobody had recognised. Madame Ruby beckoned to her, but could hardly hide her surprise as the slightly plump, awkward girl approached.

'And you are?' she enquired in an intimidating tone.

'S . . . S . . . S . . . Sally Sudbury, Madame,' the girl stammered.

'Sally Sidekick more like,' whispered Maria to Eddie and Molly, who grinned in agreement.

For the audience on the driveway, the whole scene

was as ridiculous as it was spectacular and heads bobbed from one direction of conversation to the other, as though they were watching a mixed doubles final at Wimbledon.

'Welcome, Miss Sudbury, to our school of excellence.'

Sally shrank at the mention of the word 'excellence'. She'd never been particularly excellent at anything. Sally was the daughter of Maggie Sudbury, the Marcianos' housekeeper. Maggie had come to work for the family as a struggling, single mother, with baby Sally, who the family were kind enough to accommodate as part of her domestic arrangement. As the years went by, Sally had become a sort of playmate for Lucinda. Now she was burdened with the role of 'companion' and had spent her entire life in Lucinda's shadow. Blinded by the privileged life that she thought Sally was experiencing alongside Lucinda, Maggie was unable to see the damage that this was doing.

'Erm, thank you, Madame . . .' she mumbled. But no sooner had she finished speaking than Lucinda yanked her by the arm.

'Move it, Sally – since when did this become about you? You've got my unpacking to do!'

And with that, the whole Marciano clan, plus

poor Sally, were marched off through the main L'Etoile entrance by Madame Ruby, brushing past the gold star knocker as they went, obviously getting a private tour before being shown to the 'best' Garland accommodation.

Only Maria, who had regained her calm, broke the stunned silence. 'Come on, Molly . . . let's check out our room – I'm sure it's just as fabulous. Who does that little Lucifette think she is? She'll keep – she'd best hope we don't run into each other too often!'

But you know, and I know, Story-seeker, that that would be just too easy!

2

And Then There Were Three

'I know we haven't seen Monroe House yet, but isn't Garland beautiful?' exclaimed Molly dreamily as she sat at her new dressing-table brushing her long, blonde hair.

The girls counted themselves very lucky so far. Their new housemistress, Miss Coates, had greeted them in the entrance hall and had been really sweet – a real 'mummy' type who Molly had instantly felt she could turn to if she was homesick – and who Maria knew she could run rings around! The only thing they hadn't foreseen was that there was a third bed in their room.

'Who do you think we'll get?' asked Molly thoughtfully.

'Whoever it is, she'll be hard pushed to beat Lucifette in the annoying stakes, so I'll take my chances. Anyway, you love a project, Moll – I'm sure you'll be able to dress her up and do her hair just how you'd love to still do mine!' Maria answered triumphantly from under the bed.

'Maria – what are you doing under there?' asked Molly, chuckling at how her sister still had the price tags stuck to the bottom of her shoes. Some people have no idea, she thought quietly to herself.

'Huh?' Maria wriggled out onto the bedroom floor, looking as if she'd been dragged through a hedge backwards. 'I wish I'd spotted how few plug sockets there were before Eddie left. How am I going to run a business from here? I'll have to email Dad and ask him to post me a multi-socket tonight.' She began picking balls of dust and who knows what else from her cardigan.

'You are funny, the way you talk. You're hardly running a business . . . it's more of a hobby,' Molly said, looking in disbelief at Maria's cardigan. How could she get so messy, so quickly?

'But,' said Maria, ignoring Molly's look, 'someone's got a responsibility to dig out the truth and keep the rest of the school informed, haven't they? I think that running an online blog here under the radar is a great idea – and as far as I'm concerned it *is* a business – everyone's business is my business – so, ha!' And they both laughed.

Maria's life-long dream was to become one of the world's hottest, finger-on-the-pulse journalists, and in her eyes she wasn't too young to start gaining some work experience. At the beginning of the summer holidays, she'd convinced her dad to set her up with a basic website that she could update by herself. She'd sold the idea to him as an *online community website* to keep their village up-to-date with what was going on.

Her dad – perhaps somewhat naïve about his daughter – had considered it a good way for her to learn about people in her community and keep them abreast of village events such as the Summer Fête, the St Mary's Charity Fun Run, and to help promote local businesses by raising awareness of their services. That summer Maria had made sure she accompanied her mum to various village meetings and experimented with her talents by interviewing community members, such as the farmer during lambing season, the butcher about his award-winning pear-and-pork sausages, the florist working on a local celebrity wedding, to name but a few. She wrote articles about her findings, with a little bit of community gossip thrown in for good measure, and by the time she left Little Hampton, she had managed to acquire quite a name for herself.

Her village website had been called *See it Like Maria*, but now that she no longer considered herself an amateur blogger, and was about to enter a new school community, she decided it would be much more fun to run an anonymous blog called 'Yours, L'Etoilette' – a report written by a mystery student, for the students. She'd have to spread the word about the site somehow – under the radar, of course, to avoid unwanted teacher attention – so that the girls would know where to go to get their fix of genuinely useful info about school events but (more importantly) a good bit of gossip as well. An additional feature she'd been toying with was to find a way for students to contact the mysterious 'Yours, L'Etoilette' with their comments or needs so the site could have an agony-aunt element to it, or an 'advertise for help' service. But she'd have the whole term to perfect that.

To put it bluntly, Story-seeker, Maria was more excited about this little project than any musical feats she might achieve at L'Etoile!

While Maria busied herself setting up her 'home office', Molly unpacked for both of them, filling every available drawer with clothes and toiletries and laying out their new school uniforms ready for the first day of term tomorrow.

'What do you think of these school skirts, Mimi?' she asked, using her favourite pet name for Maria.

'A skirt's a skirt, isn't it?' answered Maria, who was busy untangling about a thousand charger wires from Molly's hairdryer. She'd labelled them all clearly but couldn't account for Molly's erratic 'stuffing into a bag' method of packing.

'Are you kidding? Look how long these skirts are. Do you think we'll get away with rolling them up a bit? These are sooooo long and gross!' Molly said in despair, already dreaming up ten different ways she could make these blue and grey uniforms look cool. The girls had worn what they liked at their junior school, so this was a new experience for both of them. Molly was even more fashion-conscious than she was beauty-conscious – if that was possible – and it was fair to say that she had a natural flair for what was hot and what was definitely not!

'Oh well – at least I won't have to hold you up in the mornings now deciding what to wear,' said Molly, half-regretfully, as she stared down at the grey pleated skirt, grey tights, pale blue-and-white check shirt and navy blue V-neck jumper.

There was a knock on the bedroom door and Miss Coates appeared.

'Molly . . . Maria . . .' She looked from left to right, commanding the girls' attention. 'I'd like you to meet your new roommate for the year, Pippa Burrows.'

Pippa peered at them from behind Miss Coates and smiled shyly at the girls.

'Hi,' she whispered.

Molly jumped up from her suitcase which, despite her best efforts, still looked as if it had just thrown up on the floor by her bed. 'Hello Pippa. Really pleased to meet you. This is my sister Maria. We've been wondering who might be sharing with us. We're so happy it's you.'

Maria stifled the desire to roll her eyes at Molly's immediate tendency to *love* at first sight and managed a genuine smile of acceptance. Pointing over to the bed under the window she said, 'Molly and I left you the nicest bed as we already know each other, obviously, and don't mind being quite close together.'

It wasn't a huge bedroom so Miss Coates was

delighted to see that the twins had been generous and thoughtful to their new roommate.

'Thank you very much,' said Pippa and started dragging her beaten-up old suitcase over to her bed.

'We'll help you,' said Molly. 'Probably best if we put it straight on the bed. We've got ourselves in a bit of a mess already in here.'

'OK, girls. I'll leave you three to get to know each other. It's a picnic supper of jam sandwiches in your rooms tonight while you settle in.' And Miss Coates handed Molly a large paper bag filled with squidgy packages. 'Bedtime is at eight o'clock sharp. You'll all be exhausted after the excitement of this afternoon and ready for a good night's sleep. You'll hear the bell chime five minutes before lights out. I'm in the room at the end of the corridor if you need anything. My name is on the door.' And with that she left the girls alone, clicking the door shut behind her.

Molly, Maria and Pippa stood and looked at each other for a moment. They could hear other students in their rooms laughing and shouting at the top of their voices; things like, 'Has anyone got a spare toothbrush?' and 'Oh no, I've forgotten my school tights. Does anyone have a spare pair?'

Maria was the first to break the awkward silence.

'Molly, if you even think about rushing down the corridor with our toothbrushes so we have to use our fingers – or share poor Pippa's – I'll kill you!'

Without hesitation, Pippa shot Maria a look of understanding and dived on her suitcase as if to protect her toiletries and underwear with her life. After unpacking, all three girls joked and shared sandwiches until lights out.

So there you have it, Story-seeker. If only they knew on that first night that they would become the three corners of a triangle of friendship which would last for a lifetime.

Learning the Ropes

The school bell rang at the end of the first day at L'Etoile. And what a day it had been. All the first-years had been running around the school like headless chickens working out the quickest route to this class and that.

The twins had quickly realised that Lucinda had been right about one thing – there were loads of really talented people in Garland House. It was easy to tell one house student from another as the Monroe L'Etoilettes were in the exact same grey skirts and tights but wore yellow check shirts and V-neck jumpers. Molly, needless to say, was delighted when it dawned on her in assembly that morning how close her blonde locks had actually come to clashing with a luminous canary-coloured sweater.

Assembly had been held in the school theatre – aptly named the 'Kodak Hall' for obvious Oscar reasons. Indeed, the school had ridiculously over-inflated, celebrity-league names for most of its rooms. The music rooms were called the 'Royal Albert Rooms'; the sports hall was called the 'Athenae Olympic Quadrant'; the science and maths block, the 'Einstein Quarter'; the dance studio the 'Bolshoi Suite'; the English and foreign language rooms the 'Shakespeare and Latin Quarter' – the dining room was even called the 'Ivy Room', for goodness sake. Maria's eye-rolling was even beginning to get on her own nerves, but Molly and Pippa were in awe of everything – appreciating every not-so-subtle reference to the great and good. Maria took pleasure, though, in seeing her sister happy and, to be perfectly honest, their new-found friend Pippa as well. At least with her there, she didn't have to join in with Molly's every dreamy whim. Thank goodness for Pippa Burrows.

The whole school, approximately a hundred students at any one time, had all filed into the hall, split according to Garland and Monroe houses. Madame Ruby was joined on the stage by all the teachers. For Maria – who was desperately trying to remember every single face to write her first blog of the year – it was the perfect line-up to start off the proceedings.

Miss Hart sat to Madame Ruby's right – although set slightly back so as not to be seen to be 'on the same level' as Madame.

The girls' Garland housemistress, Miss Coates, and Mrs Bell, the housemistress for Monroe, sat to her left. The other teachers sat in rows behind. Beyond their striking appearance as a somewhat eccentric collection, they remained a bit of a mystery to the first-year students. Maria had made a mental note to start filtering through past years' student magazines to check what the teachers were really like.

'My L'Etoilettes,' Madame Ruby addressed her audience, 'On this, the first day of the new school year, there are those among you for whom this is the beginning of the rest of your star-seeking lives, and there are those who are already in that star-seeking process, but you have one crucial thing in common. You are in the world's very best establishment to mould your careers as superstars.' She drew a short breath.

'May I share with you a piece of advice passed on to me as a starlet by my great grandmother and founder of L'Etoile, the great Lola Rose D'Arcy . . . Be true to yourselves and your talent and in doing so you will achieve your potential. Reach for the stars, L'Etoilettes, reach for the stars!'

A round of applause erupted. Only Maria sat manically scribbling away on the notepad she'd smuggled in between the band of her rolled-up skirt and her hideous grey tights.

'From this moment on,' Madame Ruby continued, 'we, the loyal, talented teaching staff at L'Etoile, promise to guide and develop your individual artistic talents to their utmost potential. And in return we ask that you are receptive to every criticism and note. So go forth, L'Etoilettes, and become the stars your namesake school can be proud of for years to come.'

Another enraptured round of applause followed. For all the dodgy make-up, even Maria couldn't deny the excitement and zeal Madame Ruby made her pupils feel.

After assembly, the girls made their way to the classroom numbers they had been given that morning by their housemistresses.

Thankfully, Molly, Maria and Pippa had once again been banded together in Form 1 Alpha under the tutelage of the slightly alarmingly named Mrs Rene Spittleforth.

Mrs Spittleforth had horn-rimmed spectacles and

was wearing what could only be described as a violet and daffodil print tabard! She was, to all intents and purposes, a very nice lady – the girls thought she was about forty years old – but then, to them, anyone over twenty-one seemed about forty years old.

Their first hour in the classroom began with Miss Spittleforth standing in front of a large whiteboard, explaining their timetable.

A school day at L'Etoile was divided into two sections. Morning classes were sciences, languages, history and geography. Then each afternoon would focus on the special L'Etoile arts of music, dance and drama. During the enrolment process, every student had had to demonstrate a particular skill to an exceedingly high level before they could be awarded one of the 'gold-dust' places at the school. These skills could take the form of being a budding concert musician, an exquisite classical or modern dancer, a talented actress of stage and screen or an incredible vocalist. Or, like Lucinda, you had to have a face that fitted and parents with bulging bank accounts and friends in high places who could benefit the school's standing.

Next there was class registration – students had to report to their assigned class tutors at nine o'clock every morning. Each member of the class was given a number between one and ten, according to where their names fell alphabetically, to call out as proof that they were in the room. Maria had thought how easy it would be for Molly to answer twice while she was up to mischief elsewhere.

Molly and Maria were numbers four and five. Just for that morning's registration, every girl was asked to stand up when they called their number, and give their name and their artistic talent by way of an introduction to their fellow pupils.

Form 1 Alpha was a mixture of Garland and Monroe students:

♪ Form 1 Alpha ♪

Lydia Ambrose	Monroe Cellist & Double Bassist
Belle Brown	Garland Classical Ballet Dancer
Pippa Burrows	Garland Singer/Songwriter
Maria Fitzfoster	Garland Pianist
Molly Fitzfoster	Garland Singer & Actress
Amanda Lloyd	Garland Dancer
Daisy Mansfield	Monroe Bassoonist
Alice Parry	Garland Singer & Actress
Sofia Vincenzi	Monroe Singer & Actress
Lara Walters	Monroe Drummer & Percussionist

Believe us when we tell you, Story-seeker,
that you should make a note of these names –
for most, if not all of them, will walk the halls
of fame for generations to come.

It is true to say that Molly had the voice of an angel and a delicate subtlety as an actress, which one is born with rather than taught. Maria, in her expert knowledge of, well everything, recognised and appreciated that L'Etoile was the only place in the world that could harness and nurture her sister's natural ability, which is why she hadn't put up much of a fight when it was decided the girls would both apply to be L'Etoilettes. Maria's musical speciality was playing the piano. She was, of course, as much of a genius at that as at everything else she did. No one could argue that she had been given a place because of the social standing of her family. She really was a very clever girl.

As luck would have it for the whole of 1 Alpha, Lucinda and Sally Sudbury were in the other class, 1 Beta, with eight other girls who would no doubt be endlessly tormented by Lucinda's taunts and boring chatter. Their class registration session ran as follows:

♪ *Form 1 Beta* ♪

Nancy Althorpe	Monroe Actress
Autumn Costello	Monroe Pianist
Betsy Harris	Monroe Pianist
Elizabeth Jinks	Monroe Dancer
Charlotte Kissimee	Monroe Singer
Lucinda Marciano	Garland Singer & Actress
Corine Sequoia	Garland Singer & Actress
Heavenly Smith	Garland Dancer
Sally Sudbury	Garland Actress
Faye Summers	Garland Fashion Student

And so it was that our three heroines had so far that day magnificently managed to avoid any direct contact with the undesirable Lucinda Marciano. Pippa had narrowly avoided a situation earlier that evening when she had nearly bumped trays with Lucinda in the Ivy Room during the mad scramble for dinner. Luckily for her on this occasion, the rotund, red-faced, head dinner lady, Mrs Mackle, chose that exact moment to haul a mortified Sally Sudbury out of the dinner queue directly in front of their collision after observing her queuing up for seconds. This distraction gave Pippa just enough time to bomb over to the opposite side of the dining room to the safety of the Fitzfoster twins before Lucinda noticed. Thank goodness for small mercies and busybody cooks!

4

Midnight Feasts and Girly Chats

That night after lights out, Molly, Maria and Pippa had decided on a torchlight *not-so-midnight-more-like-nine-o'clock-but-who-cares* feast to mull over the day's events.

'So, Pippa . . .' Molly said, as the three girls lay snuggled up in their beds munching on fondant fancies.

'Hold on . . .' Maria interrupted. 'I can't see a bloomin' thing in this tuck box Mum packed, and my torch doesn't seem to want to work with or without batteries!'

Pippa reached an arm from the warmth of her duvet, leaned over to the window and yanked the curtain back to allow a little moonlight into the room.

Maria looked up, impressed at Pippa's solution, and Molly continued, delighted not to have been delayed for another ten minutes, while her ever-efficient sister worked her way through an entire battery pack.

'Tell us about you, Pippa. It suddenly dawned on me while I was brushing my teeth tonight that I don't know anything about you really – other than you're pretty cool!'

'What do you want to know?' Pippa asked through a mouthful of pink sponge cake.

'You know – where you grew up, what your mum and dad are like, whether you have any brothers or sisters, where you went to school – that kind of thing,' said Molly.

Pippa took a deep breath. This had been her biggest fear before coming to L'Etoile. She was confident enough in her talents as a singer/songwriter, but she thought her rather impoverished family roots might prevent her from fitting in with the more privileged girls. And here she was, having a mid-evening feast with two of the most glamorous students in her year, and being asked to talk about herself.

'I'm on a scholarship,' she blurted out. Molly looked blankly at Maria, who was nodding warmly in Pippa's direction, willing her to go on.

'A scholarship, Molly,' Pippa continued, 'is for students whose families can't necessarily afford to send them to an incredible school like this because it costs too much money. But rather than both the school and the student missing out on each other – for, as we all know, both benefit from talent – the school sometimes offers one or two places a year free of charge to someone who deserves a chance. That's what happened to me and my family – or I should say to me and Mum – there's just the two of us at home.'

'Where's home?' asked Molly, absent-mindedly, as she struggled to extract a boiled sweet which had stuck to its own wrapper.

'Oh, do put a sweet in it, Moll,' shushed Maria. 'Let the girl speak, for heaven's sake. You've already asked enough questions!'

Molly, realising her insensitivity, sat back and put both the sweet and the wrapper into her mouth.

'Home,' continued Pippa, 'is near Clapham Junction in London. Mum's a special needs teacher by day in a local school, and a legal secretary by night. She's always worked long hours to try and bring in as much money as she can for us without losing out on doing what she really loves, which is working with the children who need her most.'

Molly could feel tears in her eyes – thank goodness it was dark.

At that point, Maria jumped in. 'Well, to be honest, Pips – that's not entirely unlike us. We just had a few more people around. Dad runs the family diamond business and works all the hours under the sun – in fact we only really see him on holiday, and Mum, although she's around all the time, spends hours on local charity and council work. Sounds like we all come from really kind families though, which is why we probably get on like we do.'

Bless her, thought Pippa, bemused but touched. You couldn't get two more different families; but she loved Maria for trying to put her at ease.

'When you put it like that, I suppose you're right. I hadn't thought of it that way,' she said.

Maria was on a roll. 'Look at it another way, there's a glaringly obvious case of it's not WHAT you have that makes you a good person, it's WHO you have around you in life. That awful Lucifette comes from money like Molly and me but the difference is that no one around her cares about anything other than money and fame. That's what makes her such an insensitive, self-absorbed little witch.'

'All right, Maria, we get your point,' Molly said.

'Carry on, Pippa. How did you come to apply for L'Etoile then? Have you always wanted to be a singer? Can't wait to hear you sing, PS!'

Pippa laughed. Molly's little Mollyisms were so adorable. She abbreviated everything where she could get away with it: BTW – by the way . . . FYI – for your information . . . FGS – for goodness sake . . . and they were just the few she'd used today.

'Well . . .' continued Pippa, 'or should I say FYI, Miss Molly? L'Etoile actually approached me!'

'What?' The twins sat bolt upright in tandem, Maria knocking a bag of cola bottles all over the floor as she did so.

'I know!' exclaimed Pippa. 'It was completely crazy. I'd just got in from school on the day we broke up for the summer and the phone was ringing. Mum was still at work so I answered it and you'll never guess who was phoning.'

'Not the Grand Madame herself?' Molly gasped, wide-eyed and incredulous.

'Not quite,' answered Pippa. 'But second best. It was Miss Hart, the deputy head. She's really nice, by the way.'

'I know, BTW,' said Molly who had now hopped onto the end of Pippa's bed and helped herself to some duvet. 'She's the one who first checked us in on the drive yesterday. I picked her as she looked the nicest teacher. So then what happened?'

'Well,' said Pippa, happy to be sharing her story at last, 'Not sure if I told you or not, but I write songs as well as sing. My Uncle Harry has a little studio at the bottom of the garden so I used to spend the weeknights while Mum was at work, writing lyrics and singing into the voice recorder on Mum's computer. Then on a Sunday afternoon, I'd go over to Uncle Harry's and we'd try and lay down onto track what I'd been working on. He always seemed quite excited by what I'd done. I had no real idea – you can't really gauge how good you are yourself, can you?'

'Oh, I don't know,' Maria joked. 'Moll never seems to struggle with that kind of humility!' Molly swiped at Maria's duvet and another bag of sweets emptied itself all over the bedroom floor. 'Ooops,' she said and turned back to Pippa. 'Go on, go on.'

Pippa giggled at them. 'Sorry, where was I?'

'Uncle Harry's shed,' said Maria.

'Yes, Uncle Harry's *studio*,' she said. 'So anyway, after a few months, my Uncle Harry said that there was a website where you could create your own page and upload songs and performances for people to rate, so I did, and next thing I know Miss Hart is on the phone saying that she's heard me singing online, asking me if I really wrote the songs myself and could she make an appointment to come over to meet me and my mum!'

'What, just like that?' Maria asked.

'Just like that,' Pippa finished.

'Wowsers, it's so perfect and romantic. What a way to get discovered. To be recognised for your true talent and potential. It's just fabulous,' said Molly, scooping up a handful of dusty cola bottles from the floor.

'Wait until Lucifette hears your story. It will infuriate her into orbit,' chuckled Maria. At which point the very useless torch on her lap miraculously started throwing out enough light to illuminate a small stadium.

'Maria, turn it off, we'll get totally busted!' Molly scrambled back into her own bed in a panic.

A mixture of full tummies and tales of stardom had tipped the girls over the edge and within seconds of Maria switching off the super-torch, they were fast asleep, dreaming of over-achievement!

5

Mackle the Jackal

*A*fter an endlessly long week of boring mornings and fun afternoons spent doing what each girl loved to do best – perform – Forms 1 Alpha and 1 Beta learned that they were finally going to get together for the weekly Friday Afternoon Entertainment Session. This was an opportunity for each of the twenty students in the first year group to put on a display for her classmates of her favourite achievement of the week. The girls were told during classical ballet (on the first Thursday of term), which immediately sent them into a massive panic at the thought that they had less than twenty-four hours to prepare. Luckily though, the performance was to start the following

Friday so they had plenty of time to discuss and think about what they'd do.

'If I never see or hear that sickly sweet Seminova woman again, it'll be too soon,' Maria groaned, launching her ballet shoes into the bedroom so violently that they landed in a puddle in the sink.

Miss Natalia Seminova had spent most of her life training and performing for the world-famous Bolshoi Ballet in Moscow and most recently in New York. She had the most immaculate credentials of any ballet teacher, and the sweetest nature. She would put the girls through their paces every second Thursday; modern dance, hip-hop, tap and jazz. Miss Seminova had told them that L'Etoile's dance focus was mainly on ballet for discipline and posture. The more fun genres of dance could be added to a L'Etoilette's repetoire with ease at any time.

'Well, I think she's the perfect ballet mistress,' said Molly.

'Me too,' agreed Pippa. 'I've never done ballet before in my life and I was completely dreading it. I mean, be honest, girls – look at me – it's more suited to Maria, and that's saying something!' Maria grimaced. She was not, nor did she ever plan to be, a ballerina!

Pippa did kind of have a point though. She was taller than most of the other girls in her class, with a slender, willowy body, dark eyes framed by luscious black lashes, and long raven-coloured hair which tumbled wildly down her back. She was striking in a way that no amount of styling could create. Her wild-child appearance just needed taming slightly – or perhaps *refining* would be a better word, and then it'd be a case of 'watch out L'Etoilettes – here comes Pippa Burrows!'

Molly, had of course, been desperate to get the straighteners out and untangle those crazy locks. One good thing to come out of Pippa's arrival, though, was that Molly had officially become thankful for school uniforms, after seeing – and in fact successfully enduring, some of the outfits Pippa had in her wardrobe. It had taken some strength of character for Molly to hold back, but her sensitive side won the battle and she temporarily put her thoughts on ice. She needed to feel confident that their friendship was completely cemented before she would tactfully attempt to transform this little wild duckling into the swan she knew Pippa could be.

The happy trio changed out of their ballet things and, half-starving after two hours – or near enough –

of relentless pliés and pirouettes, flitted like gazelles to the Ivy Room for supper.

'Come on, let's eat. I'm sooooo hungry,' pleaded Molly. 'And let's use dinnertime to talk about what on earth we're going to perform at the group session next Friday. Eeeek!'

They were pretty late for dinner, which on the one hand meant no queue, but it also meant that most of the decent food had already been scoffed.

Molly, who was a fussy eater at the best of times, and certainly no fan of L'Etoile school dinners, had been mostly living on a diet of bread and cola bottles the whole week. Maria, on the contrary, was concerned that she was starting to put on a few pounds. Every mealtime she was trying to clear Molly's plate and her own to avoid the wrath of Mackle the Jackal, L'Etoile's infamous dinner lady!

It was poor Betsy Harris who had so brilliantly nicknamed Mackle, because of the way she scavenged through the leftovers, as a jackal would an old carcass. Like Molly, Betsy was also finding mealtimes hard to swallow, but she didn't have a Maria to protect her, and was always left sitting at the table by the exit doors, as an example to everyone, being made to stomach every last morsel. Mackle the Jackal would stand, with one fat elbow resting on the work surface, just at the point where the girls put their trays down on the runners to scrape off the leftovers. Her beady, shark-like eyes darted over every plate that passed under her nose, checking for anyone who'd left too much food.

The twins and Pippa entered the dining room just in time to see Mackle the Jackal's fat hand come down on Betsy's plate for the fourth dinnertime that week – or near enough eighth if you included lunchtimes as well!

'Betsy Harris!' Mackle spat, and as she did so a bit of semi-chewed food escaped from her mouth and sat on her top lip – moving up and down in a disgustingly hypnotising manner every time she spoke.

'Betsy Harris,' she repeated. 'How does it feel, Betsy, to be the most famous student in your year? Hit the giddy heights of fame a little sooner than expected, eh!?!' In her excitement, Mackle had produced a little too much saliva, which thankfully dislodged the piece of rogue food from her lip – but made her look like a drooling, rabid animal hovering over her kill.

'I . . . I . . . I beg your pardon, Mrs Mackle. Famous, you say?' said the terrified Betsy.

'Yesssssss, Harris!' Mackle hissed. 'Yours is the only name everyone hears day in, day out, in this dining room. When are you going to learn to eat up! Those sprouts will put hairs on your chest!'

The whole dining room winced in horror.

'What, and have a hairy chest – and top lip . . . and chin – like her!' Daisy Mansfield the bassoonist stage-whispered to the other Monroe girls behind her in the queue.

'Daiissseee – careful,' hissed Lydia Ambrose (cellist) who was a couple of places behind Daisy in the dinner queue. She'll hear you and then you'll be for it!'

'She won't hear me from all the way down there – she's probably eaten so much of the decent stuff and cooked up all the rubbish that's left for us, her body can't take any more. Did you see her spitting food as she spoke? It's coming out of her mouth, her nose, even her ears!' Daisy continued daringly – delighted to be getting some sniggers from her peers.

'Oh, so that's what they call cauliflower ears!' Maria said – with perfect comedy timing. At which point, the seven girls now left waiting to collect their meals dissolved into muffled, *you-know-you-shouldn't-be-laughing-but-you-just-can't-stop* hysterics.

Betsy's roomate, the pianist Autumn Costello, jumped up from the table where she was struggling to eat her own supper. 'Oh please stop, girls – poor Betsy will think you're laughing at her – or worse, Mackle will think she's the one being humorous and continue the torture. It truly is bullying of the most horrible kind.'

Pippa, who hadn't uttered a single word during the whole horror show, was deep in thought about how to beat the Jackal so that she'd never be able to bully anyone ever, ever again. She'd been subjected to bullying at her junior school and when she'd left those small-minded Jenson brothers behind, she had vowed that she'd never be a victim again and would always help others in need.

'Guys . . . guys . . .' She grabbed Maria and Molly. 'We've got to help her. Any minute now she's going to throw up – and then she'll probably be forced to eat that too!' Molly gagged at the thought.

'Welcome to my world,' said Maria sharply. 'Except I'm having to plough through two dinners every mealtime.'

'No way!' exclaimed Pippa. 'I'm surprised at you, Maria – had you pinned for a bright spark! Why are you putting yourself through that misery? It's not rocket science! See here.' She pulled a small freezer bag from her sleeve.

'You've gotta be kidding me,' whined Maria. 'Have

you been doing that all week? How have we not seen you?!'

'Cos I'm the Queen of Cool, dufus! And besides, sometimes you two are so caught up in your own twin world, you wouldn't notice if I sat here for an entire meal with my knickers on my head!'

'Now, you think of something to distract the Jackal and I'll fly by and clear Betsy's plate into the bag and then we're all out of here. I'd rather do cola bottles and cake again tonight anyway – there's nothing decent left.'

Pippa stuffed the plastic bag back up her sleeve and slinked down the dining room to position herself ready for the swoop.

Molly looked at Maria. 'What are you going to do?' she asked urgently. Maria thought for a second and then grinned. 'Do you remember that stunt we pulled last Christmas to get out of performing at yet another boring drinks and canapés party Mum and Dad had?'

Molly paused for a moment and then the realisation of what lay ahead dawned. 'Oh no, not again, really? That took all of my acting strength and I'm not quite sure I did it justice the first time round!'

'Come oooon, Molly!' ordered Maria and rushed

over to grab a huge ugly sprout from an unsuspecting Belle Brown's plate. 'Ready?' she asked.

'Ready,' answered Molly, and as she thrust the disgusting green vegetable into her mouth, Maria started flailing her arms and screaming.

'She's choking . . . quick, somebody help! She's choking!' Maria threw her arms around Molly's waist from behind and began squeezing her hard (something she had once seen in a film), heaving in and out as convincingly as she could without actually hurting her sister. Molly meanwhile was putting on a choking display worthy of an Oscar. Between them, they were making quite a scene.

Lucinda had been watching the plot unfold, and was wondering how she could best expose their little show and get them into the most trouble. But before she had time to interfere, Mackle the Jackal was on the move, up the centre of the Ivy Room, throwing students left and right, obliterating any chair or table in her path. Then Molly, mid-splutter, to her absolute horror, saw Lucinda run over to Sister Payne, who turned and made a beeline for them.

Well, with a name like that, Story-seeker, she could only have been the school nurse, couldn't she!

As soon as the Jackal's back was turned at the other end of the dining room, Pippa was on Betsy's plate faster than you could blink, shovelling her leftovers into the bag, then out through the exit like a rat up a drainpipe.

Betsy had absolutely no idea what had happened and just sat staring at her clean plate in grateful astonishment.

Maria, seeing that their mission had been accomplished, whispered in Molly's ear, 'NOW!' and with one last convulsion, Molly expelled the enormous, amazingly untouched sprout with such violence that it hit the dining-room window and rolled down the pane, leaving a slimy trail in its wake. The room erupted into whoops and applause from the girls. Molly, still in character, collapsed in a heap on the floor gasping for breath and tearfully uttering, 'You saved me . . . you saved me.' Sister Payne had arrived in time to see the sprout make its miraculous exit and was now on her hands and knees stroking Molly's hair.

'Well done, Maria. I must say, I couldn't have done better myself.' Then she turned to the rest of the students and scolded, 'This is why you should all make time to attend my first aid club on a Monday lunchtime. You never know when disaster may strike. Let this be a lesson to you all!' And on that note, she scooped Molly up, and marched her off to the sick bay.

'Come on everyone,' exclaimed Maria with glee, although full of sympathy for Molly. 'Let's get *sprout* of here.' And the girls once again collapsed into fits of giggles.

Pippa, Maria, Daisy, Lydia, Belle – and Betsy and Autumn, who had sneaked over from Monroe to thank everyone – waited anxiously in their bedroom at Garland for Molly to get back from the san.

'Pippa, that's so clever. I've just been rolling mine up in toilet paper and stuffing it down the back of the radiator,' exclaimed Lydia in awe.

'Well, that's just brilliant, Lyds – the whole place is going to be stinking to high heaven in a week with the heat those radiators are throwing out,' sniped Maria – worried about what Molly was going through and slightly put out that Pippa had usurped her 'genius' title.

'I don't even want to admit what I've been doing,' confessed Belle, the ballet dancer, going redder by the second. 'I was so desperate. I've been putting it in a napkin too and then tucking that hideous, soggy mess up my sleeve.'

'Gross!' giggled Pippa.

'That's not the half of it – you try flushing that lot down the toilet after every meal! It doesn't all usually ...well, you know, go down, without a bit of prodding!' Belle finished, mortified, and the girls exploded into laughter all over again.

'Yuk! You guys are totally disgusting!' A bedraggled Molly appeared at the doorway.

'Molly!' Maria cried out. 'Are you OK? You've been ages!'

'Well, I've been pushed and prodded in places I didn't even know existed, but I'm fine.' She shuddered and Maria squeezed her sister's shoulder in a reassuring *well done* kind of way. 'Anyway, never mind sick bay! Wasn't that totally brilliant? The best fun I've had in ages. I think I was particularly convincing that time, wasn't I?'

Maria began to roll her eyes and then checked herself. 'You were fabulous,' she said proudly.

'I don't know how to thank you all,' said Betsy, almost in tears.

'Well, it was Pippa's idea,' said Maria gallantly.

'Oh no – I just brought the bag along – you guys

did all the work with your dramatics. You might be a bit slow on the uptake about how to remedy a seemingly impossible situation, but boy do you know how to carry out a plan!' Pippa praised them.

'Well, thanks so much,' said Betsy again from the heart. 'We'd best be off before anyone discovers we're missing. First thing I'm going to do when I get back to Monroe is put in a massive order for freezer bags! See you in the morning, my friends.'

'Byeee,' the remaining group called as she and Autumn disappeared down the corridor, back to Monroe.

'We'd best get back to our rooms too,' said Belle. 'Thanks for a brilliant afternoon, girls. What will we think of next?' Lydia, Daisy and Belle hugged the Garland girls goodbye.

What next indeed, thought Maria to herself later that night when she was tucked up in bed with her laptop, writing her first blog of the term. This evening's dinner shenanigans had inspired her. *I know*, she thought to herself, a contented grin on her face. *I'll call it 'Better Sprout Than In!'* Brilliant!

There was one thing though which had stuck in her throat . . .

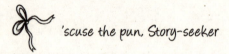

'scuse the pun, Story-seeker

. . . about the evening's events. It was Pippa's comment that she, Maria *the brains*, had been slow on the uptake about finding a solution to the nightmare that was Mackle the Jackal and her Ivy Room patrol. Pippa was right, she had been completely useless; she'd even been eating two meals at a time, for goodness sake. That's it. From now on she'd have to sharpen up and be prepared for a crisis.

6

An Important Announcement

Maria had sneaked out of Garland super-early the following morning to deliver printed slips of paper with the 'Yours, L'Etoilette' website address and a brief description into everyone's pigeonholes. By the time 1 Alpha had reached the second hour of their technology lesson, which was the practical half of the lesson, Maria was delighted to see at least half the class secretly logging on to her website and reading her account of the dining-room rescue episode. Several of them were giggling so much, they nearly got caught by Mr West who was pacing up and down the aisles, monitoring monitors! She thought she'd better log on herself so people could see her looking too. It wouldn't do to be exposed this early in the game! Maria smiled to herself. This made ballet so much easier to stomach.

Lunch that day was fairly uneventful, given that most of the girls had now cottoned on to the fail-safe way of disposing of their unwanted leftovers. Mackle the Jackal could barely hide her frustration as she eyed up clean plate after clean plate as each girl filed past her looking smug.

'Something's going on around here!' she drawled to one of her fellow jackals. 'And I'm going to find out what it is. Them girls think they've got the better of me, but no one beats the Mackle at her own game.' And for the first time in her cooking career at L'Etoile, she retired to her office kitchen before lunch was over.

'I don't know how long we've got before Mackle busts us!' Molly said as she held her nose and emptied her two freezer bags full of disgusting brown slop into the toilet. 'She knows something's up and it's killing her. I'd even go so far as to suggest she's lost weight!'

'Fat chance! Ha!' exploded Pippa, as she flushed the loo and followed Molly back to their bedroom.

Maria looked up from her laptop as the giggling girls entered.

'Moll, there's an email here from Albie. He reckons

he'll be able to get here for about half-past twelve on Friday – blimey, that's tomorrow – but you'll have to sneak out and meet him up the drive somewhere. If he gets caught bringing deliveries into the school, Ruby'll be sure to have something to say about it,' she warned.

'Who's Albie?' Pippa asked.

'Molly's lifeline to Vogue and cutting-edge fashion!' Maria replied.

'Well, you don't seem to mind so much when I'm kitting you out in the latest fashions. And anyway, Mummy's always giving him little extra things to bring down for us – including extension plugs for you!' Molly retorted in annoyance. 'Albie, Pippa, is my little delivery friend. I've been placing weekly orders on www.looklikeastar.com for the last six months or so and he's never missed a drop yet. Why don't you come with me tomorrow when I pop out to meet him?'

'Sure, why not?' Pippa agreed, up for a little excitement.

'Brill!' Molly exclaimed. 'And when we get back with all the new stuff I ordered, we can have our own little fashion show . . .' Pippa opened her mouth to protest but was suddenly interrupted by a voice on the school intercom:

DING DONG

Attention all First-Year Students.

This is Madame Ruby speaking. I have a very exciting announcement for you all, so please pay attention as it involves every single one of you. There is to be a Christmas gala on the evening of Friday 13th December in the Kodak Hall. Each of you will be required to perform in front of an audience made up of parents and talent scouts from across the globe. I cannot impress upon you enough how important a platform this is to get your talent noticed and ask that you sleep on it and come up with some ideas for tomorrow's Friday Entertainment Session which, incidentally, this week will be with me and Miss Hart.

Good Night, L'Etoilettes.

 # DING DONG

Molly's jaw almost hit the floor.

'Did you hear that, Mimi? Did you?' Molly screeched.

'Of course I bloomin' heard it,' Maria replied. 'We all did.'

'A Christmas gala! Oh how wonderful.' Molly was all of a daydream. 'I can't wait to invite Mum and Dad to L'Etoile.'

Maria looked over at Pippa, who appeared to be in a complete panic.

She tossed her laptop aside and sprang over to Pippa's bed. 'What's worrying you, Pips?' she enquired, concerned.

'Two things, really. I know for a fact my mum won't be able to make it, as the school where she teaches has its own Christmas production that day. They've been rehearsing for weeks. Plus, I've never really sung in front of anyone before. Not in person anyway. The internet's different – you can't see a thousand faces looking at you. What if they don't like my music, what if they don't like my voice, what if I totally clam up and no sound comes out?'

Molly, who had now come back down to earth, was at Pippa's other side, holding her hand. 'You'll be amazing, Pippa. You've got more natural talent in your little finger than the rest of us put together. And anyway, by the time I've finished your makeover, all your confidence issues will just melt away.'

'Makeover?' Pippa stammered, her big eyes searching Molly's.

Maria raised an eyebrow. 'Here we go again . . . can't believe it's taken you this long, Moll,' she said with a grin. 'All I can say is, brace yourself Miss Burrows, and get ready to be plucked and painted to within an inch of your life!'

'Oh, Mimi!'

'Only kidding, Moll! Pippa, my sister is nothing if not a beautificating genius. I suggest you sit back, relax and plug in to my iPod. This is going to take some time, but I guarantee you'll be totally made-up! Ha, made-up – get it? Ha!'

And with that, Molly had leapt out of bed and was busy untangling her hair straighteners. It was time to pull out all the stops and make this divine diva look like a star!

7

Beware the Wolf in Sheep's Clothing

*P*ippa, absolutely desperate for the loo – or, if the truth be known, to have another quick look at herself in the mirror since Molly's overnight transformation – had shot out of drama class as soon as the bell rang. Molly had somehow managed to tame her wild mane of black hair, leaving her looking more sleek and sophisticated than she could ever have imagined. She felt like a true superstar. In fact she was so caught up in her own thoughts that she hadn't noticed Lucinda steal away after her.

When she emerged from the cubicle, Lucinda, who was standing in front of the mirrors re-plaiting her hair, swirled round and made her jump.

♥ *63* ♥

'Oh!' Pippa gasped, shoving the little pink comb Molly had given her into her bag. 'You scared the life out of me. I didn't realise anyone else was in here.'

'Hello Pippa,' Lucinda began, her eyes transfixed by Pippa's. 'Actually I followed you in. I've got something for you that I didn't want the others to see.'

Pippa looked at her, at first alarmed, and then suspicious. 'For me?' she said, puzzled. 'What do you mean?'

Lucinda reached into her designer Prada bag and pulled out a white envelope with a yellow and blue logo in the corner.

UNIVERSAL MUSIC PUBLISHING

And in the centre of the envelope was written:

PIPPA BURROWS

L'ETOILE, SCHOOL FOR STARS

She thrust it in Pippa's direction. 'Daddy was given this to pass on to you.'

Pippa, totally bewildered, stared at the envelope in silence, all manner of things going through her head – mostly, *what is Lucifette playing at?*

'Aren't you going to open it then?' Lucinda said impatiently.

'Right . . . yeah . . . erm . . . what is it?' Pippa replied, gingerly turning the envelope over in her hands, as if it contained some kind of ticking bomb.

'Oh, just open it and find out,' snapped Lucinda, in total frustration.

Just then, Belle Brown and dancer Amanda Lloyd, both Garland girls, burst in, singing at the tops of their voices. They stopped dead at the unusual sight of Lucinda talking to Pippa.

Their entrance seemed to send Lucinda into a fluster. 'As I was saying, Pippa . . . if you could just, er . . . help me pitch my harmonies for Friday's Entertainment Session that would be great. I just can't seem to get them right. Have you got a sec to go to the Royal Albert rooms now?' she asked.

'Um . . . sure,' Pippa replied, still bewildered. Before she knew it, Lucinda had grabbed her by the arm and whisked her off down the corridor to one of the piano rooms, where Pippa tore open the envelope and read:

Dear Miss Burrows,

It has been brought to my attention via the Marciano family that you are a lady of some considerable vocal and songwriting talent.

I understand that as an attendee of L'Etoile, you have aspirations to become a singing sensation and having listened to some of your material through your web page, I, and my team here at Universal Music, feel that we could work together to develop your talent and potentially launch you onto the world's stage.

I would very much like you to come to my London Office at Universal Music Publishing for a meeting on Friday 13th December at 5 p.m. I will make all the necessary travel arrangements and send a driver to collect you from school in the morning and return you the same evening. All I ask is that you clear this with the relevant staff members and confirm your attendance with me via the Marciano family as I shall be working with Mr Marciano for the rest of the week finding artists to score for his next blockbuster.

Yours sincerely,

Emmett Fuller

President, Universal Music Publishing

Pippa looked up at Lucinda, aghast at what she had just read. 'W-what the . . .?' She just didn't understand.

'Oh, give it here.' Lucinda snatched the letter and scanned it. 'Wow!' she said, 'that's quite an invitation! Shame it clashes with the Christmas gala though.'

Pippa's face drained of colour. She'd never be allowed to get out of that one. Miss Hart would never agree to her absence, not with all that was at stake. What a decision – a real *crossroads moment*. Which route should she take? Should she put all her eggs in one basket and head up to Universal Music, or take her chances and perform to dozens of world-famous talent scouts in attendance at the gala – but risk being outshone by the nineteen other girls in her year who would also be performing as if their lives depended on it?

'I know what you're thinking,' snapped Lucinda again. 'But really, Pippa – it's a no-brainer. Opportunities like this don't come along every day – or perhaps they do for the great Pippa Burrows?'

'Oh no!' Pippa exclaimed. 'I truly am so, so grateful for this, Lucinda. Really I am. It's just . . .'

'Just what? Just that you'd prefer to sing in some little school concert for your family – or that you'd like to change your family's fortune forever by becoming a worldwide superstar? I know what I'd do if I was given such a golden opportunity. Do you think these kinds of offers grow on trees, Pippa?'

Pippa shrugged. 'How did they even find out about me in the first place?' she asked again. 'I just can't quite believe that they would be interested. They must see thousands of artists all the time. What makes me so special?'

'Because of me, stupid,' Lucinda spat, exasperated. 'As the letter says, Mr Fuller is working with Daddy to produce a soundtrack for his latest film. He's at the house all the time, and last weekend when I went home, the whole 'U' Music team was there. They asked me who was the most talented star in my year and I, of course, told them all about you, Pippa.'

'Oh, Lucinda – did you really?' Pippa said, not quite believing what she was hearing. 'I'm so sorry – I had you all wrong. Now I see that you have just been very misunderstood. Wait until I tell the others how wonderful you've been to me.'

Lucinda immediately turned serious. 'I wouldn't do that if I were you, Pippa,' she warned. 'Especially not the twins. You know how desperately Molly wants stardom for herself. One word from her to the great Mr Fitzfoster and he'll be straight on the phone to Emmett Fuller asking for the same audition. Do you really want to risk that?'

Pippa immediately felt upset. Molly wouldn't do that to her. Not her dear friend Molly. But it was too late. The doubt had already crept in.

'No, I s'pose not,' she responded.

'And anyway,' Lucinda continued, 'you've got me to talk things through with and rehearse with. I've seen a million of these sorts of auditions and can tell you exactly what to expect.'

Mentally, Pippa felt as if she'd gone ten rounds in a boxing ring. Even though she had in her hand a letter, displaying the facts in black and white, something didn't quite add up. Here was Lucinda, the enemy, standing before her, giving her the chance of a lifetime – and not only that, but offering her friendship, support and to coach her through it.

'Thank you,' she said meekly, beaten into submission by the one girl she had said she would never let get the better of her. She pushed the nagging feelings of suspicion to one side and decided to put her faith in Lucinda. What choice did she have?

'Oh, but what about Miss Hart? She'll never let me miss the Christmas gala.'

Lucinda paused. 'I wouldn't tell the teachers either.'

'What? I can't do that. I'll be expelled!' answered Pippa in a complete panic.

'There's more ways than being honest to get out of school,' Lucinda replied. 'And you said yourself, they'll never let you go willingly. How about this for an idea? What if Miss Hart receives a phone call from your mother the morning of the gala saying that your Uncle Harry has been taken ill and that she is sending a car to collect you immediately? What could she possibly say in answer to that? So long as the car turns up as promised, she'll have to let you go.'

Pippa's face fell. 'But my mother wouldn't lie for me – and neither would Uncle Harry,' she protested, feeling as though the whole plan was falling down around her ankles.

'Oh Pippa, Pippa,' Lucinda taunted. 'Where is your ingenuity? Where is your courage? Where is your brain? Do you think any of the great stars of stage and screen made it without a little bit of cunning along the way?'

Pippa felt completely out of her depth and, for a second, sorry for all the mean things she'd said about Sally Sudbury. That poor girl didn't have a hope of having a mind of her own with Lucinda around. She really was so persuasive.

'It won't really be your mum phoning – it'll be me on the other end of the phone – pretending to be your mum,' Lucinda said.

'But you don't even know what my mum sounds like,' stammered Pippa.

'And Miss Hart does? Oh please, Pippa – do you honestly think that Miss Hart is going to remember what your mother sounds like from the two-second conversation she had with her on the drive on the first day of term and a couple of chats on the phone? Of course she won't! If I put my mind to it, I can convince anyone of just about anything,' Lucinda finished ominously.

Pippa took the letter back from her and stared at it. The elation, confusion and now fear that she felt about what all this deception meant made her eyes prick with tears. She fought hard to hold them back, not wanting to appear weak in front of Lucinda. As she read the words over and over, they seemed to be swirling in front of her as if to create a big black hole in the centre of the page. Was this where she was heading if she followed Lucinda's advice? A big black hole of lies and deceit? Or would there be light at the end of the tunnel – a singing career for her and financial security for her family – no more night job for Mum – and a real music studio for Uncle Harry?

'Listen,' Lucinda broke into her thoughts. 'You have a think about it, but take my advice and tell no one! Meet me back here during study time tomorrow at four o'clock and let me know what you've decided. As I said, I'm more than happy to help you prepare. In fact, do you have a CD of your full vocal and backing tracks on you now that I can familiarise myself with tonight?'

'Sure,' said Pippa, quite overwhelmed by Lucinda's attention to detail and enthusiasm. And she scrabbled around in her rucksack. She handed over the two discs, which she'd been carrying around for any spare gala rehearsal time.

'Great, I'll have a listen to everything tonight and tomorrow we'll pick the best one for you to perform. I'll even learn it so that we can rehearse together tomorrow.' Lucinda turned on her heel and left the piano room.

'Oh my goodness, oh my goodness,' was all that was running through Pippa's mind as she ran off to the library to meet the girls for study. What had just happened? How could she keep this huge secret? All being well, she'd come back and surprise everyone with a signed record contract. And if the worst came to the worst, no one would ever know she'd failed. She needed to keep it simple in her mind, all the better for the truth to remain between her and one other – even if it was Lucinda. Too many cooks spoil the broth and all that.

8

Hook, Line and Sinker

When Pippa entered the library looking for the twins for study time, she didn't see Lucinda deep in whispered discussions with Sally in the fiction section.

'Hook, line and sinker!' Lucinda snorted to Sally, who was sneaking a brownie she'd pinched from yesterday's pudding selection. 'Wow, I'm good, brilliant even. She fell for every word. There's no way she won't turn up tomorrow ready to rehearse. I even got her to hand over all her tracks!' She flashed the silver CDs.

'She didn't, did she?' Sally frowned through a mouthful of chocolate sponge. 'Oh, Lucinda, I'm not sure. I've got a bad feeling about this. What if she tells someone?'

'Do shut up, Sal – she wouldn't dare now – not after the number I've done on her.' Lucinda hated it when Sally questioned her mastery. 'My idea of saying that a driver would be sent for her was the icing on the cake in terms of giving the whole plan authenticity. I'll just arrange that with Daddy's secretary and make out I need to be picked up and dropped back that night. She's too scared of me to ask any questions or run anything past Dad since she forgot my hair appointment. When Miss Hart sees a car arrive for Pipsy she won't even question that her family haven't really sent it to take her straight to the hospital. I am, officially, a genius!'

Sally, covered in crumbs, glanced up at her and agreed. Part of her wished she could be so clever and so without conscience.

But the truth was, Story-seeker, that Sally Sudbury, no matter how much she tried to bury it, had a good heart.

It wasn't her fault that she had been born into a life of subservience to the bullying Lucinda Marciano. She'd never known anything different and Sally had quickly learned that it was far better to be on Lucinda's side than not. There had been one time at their old school when Sally had, from nowhere, taken a shot at goal during a crucial netball match, something, which is nigh-on impossible for the Goal-Keeper to do, and it had flown through the net, like a knife through butter. It was just one of those moments in life where you see a target and go for it, just knowing that it's going to work and, boy, did Sally succeed. The whole team, and most of the spectators, came running on to the court to hug her, as the perfectly timed goal coincided with the final whistle. For those two or three minutes, Sally had finally felt what it was like to be popular, to be adored and to be praised for having talent.

As you can imagine, Lucinda, who was team captain and held the shooter position of Goal Attack, was incandescent by the time they got back to the bus. How dare Sally steal even a second of her limelight? Who did she think she was? Well, it would be the last time! And Lucinda had been the vilest of the vile to Sally for the rest of term.

'You're quiet tonight, Pips,' said Molly, doodling on her jotter.

'Huh?' Pippa looked up. 'Just tired, Moll.' She yawned. 'Drama really took it out of me today. I just don't get Shakespeare.'

'I did *Romeo and Juliet* last year and still have all my notes,' said Maria. 'So just shout if you need a hand.' Jokingly, she held out a hand to Pippa.

Pippa felt tearful again. She really did love the twins. They were always looking out for her. Molly had made her look like a princess and Maria treated her as an equal, which she knew wasn't a compliment Maria gave lightly.

As the supper bell went, Pippa thought she'd keep her news to herself overnight and then decide what to do in the morning. Who knew what might happen before her meeting with Lucinda? Maybe she'd get lucky and Maria and Molly would somehow guess why she was so quiet. Highly unlikely though, she realised, surprised by the disappointment she felt. She almost wanted to get caught – then there'd be no choice to make.

The weekly Friday Entertainment Session had now been allocated as rehearsal time for the first-year students to make sure they were as prepared as possible for their big moment on 13th December – or Doomsday as some had coined it when they'd worked out the day fell on a Friday. Parcels of pink knickers arrived in armfuls from superstitious parents, for their girls to ward off any Friday 13th bad luck.

The first-years were spread around the Kodak Hall with Madame Ruby at the helm spelling out what this golden opportunity meant for them all.

'A moment's hush now, L'Etoilettes. I need not impress on you how important your choice of performance is. Friday 13th is the day when talent scouts and critics flock to L'Etoile from all over the world to see you, the new crop of up-and-coming stars. You each have a very short time to shine and impress. They will be watching your every move. May I also take this opportunity to say that you need not only sound your best, but you must also look your best.'

As Lucinda shot Sally a scornful glance, Molly glowed with pride as she looked at Pippa who sat there, groomed to breathtaking perfection.

'I have made arrangements for the very best hair and make-up people – or the glamsquad as we refer to them in the industry – to be on standby that day. It will, however, be entirely up to you to make sure that you look fabulous.'

Betsy Harris winced and whispered to Autumn in a panic, 'What am I going to wear? I've already been through my whole wardrobe this morning and there's nothing in it which will even slightly pass for fabulous!'

'Don't worry, Betsy,' Molly whispered over her shoulder. 'Come over to Garland on Sunday afternoon and we'll find you something. Pips and I have just picked up a new order from Albie. There'll definitely be something for you there. And Faye Summers is a complete star with the sewing machine – she'll be able to take anything in or up for you. She's totally going to be the next Vivienne Westwood!'

Blonde-haired, blue-eyed Faye, who was sitting a few rows in front, too close to Lucinda for her liking, turned round and winked at Betsy.

Lucinda rolled her eyes and sneered. 'Yes, I'm sure she can do wonders with a pillowcase for you, Betsy – no one will ever know – NOT! Just make sure you send it to the laundry first, Faye . . . Betsy won't look great wearing an outfit with your dribble on it!'

Maria fizzed with anger. 'Put a sock in it, Marciano. And I suppose you'll be having something flown in from Milan.' Lucinda smirked at Maria and nodded in agreement.

'Oh, that's too bad. Mum says it's Paris or nothing this season,' Maria shot back.

Lucinda pouted in her direction then turned her back on her. She never seemed to answer Maria back. And quite rightly too – Maria's razor tongue was at its sharpest against her enemies.

'And so, my L'Etoilettes, I leave you now in the capable hands of my deputy, Miss Hart and her team,' Madame Ruby said.

She exited stage left and through the back entrance to the theatre.

'Off she goes . . .' giggled Molly, 'back into make-up for the forty-fourth time today.' Her classmates roared.

'Girls!' exclaimed Miss Hart. 'May we all share the joke?' She looked expectantly at Molly and her gaggle of friends. For once they were as quiet as mice.

'Right then,' she continued, uninterrupted. 'Time for you to split up into your performance categories. Instrumentals – you will be with our Musical Director, Mr Potts, to the right-hand side of the stage by the piano. Actresses, you will be with Miss Fleming at the back of the hall to my left.'

The girls started to grab their things and manoeuvre.

'Wait a second, ladies . . . please let me finish,' she scolded. 'Dancers, you will be under the excellent supervision of Miss Seminova at the other side of the hall to my right, and singers, you will be with me down here. Best of luck to you all.'

Twenty girls started scrambling in four different directions, desperate to get to their respective teacher first for advice. Or should that be nineteen girls, leaving one very confused Faye Summers still sitting in the middle of the theatre alone. She put her hand up. 'Miss, Miss,' she called out to Miss Hart, her voice rising anxiously.

'Oh Faye, I'm so sorry. I quite forgot. We would very much like you to style the whole event.' Fashion Faye's mouth dropped open in shock.

'As you know,' Miss Hart continued, the other girls now listening intently, 'L'Etoile usually only takes on performance students, but with your brilliant flair for textile design, Madame Ruby was only too happy to host one of the country's budding fashion designers.'

Faye beamed as there were a few whoops of congratulations from the Garland girls. Lucinda elbowed Sally spitefully as she started to clap, and waved her hand in the air for attention.

'Erm . . . Miss Hart, my mom is sending my stage costume over from Mil . . . er . . . Paris.' Maria noticed with glee how the very stupid Lucinda had taken note of her lies about Paris. 'Will I be subjected to one of Miss Summer's designs? I'm not sure Mom would be too pleased about that.'

Faye looked wounded but not surprised, while an irate Miss Hart tried to smother her frustration with the favoured celebrity student.

'That, Lucinda dear, is a question for Madame Ruby. I very much doubt that you will be eligible for any special treatment regarding costumes . . . but I will of course raise your query at the next staff meeting.'

Slightly unprofessionally, Miss Hart hoped that Faye would have the opportunity to dress Lucinda in any way she deemed fit, but somehow felt that Madame Ruby would sooner come to the gala without her lipstick than risk upsetting Mrs Marciano! Lucinda gave a triumphant, smug nod.

The vocalists, consisting of Pippa, Alice, Sofia, Corine, Lucinda and the divinely named Charlotte Kissimee, crowded around Miss Hart, who was handing out sheet music.

'What are you going to sing, Pippa?' asked Sofia Vincenzi.

Pippa shot Lucinda a guilty look and mumbled something about not having completely decided yet. Sofia Vincenzi was an opera student of Italian descent.

While it would take years for her voice to mature to a true operatic standard, she already possessed the most exquisite soprano range and was a definite contender among the singers. She had been born in Venice to a theatrical family, but had moved to England when her father, Antonio Russo, a world-famous Italian chef, had come over about ten years previously, to open some very exclusive Italian restaurants.

Sofia babbled on. 'Charlotte and I would LOVE to do "The Flower Duet" from the opera *Lakmé*. But I'm not sure if we'll be allowed to perform together.'

Charlotte Kissimee and Sofia were roommates at Monroe and had been inseparable since their arrival at L'Etoile. Their beautiful voices could be heard at all hours, floating around the school.

'That's a great idea!' said Pippa. 'I totally love that song – it's the one from the advert, isn't it?' she asked, desperate to keep the focus away from her.

'Si!' bubbled Sofia, brimming with excitement. 'Charlotte and I have already been practising it!'

'So we've all heard,' growled Lucinda, unimpressed.

Miss Hart, who had been sitting back, listening to the girls' ideas with interest, entered the conversation. 'I'll have to check with Madame Ruby, ladies, but I think that song would combine your voices beautifully and really show off your abilities. Why don't you put something together and we'll see what she says.'

Sofia and Charlotte hugged each other and ran off to a quiet corner to practice.

Alice Parry, who had been nearly as quiet as Pippa, suddenly jumped up. 'I've got it!' she declared, nearly knocking Corine off her chair. 'Ooops – sorry, Corine.'

'I'm gonna . . . going . . . to sing Wouldn't It Be Loverly from *My Fair Lady*. I was in that at my old school and it was such fun. I'll have to work on it, Miss – but I fink – I think – that I could do a really good cockney accent. What do you fink?'

Pippa had to muffle a giggle. Alice's family had come from humble beginnings in the East End of London, but thanks to their very canny investments, the Parrys now owned Parry Parks – which consisted of most of the car-park properties in central England. Alice's father, Big Al Parry, was determined that his daughter should not be held back by his lack of social know-how and had sent Alice to every finishing school and elocution specialist in the country in an attempt to disguise her cockney roots. The result of all this training was that unlike Pippa, who understood and accepted that no amount of success would make her sound like the Queen, Alice was convinced that years of elocution lessons had banished her cockney accent forever.

'Wonderful idea,' agreed Miss Hart. 'It's perfect for you, Alice – I know you'll do it complete justice.'

'All she wants is a room somewhere. . .' sang Lucinda maliciously. 'But who's she kidding? This is one flower girl who'll never pass for a lady!' She turned sniggering to the rest of the group. 'Who's she kidding?'

A mortified Alice scurried off with her laptop to download the lyrics.

Miss Hart turned her attention to cruel Lucinda, to put a stop to the taunting.

'And what, may I ask, have you come up with, Miss Marciano?' she said, coldly.

Lucinda was a little taken aback by Miss Hart's tone. How dare she talk to her like that in front of her classmates? But the truth was that Miss Hart had caught her unawares, as she hadn't planned far enough ahead to think of a response to this question. She planned to steal one of Pippa's songs, but she could hardly say that. Thinking on her feet, and not too successfully, she said that she was in the middle of writing something spectacular. 'You can't hurry perfection,' Lucinda drawled. 'I shall come and see you separately with my chosen piece, Miss Hart.'

Miss Hart eyeballed her and then nodded in annoyance. Looking around her group she summarised, 'Right then – so that's you, Lucinda, and Pippa who need to come back to me with a solid idea ASAP. As it is, you only have three weeks to rehearse, so time really is of the essence. I'm happy to make some suggestions if you are short of ideas, girls.' Pippa looked away in shame and Lucinda reddened at the insinuation that she had come unprepared.

'Anyone else – oh yes – Corine.' Miss Hart looked at her.

Corine didn't flinch. '"Memory", from the musical *Cats*,' she said. 'I've some terrific ideas for a catsuit which I'll speak to Faye about.'

'Oh pullllease . . .' groaned Lucinda again, incensed by the idea that Corine would look simply fabulous in a catsuit.

'OK, L'Etoilettes . . . that's enough for today. Pippa, Lucinda, I shall expect to hear from you imminently. As for the rest of you, well done, girls. I'm really very impressed with your efforts so far and look forward to hearing you all in rehearsal.'

As she disbanded her group of vocalists, Mr Potts, with one arm bent at the elbow, his hand resting on his waist, and the other hand flailing around – looking very much like a *teapott* – did the same with his musicians. The pianists, Maria, Autumn and Betsy, had all chosen classical pieces which would show off their command of the keys. Daisy had selected the famous bassoon solo from *Peter and the Wolf*, Lara had chosen a very noisy drum piece which was slightly too rocky for Mr Potts' old-fashioned taste but a superb example of rhythm, and Lydia was to send everyone to Dreamland with Johannes Brahms's masterpiece, Wiegenlied, known to everyone as Brahms's Lullaby.

The dancers, Belle, Heavenly, Amanda and Elizabeth had discussed the styles they would most like to perform under the guidance of Miss Seminova. It was slightly more difficult to discuss which pieces these would be, as each wanted to choreograph her own routine. These four girls had perhaps the most work to do in the coming weeks and had left the hall early for some time at the barre in the Bolshoi Suite.

Last, but by no means least, were the actresses – Molly, Nancy and Sally.

Sally had mentioned something about reciting

one of her own poems, which had raised an eyebrow or two among the girls, but Miss Fleming seemed delighted by her originality.

Nancy had chosen Shakespeare's monologue by Lady Macbeth after she's just helped her husband to murder the king. This had slightly annoyed Molly as she had been prepared to do Juliet's 'Wherefore art thou Romeo?' soliloquy from *Romeo and Juliet*, but when Nancy had got in there first with *Macbeth*, she quickly had to change tack.

'Oh no!' cried Maria later that night, as Molly recounted who was doing what among the drama group.

'I know, WATC eh?!' Molly exclaimed in a huff.

'WATC?' asked Maria, confused. Even she sometimes struggled to translate every Mollyism.

'What are the chances?' Molly cried, wondering why she couldn't work that out.

'So what are you going to do now, then?' Maria said.

'Well, I explained to Miss Fleming what had happened and that I need a bit of time to come up with something. I was thinking though about doing that split-personality monologue I did for my final exam.'

Maria exploded into laughter . . . remembering Molly on that huge stage all by herself, lit by a single spotlight, jumping up and down pretending to be five different personalities. She'd been so convincing that their mother had even taken her to the doctor the following week just to make sure that Molly didn't actually have a multiple personality disorder!

'Oh Molly – that would be superb and will blow everyone else out of the water. Shakespeare, Schmakespeare. Wait till they get a load of Molly the schoolgirl . . . and Marilyn, Queen of Hollywood, and Mary the Welsh shepherdess!' Tears of joy were rolling down Maria's face.

'Don't forget Marlene the school teacher and Mildred the murderer!' Both girls giggled as they reminisced and Molly acted out little snippets on her bed.

'Yo! What's so funny?' asked Pippa as she arrived back, collapsing onto her bed.

'Oh do it for her, Moll – pulllease!' pleaded Maria.

'Not now, I'm pooped and we haven't really got time before bed.'

'How'd you go, Pips?' asked Molly through a mouthful of toothpaste.

'Oh, you know . . . not bad,' Pippa said coyly.

'Not bad – what are you talking about?' Molly

asked in surprise. 'I would have thought you, out of everyone, would have had the easiest decision. You've written so many fab songs. Any one of them's a winner IMB.'

Pippa threw Maria a confused glance. 'In my book,' Maria translated.

'Ah, thanks, Moll. I just need to have a think which will be best.'

Pippa felt awful about keeping a secret from her BFFs. As she put her head on her pillow, she knew she had some hard thinking to do before her meeting with Lucinda in the music room tomorrow afternoon. Once she'd agreed to accept her help, there'd be no going back. She just hoped her friends would forgive her in the long run, once she came back to L'Etoile with a signed music contract in her hands.

9

Life's a Dream

*L*ucinda was already waiting in the music room when Pippa arrived. Poor Pippa hadn't had a wink of sleep and felt exhausted.

'I was beginning to think you weren't coming,' snapped Lucinda, her usual charming self.

'Yeah, sorry, got held up,' Pippa mumbled.

Lucinda looked at Pippa thoughtfully. She couldn't help but notice how naturally attractive Pippa was – and perhaps even more so now with her face betraying a certain vulnerability. There was no denying it – this girl was a threat, and much better out of the way.

'Well, Burrows, are you in or out?' demanded Lucinda.

Pippa took a deep breath. 'I'm in,' she answered quietly, and as she did so it felt as if the sun had chosen that moment to disappear behind a cloud on purpose.

'Don't look too happy about it!' cried Lucinda. 'I'm about to hand you the keys to the rest of your life!'

Now it was Pippa's turn to study her new partner in crime. Lucinda was stunning but had a permanently spiteful look – even when she was trying to be nice, her face was pinched and mean.

'So what's the plan then?' Pippa gathered herself.

'I'm glad you asked. I've added a bit since we last spoke to make sure that you're not putting all your eggs in one basket,' Lucinda went on.

Pippa raised an eyebrow – was this girl really trying to help? It was all getting a bit much now.

'I've had a long think to see how we can work this so that you don't completely miss out on showcasing your talent at the gala while you're up in London schmoozing Mr Fuller.'

'Go on . . .' Pippa murmured hesitantly.

'I think that I should sing one of your songs, Pippa.'

And there it was – the trade-off that Pippa had known there would be behind all this kindness, but hadn't so far managed to foresee.

'One of my songs? One of the songs I've written?'

'Yep.' Lucinda jumped in quickly while she had Pippa on the hop. 'I listened to all of your tracks last night and there's one which really stands out from the rest. I think I could do it real justice at the gala. What have you got to lose? At least the audience will get to hear it – even if you're not there singing it yourself. It'll get your songwriting noticed.'

Pippa's mind was reeling. No one else had ever sung any of her songs. She'd hoped to reveal them one by one, as and when each was ready to be heard – but then again, at this moment she was completely terrified about singing in front of a huge audience. This could be an easy way out for her. She felt she was losing control of the situation.

'Which one do you want to sing?' she asked, her voice trembling slightly.

'"Life's a Dream",' Lucinda said without hesitation.

Pippa gasped. '"Life's a Dream"? Oh no, Lucinda. Really, that track is private – I didn't even realise it was on the CD I gave you – it really shouldn't have been. No one's heard that one yet. It's not even ready!'

'Life's a Dream' was the first song she had ever written. It summed up every single one of her hopes and fears and was the most personal of all her tracks. She had to try and put Lucinda off.

'Er . . . I'm not sure that one . . . I mean . . . that's so obviously about someone who comes from nothing . . . I'm not sure it'll suit your . . .'

'Nonsense,' Lucinda snarled. 'It'll be perfect . . . the irony of the words against me singing will give it the edge it needs. If you sang it, people would just pity you . . . if I sing it, my story of fortune and glory will bring it to life. You're the girl at the start of the song – I'm the prize. I'm the aspiration here.'

Pippa gasped again, fighting back the tears.

'Look, the way I see it is that you have two options. Number one – you take the chance of a one-to-one audition with Mr Fuller at Universal Music, or number two – you take your chances against the rest of the pack here at the Christmas gala. I can't understand why it isn't blatantly obvious what to do!'

'I know, I know,' bleated Pippa. 'I just always dreamed of having the confidence to sing my songs in front of an audience myself – and now it'll be you singing them.'

'So what's your point, Pippa? I only suggested this to help you out!' said Lucinda. 'Forget I even mentioned it. There are much better songs I can sing anyway.'

'No, no . . . I didn't mean . . . it's fine, really, Lucinda. I'm OK with you singing "Life's a Dream". Want to have a practice now? Maybe I can give you a few pointers.'

'Sure,' grinned Lucinda, triumphantly. 'We can rehearse together and I'll give you the low-down on old Fuller so you're fully briefed. Come on – we've got half an hour before supper.'

And so it was that Lucinda Marciano and Pippa Burrows set the wheels of deceit in motion.

10

Rehearsals and Deceit

The next few weeks whizzed by in a flurry of theatrical activity. Perhaps more run off her feet than most was Faye Summers. Madame Ruby had of course said that both Lucinda and Sally could wear whatever Mrs Marciano had selected for them in Paris, but that still left seventeen other girls turning up at Faye's door day and night.

In a desperate attempt for Faye's roommate, Alice Parry to be allowed to sleep without interruption, Miss Coates, the housemistress, had cleared out one of the large storage rooms at Garland so that Faye could relocate to a place where she could eat, sleep and drink costume design. Alice was sad to be losing her best friend, but equally delighted that she could rehearse, trade tuck with the other girls and sleep in peace.

Maria's blog was getting more hits than ever with all the details she was managing to glean about the gala. The first few weeks of publication had been a bit slow as it took a while for word to get round that there was an anonymous blogger in their midst. Now, though, it was *the* place to go for up-to-the-minute information about the show, rehearsal tips, rehearsal-room schedules and gossip. As Maria could play the piano piece she'd chosen standing on her head, she had plenty of time to make everything and everyone her business. If you looked closely enough, you would have seen her everywhere, ducking down behind desks, creeping behind bookcases in the library, listening in to anything that could feather her 'scoop'. She'd had a great response to her headlines:

'Hair Curly or Straight – the Big Debate'
'Music Room Battles – Use it or Lose it!'
'Tonsillitis Strikes Gala Stars – Top Up Your Vitamin C'
'Mystery Midnight Rehearser Revealed'
'Sequin Shortage Threatens Costume Completion'

'You're so clever, Mimi,' said Molly as she finished reading that morning's update entitled **'No More Nerves: How to Fight the Fright!'**

'But I do feel bad that we have to wait for Pippa to go off to morning rehearsal before we can talk about the blog. Do you think we can bring her in on it soon?'

'I just don't know,' confessed Maria, who had been feeling equally guilty that she was keeping a secret from Pippa. 'I don't know what to do about telling her. We agreed before we came, that no matter who we met, we'd keep this to ourselves rather than risk being discovered. It just works much better as an anonymous blog. People are more inclined to contact *Yours, L'Etoilette* with their thoughts if they don't know who's on the receiving end.'

Molly looked thoughtful. 'I s'pose you're right. Hadn't considered the email contribution side of things. That anonymous address you set up is a stroke of genius, BTW,' Molly continued. 'You were right about students needing an outlet to vent their feelings, or just to ask for help. Has anything new come in from anyone today?'

'Oh, good point, Moll. Haven't had a chance to check it yet,' Maria answered as she logged on to haveyoursay@letoile.co.uk.

She scrolled down about eight new messages – one from Faye asking Yours, L'Etoilette to put up a notice calling for any students who had not yet come to her for their final fittings to do so by the end of the day. With only two days to go until the gala, she was nearly at breaking point with the number of alterations she still had to make. Then there was another one from Alice Parry, asking Yours, L'Etoilette to ask if anyone had some silk flowers she could borrow for her *My Fair Lady* hat.

'Nothing particularly exciting,' Maria commented as she uploaded the student requests onto the main blog. 'It's amazing, isn't it, how much faith people put in Yours, L'Etoilette to fulfil their requests when they've no idea who's responsible.'

'That's because you've been so helpful, Mimi. No sooner do they ask, than their requests appear for the whole school to see.' Maria felt proud.

You see, Story-seeker, to all intents and purposes, she was there primarily to help and secondly to have fun, but never at anyone's expense. She was there to provide the facts, not fiction.

'Hold on a sec, Moll – look at this one!'

Molly looked up from her laptop. 'Who's it from?'

'Well, that's just it. It's from a totally random email address – not a standard student@l'etoile address.'

Molly tossed her laptop to one side and leapt over to her sister.

'This one here,' Maria pointed. 'From email@starservice.com.'

Both the girls waited patiently for the email to open and pored over its odd contents:

To: haveyoursay@letoile.co.uk
From: email@starservice.com
Date: Wednesday 11th December – 7:04 a.m.

One little rabbit new to the scene
Met another who wanted to reign supreme
Like one in the headlights,
She'd follow her blind
What happened to that rabbit, we'll find out in time.

Maria was puzzled. Was it a joke? Or a riddle? Either way, it wasn't a very nice message – more of a threat, to be honest. One thing Maria was confident about was that she'd get to the bottom of it – this mystery writer was no match for *Yours, L'Etoilette!*

'Molly, I'm not really sure what this means at the moment. Look, let's give it some thought and talk about it tonight. One thing I would say though – let's keep this to ourselves for now. No one's supposed to know I'm the blogger, remember, and seeing as we've no idea who sent this, if we start asking questions, we might just ask the wrong person and then my cover will be completely blown.'

'OK, Mimi, but I have to say it's a bit weird. It feels like a warning or a threat or something. What if someone's trying to tell you something serious? It's totally up to us to figure this thing out. Eeek, I've got a RBF about this one.'

'Don't worry. We'll work it out – when have I ever let you and one of your Really Bad Feelings down?'

Molly threw her arms around her twin and planted a big kiss on the top of her head. 'What a team! Come on – we'd better get to class. We've got history this morning and old Butter-boots is gunning for me after my disastrous essay last week!' Maria sighed at her hopeless sibling and followed her out of the dorm.

Geography followed history and needless to say neither twin had been able to concentrate on what they were supposed to be doing. By the time they got to drama after lunch, Molly was so consumed with visions of baby rabbits running to their doom in blinding headlights that she was practically in tears.

'Maria! Have you thought any more about who might have sent that horrible email this morning – and, more importantly, who it might be about? The more I think about it, the more I think someone's really in trouble,' Molly whispered during improvisation.

'No!' Maria whispered back, feeling like a failure. She hated to be puzzled by things. 'There's always the possibility that it's a complete wind-up, Moll, by someone who's jealous of the blog.'

'Molly and Maria Fitzfoster!' Miss Fleming boomed. 'If I meant you to use this session for a gossip, you'd be tucked up in your dorm rooms! Now split up and show me how a tree would move in a storm!'

Maria rolled her eyes as Pippa grabbed her hand and started encouraging her to flail around. 'What play are we doing this week?' Maria chuckled. '*Willows in the Wind*?' Pippa managed to smother her giggles by pretending to splutter out the noise the wind would make.

Drama dissolved into individual study time and the first-year students ran off to their respective rehearsal rooms. The academic subjects like history and geography were at the bottom of the pile until the gala was over. They were on a forty-eight-hour countdown to Friday 13th December and all the girls were determined to do the best they could for themselves, their families and their futures.

There was one girl, however, who, as you know, Story-seeker, was more nervous than the rest, faced with the audition of her life on Friday.

Lucinda had surreptitiously thrust a note into Pippa's hand as she passed her in the supper queue that evening, requesting an extra meeting with her before English on Thursday morning to finalise plans for Friday. Apart from their rehearsals together, Pippa had done her level best to keep out of Lucinda's way the past three weeks since they'd become co-conspirators. The whole thing had stuck in her throat but she felt helpless to change events when there was the possibility of a record deal at the end of it. It had been so difficult to keep sneaking away from the twins early every morning – pretending to have some meeting with Miss Hart, or a rehearsal with Mr Potts. She couldn't actually believe the twins didn't suspect something. The truth was that the twins couldn't believe their luck that Pippa was so busy every morning before class, as it meant they had about fifteen minutes to themselves in the dorm to update the blog and go through the *Yours, L'Etoilette* emails. Pippa couldn't work out if the twins were just distracted by their own performances at the gala, or too caught up in twinsville to ask her any probing questions. Either way, she felt a little bit disappointed that they hadn't taken more of an interest.

You see what secrets between friends can do, Story-seeker?

Pippa once again entered the music room to find Lucinda sitting on the piano stool scribbling a note.

'You took your time – we only have ten minutes before the bell for morning lessons,' snapped Lucinda. 'Right. I'll talk, you listen. Tomorrow at ten o'clock, I'm going to phone Miss Hart from my mobile pretending to be your mother to explain about your Uncle Harry being taken ill and let her know that the family is sending a car to collect you at eleven o'clock.' Pippa just stared at Lucinda, feeling sick with nerves.

'Then I imagine old Hart will come to technology class and pull you out to explain what's happened. You will need to dig deep and appear distraught at the thought of dear Uncle Harry being poorly.' Pippa's heart sank, imagining what she'd do if she ever did receive that kind of horrendous information. It would rip her world apart.

'Pippa!' Lucinda said. 'Are you listening to me?'

'Yes!' Pippa said. 'It's just not going to be that easy, Lucinda. Lying doesn't come naturally to me.'

Lucinda threw her a spiteful look. 'It's a good job one of us is on the ball enough to launch your career then, isn't it?' she retorted. 'You should rush back to the dorm and pack a couple of things with Miss Hart to make it look authentic. You won't have to worry about bumping into Dumb and Dumber . . .

Lucinda's favourite nickname
for the Fitzfoster twins

. . . as they'll be safely tucked away in class. Then just go out and wait somewhere quietly for the car to arrive. I shouldn't imagine Miss Hart will let you out of her sight so you're going to have to keep up the act the whole time you're with her. Just one extra thing though.'

Pippa looked up at her in disbelief. 'I can't do any more!' she protested.

Lucinda thrust a piece of paper into Pippa's

hand. 'You need to make sure you copy this note in your handwriting and give it to Miss Hart before you leave. Ask her to make sure she gives it to me urgently.'

Pippa took the piece of crumpled paper from Lucinda and read:

Dear Lucinda,

My uncle has been taken very ill and I won't be able to perform in the gala this evening as I'm going to the hospital now to be with him. Would you mind performing 'Life's a Dream' in my absence? You sang it so well the other day in rehearsal and at least the scouts will get to know of my songwriting ability, even if they can't hear me sing.

I hope you understand and are able to help.

Good luck.

Pippa x

Pippa couldn't hide her sorrow any longer and the tears started to fall, but she was in too deep to back out.

Lucinda ignored her. 'I'm just a bit worried they

won't let me change my song to yours at the last minute, unless you've officially asked me to.'

Pippa didn't even look up from the note. She felt as though she was signing her life away.

'Oh, Pippa, stop snivelling! Hurry and get cleaned up – we're going to be late. It'll all work out. I promise!' Lucinda said, with her fibbing fingers crossed behind her back.

Pippa ran off to the bathroom to sort out her blotchy face with some powder, and Lucinda made her way to English, grinning like the cat who'd got the cream.

11

Friday the Thirteenth

'I just can't face any more rehearsals,' said Molly, a slightly insane look on her face as she walked with Maria and Pippa to technology. 'For the first time in my life, I'm delighted to be going to sit at a computer to create spreadsheet formulae!'

Maria was thinking the opposite. She'd barely practised her piece for all the blogging and snooping she'd been doing. Still, thanks to her efforts, every student who'd written in asking *Yours, L'Etoilette* for help had been rescued. She must make proper use of the rehearsal time before lunch to give her own piano piece a good practice!

'You're quiet, Pips,' said Molly. 'You're just a bit

nervous, I expect. I can't wait to hear which one of your songs you've chosen. I love the fact you've kept it a secret from everyone. I haven't even heard all of them myself yet. Is it one of the ones that was on your web page?'

'No,' answered Pippa, trying to sound enthusiastic. 'It's actually the first song I ever wrote. No one except Uncle Harry's heard it yet.

Which wasn't strictly true, was it, Story-seeker? That should have read, no one except Uncle Harry and Lucifette.

You're right, I'm nervous anyway and the lyrics are kind of autobiographical, you know, about who I am, where I've come from and what my dreams are.'

'Oh how brilliant, Pippa. I can't wait to hear it! You're so lucky — bet you've not really needed to practise it at all, have you, if it's your own piece? What can they compare it to? It'll just come from the heart. You're so clever!' Molly said, proud of her gorgeous raven-haired friend. Pippa managed to beam through her guilt.

'What's the time, girls?' Lydia asked. 'This lesson is completely dragging. I've really got to get out of here

– my dad's dropping my cello back at ten thirty. Can you believe all four strings snapped yesterday? Talk about timing!'

'Still, better that it happened yesterday than tonight!' added Belle Brown from behind a monitor. 'It's ten o'clock.'

'Ten o'clock,' Pippa gasped. That hideous Lucinda would be on the phone to Miss Hart right now, giving the performance of a lifetime as Mrs Burrows. Pippa couldn't bear to think what was being said.

'So you understand, Miss Hart . . .' Lucinda was saying into her end of the phone, 'I simply can't leave Harry's side so will send a car to collect Pippa immediately. She would never forgive us if she wasn't there.'

'Of course, Mrs Burrows,' replied Miss Hart sympathetically. 'I can't imagine the shock and heartache you must all be going through. It is indeed a great shame, as you say, that Pippa won't be able to attend tonight's gala. The girls have all been working so hard. But there will be other chances next term. Some things are without doubt more important and should take priority. I will go myself and excuse Pippa from her lesson right away. Our thoughts at L'Etoile go out to you and your family. What time did you say the car would arrive?'

'Thank you, Miss Hart. You've been very kind. The driver will arrive at eleven o'clock. I've asked him to go to the private Garland entrance so as not to make a scene for Pippa. Could you possibly make sure she is there by eleven?'

'No problem at all, Mrs Burrows. Consider it done. Pippa will be with you shortly.' And with that, Miss Hart replaced the receiver, full of sorrow for poor Pippa, knowing what a horrible day lay ahead of her. She scanned the block of timetables on her office wall for 1 Alpha's schedule. There . . . technology . . . and off she went.

When Miss Hart appeared at the tech room doorway at ten minutes past ten, Pippa thought she might faint. Lucinda, who'd arrived mysteriously late for class, tried to catch her eye with a *don't-screw-this-up* look, but Pippa refused to glance in her direction. As Miss Hart approached, saying she needed a quiet word, Pippa could hear her heart beating in her chest. *Come on, Pippa! Pull yourself together – think record deal, think America, think superstar,* she said to herself, over and over again. It hadn't taken too much effort to be 'distraught', as per Lucinda's instructions. To be honest, distraught was the only emotion she did feel! The fact that Miss Hart was so kind and gentle, helping her to pack a bag for the journey, made it all much worse.

'There, there, Pippa,' said Miss Hart. 'Your Uncle Harry is going to be just fine. You mark my words. You're doing the right thing being with him and your mother. And nor should you worry about the gala. There will be so many opportunities for you to shine in the new year. You have such a raw, genuine talent, Pippa, I'm not at all worried about you missing your chance today and you shouldn't be either.'

The gala! The letter! Pippa had nearly forgotten. She ran over to Maria's desk and grabbed some paper and began writing the letter Lucinda could use as authorisation to sing 'Life's a Dream', should anyone query her change of song later on.

'What are you doing, Pippa?' Miss Hart asked in surprise.

Pippa stuffed the note into an envelope and handed it over. 'I've had an idea, Miss. Would you be kind enough to see that Lucifette, I mean, Lucinda Marciano, gets this, please?'

Miss Hart was bewildered but she took the letter

and promised to deliver it as soon as she could. She led Pippa down the back stairs to where her car was already waiting. 'Off you go, dear. You stay strong for your mother now. She needs you.' Pippa nodded and closed the car door.

And I need my mother, she thought. How had she allowed herself to get into such a mess?

12

How do You Solve a Problem Like Maria . . . and Molly?!

Maria was in a panic. Out of worry for Pippa and a desire to find out what was going on, she had immediately feigned a dizzy spell and the need to visit Nurse Payne. She had followed Miss Hart and Pippa down the corridor to the dorm, absorbing every snippet of their conversation, and then watched in despair as Pippa had been driven away in a very expensive-looking chauffeur-driven car.

What was going on? Poor Pippa! She had to get back to Molly and tell her what she'd seen.

Luckily, classes had finished for the day and the girls had been left to use the time before the gala commenced at six o'clock for rehearsal and general preening.

'What do you mean, she's gone?' Molly shrieked in alarm.

'Shhhh!' spluttered Maria. 'In here, quick.' She pulled Molly into one of the computer rooms.

'Gone where, FGS?' Molly asked.

'To visit her uncle in hospital, Miss Hart told her. But it just doesn't add up. That car – the one with the chauffeur that came to pick her up – was just . . .'

'Just what?!' Molly interrupted, exasperated with Maria for not being able to find the words.

'Just, er . . . well . . . too posh for Pippa's family. You know yourself Pippa said they don't have a lot of money. Why would Pippa's mum send a car like that? Anyway, surely her mum would have come to L'Etoile to break the news to Pippa herself. I know Mummy would do that if she had something horrible to tell us. It just doesn't make any sense.'

'I hardly think the car's a cause for concern, to be honest,' Molly scolded her sister, annoyed that she only ever considered the logistics of a situation – and suspiciously at that. 'I'm more worried about Pippa. I wish I was with her.'

Maria nodded. 'Why, oh why, has that girl not got a mobile yet? I told her it's only a matter of time before she gets caught with some emergency or another.'

'There's not a lot we can do about it now, is there? I suggest we go and speak to Miss Hart ourselves and find out if there's anything we can do to help,' Molly said.

'What good will that do? There's nothing we can do. Pippa's with her family and that's the best place for her at a time like this. I'd like to know more about that letter she asked Miss Hart to give Lucifette, though.'

'What letter – you never mentioned any letter!' Molly exploded.

'Didn't I? Oh, sorry. It's all been such a whirlwind. The letter Pippa scribbled in the dorm and asked Miss Hart to take to Lucifette before she left.'

'OK, now I definitely smell a rat! Pippa Burrows send Lucifette a letter? No chance! Now I'm convinced something's up!' Molly said, almost in tears herself.

'What did you just say, Moll?' Maria stopped her suddenly. 'Rat? Burrows... Rabbit... it's Pippa!' she sputtered. 'Pippa's the rabbit!'

'Slow down, Mimi,' Molly shook her sister by the arms, trying to calm her down. 'What are you talking about?!'

'The rabbit!' repeated Maria breathlessly. 'The

horrible email from this morning, the blinded rabbit in the headlights . . . it's . . . it's Pippa.'

Molly stopped in her tracks. But of course! It was a play on words – Pippa Burrows . . . Burrows – a rabbit burrows. How could they have missed it?

'Quick – get the email up again so we can have another look and see what else it'll tell us,' Molly said.

Maria was already on the computer, logging on to the haveyoursay@letoile.co.uk email account. Both girls waited impatiently for the mail to open.

To: haveyoursay@letoile.co.uk
From: email@starservice.com
Date: Wednesday 11th December – 7:04 a.m.

One little rabbit new to the scene
Met another who wanted to reign supreme
Like one in the headlights,
She'd follow her blind
What happened to that rabbit, we'll know in time.

They read the note again. It was so obvious now that they knew the little rabbit was Pippa. She was new to the scene, having won her scholarship to the school. And she'd gone off in a car – hence the headlights – but who was this person *'who thought she'd reign supreme'*? Would there be another email with more clues?

'Maria – there's got to be a way of finding out who sent this. Can't you do something?' Molly begged.

'There is a way of finding out who an email address is registered to, via the IP address – but I'm not sure I know how to do that kind of search. I've only ever seen it done once when Daddy had the IT guy over trying to find out who'd been sending those emails pretending to be him. Do you remember?'

Molly stood behind her sister at the screen and squeezed her shoulder in encouragement. If there was ever a good time for Maria to recall her techy expertise, it was now, and as she started tapping away, she opened up screen after screen of what Molly could only describe as gobbledygook.

'Ah ha!' Maria whooped. 'Here we are . . . email@ starservice.com is registered to . . .' She gasped in shock.

'Who, Mimi – who?!' Molly squealed.

'To Marciano Industries Ltd!' Maria blurted out.

Maria looked at Molly. Both girls were totally speechless. 'It's Lucifette! It just has to be. She must be using one of her father's email group addresses. Why, that over-confident, jumped-up little witch. How dare she think she can send a riddle we can't solve? And the bare-faced cheek of showing off like this.'

'But what does it all mean? What's Lucifette done with poor Pippa?' pleaded Molly. 'This whole thing is getting more awful by the minute!'

Maria paused for a moment and then started typing.

'What are you doing now?' asked Molly.

'I'm going to play Lucifette at her own game and email her back to say that unless she agrees to meet *Yours, L'Etoilette* in fifteen minutes in the Kodak Hall to explain herself, I'm going to post a blog right now exposing her to the whole school. Everyone's getting ready, so the hall will be dark and deserted – so at least we'll be able to see and confirm it's her before she sees us!' Maria hit send and sat back in her chair.

'What if she doesn't see the email in time and doesn't show?' moaned Molly, despondently.

'I don't even want to think about that, Moll. Come on – let's get there early so we can get a good view of the entrance.'

Ten minutes later, the twins were crouching under the lighting desk, which was on a raised platform at the back of the Kodak Hall. Luckily for them, there was a small tear in the black curtaining around the front of the desk, which gave them a great view of the whole auditorium. 'This had better work, Mimi!' Molly whispered.

'Shut up!' Maria shot back as she scoured the auditorium through the gap in the fabric. And then, 'Shhh – did you hear that? Someone's coming.'

Both girls held their breath as they heard footsteps tapping across the stage. And then a voice called out. '*Yours, L'Etoilette*? You here?'

Pushing Molly out of the way so she could get a better look, Maria saw the silhouette of Sally Sudbury standing in the middle of the stage.

'I don't believe it,' Maria breathed. 'What a coward! Lucifette can't even do her own dirty work – she's sent Sally to take the heat.'

'What are you going to do, Mimi? You can't talk to her – you'll totally blow your *Yours, L'Etoilette* cover.'

'Some things are just more important, Moll – like friends. Pippa's my friend and I'm going to help her, whatever the cost.'

With that, Maria ventured out from under the desk and called to Sally. 'Email@starservice? Is that you?'

Sally looked over in their direction, still unable to make out who exactly was talking to her. Maria made her way down the aisle to the stage and, as she did so, Sally's expression turned to one of relief.

'Maria!' Sally exclaimed. 'It's you!'

'And it's you, Sally Sudbury.' Maria responded coldly – not wanting to show that she was the least bit surprised at seeing Sally standing there. 'Too chicken to come out and explain things for herself, is she? Should have guessed.'

'I don't know what you mean, Maria,' Sally said timidly, and then it dawned on her that *Yours, L'Etoilette* had been bluffing when she had emailed saying she knew the identity of the email sender. 'Oh no!' Sally realised. 'You thought I was going to be Lucinda . . . I mean, that Lucinda was email@ starservice . . . I mean . . . oh dear, it's all getting very confusing. It was me . . . I sent that email.'

Molly burst out of the shadows behind Maria. 'Sally – I can't believe it. How . . . I mean . . . why did you send such an awful note about Pippa? We are right, aren't we . . . it is about Pippa, isn't it? What have you done with her?'

'Slow down, Molly!' Maria said calmly, starting to realise what might really be going on. 'Let Sally speak. Sally?'

'Oh, I'm so pleased it's you. I half-feared – well, I

won't tell you what I half-feared. I'm just so pleased it's you. It's all got so messy. Yes, Pippa is the rabbit. And I'm sorry if my email came across as threatening – I was just trying to be cryptic, in case it fell into the wrong hands. After all – you knew who *Yours, L'Etoilette* was, but I didn't! Could have been Lucinda for all I knew, then I would have been well and truly caught in the act! She'd kill me if she knew I was telling her secret!'

Maria smiled at her in encouragement. 'Never mind Lucifette, Sally. Now you know that I'm *Yours, L'Etoilette* – you do know I'm going to have to kill you, don't you?' And she laughed softly, immediately putting Sally at ease.

'Oh, Maria, Molly – it's so horrible. Lucinda's set a trap for Pippa, just to keep her from performing at tonight's gala.' Maria stood stiff, every muscle in her body frozen with fury.

'Sally, it's OK. Tell us exactly what's happened and maybe we can all try to fix it,' Molly said reassuringly.

'It's too late, it's too late . . .' Sally tailed off. She was sobbing. And, collapsing onto one of the theatre seats, she recounted the whole sordid, spiteful tale of the lies that Lucinda had spun to get Pippa out of the way so that she could sing Pippa's song as if it were her own handiwork.

'And that's not even the worst of it . . .' she sniffed. 'She managed to get Pippa to hand over one of her CDs which has both the backing track without a vocal on it to sing live to, and a full version with the vocal recorded live in the studio. She's not even planning to sing it herself – she's going to MIME!'

Molly and Maria recoiled in horror!

As Molly was stroking Sally's shoulder, which was bobbing up and down as she sobbed and sniffled, Maria was deep in thought about what to do to make all of this right. First things first, they had to get Pippa out of that blasted car, and back to L'Etoile.

'Sally,' Maria said. 'I need you to put all of your fear behind you for a minute and think clearly about how we can get a message to Pippa. You don't by some stroke of luck know who the driver is and have his number, do you?' Sally shook her head. 'It'll be one of Mr Marciano's company drivers. They're the only ones the family ever book.' Poor Sally really did look upset as she sat there hunched in her seat. But despite appearances, she was wracking her brains trying to come up with a way to help. Part of her couldn't believe she'd been brave enough to betray Lucinda. But she was glad she had.

'The only thing I do know about the drivers is that all the Marciano cars always fill up at one particular service station outside London because Mr Marciano owns it. They *always* stop there to top up – even if the tank's still half-full. We could try and work out what sort of time Pippa will be passing through there and get a message to her. Does that help?'

'Does that help? Are you kidding – well done, Sal!' Maria grabbed at the information she'd just been given as if it was the latest iPhone. Suddenly a plan began to develop in her head. It was a vague plan and it relied heavily on timing and luck, but it just might work.

'Moll, is Albie coming today with a delivery?' she asked.

'Yeah, it's Friday isn't it? He's coming at half-past one today. I can't wait.'

Molly turned to Sally. 'He's bringing those little grey suede pixie boots Kate Moss was wearing at the Brits – do you know the ones I mean?'

Sally looked vacant.

'Mollllllly! Not now. Have you got his number in your mobile?' Molly reached into her school bag and shook it like a box of tic-tacs at Maria. 'Right, call him,' Maria instructed, 'and then pass him to me!'

Molly hit speed-dial number 4. *What a saddo!* Maria thought, but quickly re-focused as Molly held out the phone to her. 'It's going straight to voicemail,' she sighed.

'You know what to do after the tone,' echoed Albie's voice . . . *Beeeeeeeep.*

Maria grabbed the handset. 'Albie? It's Molly and Maria Fitzfoster here on Molly's phone. We need to speak with you urgently – it could be a matter of life and death.' Maria hung up and looked at her watch. If the car had left L'Etoile just after eleven, by her calculations, they should be hitting the service station by about twelve-thirty. Eeeek, they had forty-five minutes to locate Albie and convince him to go and pick up Pippa on his bike. They just had to hope he was in the shower or something and that he hadn't left home yet – he'd never pick up his mobile if he was driving.

All three girls looked at each other. They felt as though a tornado had just swept through their lives – leaving a trail of destruction and uncertainty in its wake.

'I want to thank you, Sally,' Molly began. 'I can't

begin to imagine why you decided to snitch on Lucifette and save Pippa, but I'm glad you did.'

'Yeah, thanks Sal,' echoed Maria. 'Can't have been easy making a move against Lucifette. She's pretty much got you where she wants you, hasn't she?'

'You've no idea,' Sally volunteered. 'How can I ever be seen to be going against her? She'll have me and Mum out on the street quicker than you can say Coco Chanel!' Sally looked so vulnerable sitting there with her knees curled up in her enormous baggy jumper. 'I'm not sure how I'm going to get away with this one. We'll have to come up with something, girls . . . Please, I'll need your help to cover this up; she must never know it was me!'

'Don't worry, Sal,' Maria answered, impressed by the way Sally had conducted herself. 'When it all comes out in the wash, we'll make out that Pippa caved in and phoned us from the car – and as for the whole M-I-M-E situation – well, I, in my total brilliance, could have discovered that, couldn't I?' Sally knew it was inappropriate, but she suddenly felt an overwhelming wave of happiness wash over her.

'Talking about the MIME situation – what on earth are we going to do about the gala situation?' Sally asked, looking panicky again.

'Don't worry about that,' answered Maria confidently. 'Moll and I will think of something. For the minute, we just need to get Pippa back.'

Bbbbrrrriiiinnnng . . . bbbrrrrriiiinnnng . . . Molly's phone sang out. 'Albie?' she asked desperately. 'Oh, thank goodness. I'll just pass you to Maria.'

In no time at all, Maria had revealed the whole sorry story to Albie, who felt very protective towards the girls he delivered expensive clothes to every Friday afternoon. It was his favourite job of the week and he was more than happy to be part of a rescue operation for them. Even before the phone call had finished, he'd grabbed a spare helmet for Pippa and was outside his flat revving his motorbike.

'Call me when you've got her, Albie. And thanks!'

It was far too risky for Sally to be caught hanging out with the twins by Lucinda, so the new trio made arrangements to meet again at twelve-forty-five, well away from the Kodak Hall, which was beginning to become the focus for most of the school. The gala was due to start at six o'clock, so with only a few hours to go, everyone was frantic.

Molly and Maria could hear Faye shrieking.

'Who's got Daisy's skirt? What? Oh FGS, Alice! It's coral tie-dye with a pearl and feather motif . . . Oh

FGS, Lara – not you as well . . . does that look like it belongs to you? Get it off or you'll split it!'

Molly laughed. 'Who'd be Faye right now? Not me!'

Maria humoured her sister with a giggle but was too concerned with Operation Pippa to respond further.

As soon as the twins were alone in their dorm again, Maria was logging on to the haveyoursay@letoile.co.uk email account.

'What are you doing now?' Molly muttered.

'I've just emailed Sally for Mr Marciano's assistant's number – there's one thing we haven't taken into consideration. How we are going to get Pippa away from the driver? If a biker swoops in and grabs Pippa, the driver's sure to call the police and say she's been kidnapped. Somehow we need to get a message to the driver that it's OK for his passenger to go with Albie.'

Ping. Sally's emailed response flashed up on the screen.

'Ah, here we go. Molly, will you ring his secretary and pretend to be Lucifette? It's our only hope. If you're really rude and obnoxious she'll believe you're her. Just tell her that the idiot driver picked up the wrong passenger and that you've arranged yourself for a taxi bike to collect Pippa from the service station

128

and bring her back to L'Etoile. That way we're also guaranteed that the driver will stop at the services. Just hope he doesn't get the message too early, tell Pippa and panic her. She won't know what is going on!'

Molly took a deep breath and made the call to the long-suffering Elodie Wyatt. It was easy.

'Wowsers, that poor assistant. She didn't even bat an eyelid that I wasn't Lucifette. She must have had her wits scared right out of her. She was like one of those nodding dogs that sit on car shelves – all, "Yes sir, yes madam" with no mind of her own,' Molly said as she hung up. 'So what now?'

'So now we wait,' Maria announced calmly.

'So now we get thinking!' Molly protested. 'We're only halfway there, Mimi. How are we going to expose Lucifette's miming exploits during her performance?'

'Elementary, my dear Molly,' taunted Maria annoyingly.

'Oh, don't tell me, you've already thought of that too!' grinned Molly with mischief in her eyes. 'Do tell . . .'

13

The Great Escape

$\mathcal{I}$n the back of the huge, chauffeur-driven car, Pippa was full of regret. She didn't care about the stupid record company audition. If only she could turn back the clock and tell that ghastly Lucinda what she thought of her, she'd do it in a heartbeat. She had betrayed herself and, in turn, her family and her friends. Oh, her friends. How could she have been so deceitful to Molly and Maria when they'd gone out of their way to be so kind to her?

Just as they pulled up at a service station, the driver's mobile rang.

Albie, meanwhile, was astride his motorbike, eyes glued to every vehicle entering the petrol station. He was half-terrified he might have already missed Pippa — so you can imagine how relieved he felt when he spied the gleaming black Cadillac cruising onto the forecourt.

You might wonder, Story-seeker, how he knew it was the correct car? Maria had taken down the registration number of course when she'd seen Pippa get in and drive away that morning. Told you she was methodical, didn't we?

As soon as he saw the car arrive, he walked over, being sure to remove his helmet so as not to scare her, and tapped on the window. He'd only met her a couple of times at the school with Molly when he'd dropped off her orders, so he was praying she'd recognise him!

'Albie?' Pippa exclaimed with glee when she clapped eyes on him. She was out of the car in a split second, so relieved to see a friendly face. She could have thrown her arms around him but decided that might be a bit much. 'What are you doing here?'

Albie grinned. 'Pippa — the twins sent me. You've been stitched up. You've got to come back to the school with me — they'll explain everything then. It was Lucinda . . .'

'I bloomin' knew it!' Pippa cried. 'But what about the driver – he'll think I've been kidnapped if I don't get back in the car.'

'Don't worry about that.' Albie grinned again. 'The twins have sorted it. Molly cancelled the car by pretending to be Lucinda. She told 'em there'd been a mistake and you'd be getting a taxi bike back to L'Etoile.' As he explained, he waved over at the driver and gave a thumbs-up. 'Wave and smile then, Pippa!' he commanded, helping her to fasten her helmet. Pippa waved and grinned like a mad woman at the driver, who nodded and pulled away.

It was a relatively short journey back to L'Etoile. Motorbikes were so much quicker than cars, weaving in and out of the traffic. Pippa did feel a bit guilty about one thing, though – and decided there and then that she'd omit this part of the story if she ever relayed it to her grandchildren – or her mother, for that matter, who'd have killed her daughter for ever riding on the back of a motorbike!

Molly, Maria and Sally were beside themselves with anticipation. Twelve forty-five had come and gone and they'd had no text or phone call from Albie as to whether he'd managed to intercept the car successfully and grab Pippa. Albie would later be mortified about this, as he had remembered to write a text just before they set off, saying, 'Got her!', but in his haste had forgotten to press send. By one o'clock, the girls couldn't wait in their room any longer and decided it would be best to go and hide themselves behind one of the caretaker's sheds at the rear entrance to Garland where they usually waited for Albie and his fashion deliveries. By their meticulous calculations, Maria and Sally had estimated that, with the speed of motorbike travel, if all had gone to plan, Pippa should be coming down the drive by about one-fifteen . . . and, of course, they'd been spot-on!

'There she is!' shrieked Molly and all three girls sprinted towards Pippa, who was already in floods of tears. Albie and Pippa had thought it best to leave the bike hidden in the bushes halfway up the drive and walk the rest of the way so as not to alert anyone that they were there with the sound of the engine.

'Oh, girls!' Pippa gasped. 'How did you unravel all of this? How can I ever thank you? Maria, you're so clever — I bet you hatched this whole thing.' Pippa stopped short when she noticed Sally Sudbury hanging back behind the twins, trying to make herself look as small as humanly possible.

'It's OK, Pips,' Maria said quickly. 'She's with us. If it hadn't been for her spilling the beans about Lucifette's evil plan, we'd never have known it was happening.'

Pippa, whose trusting nature had taken a bit of a battering of late, looked suspiciously at Sally, and then smiled. *Oh well, just this last time,* she thought to herself and gave Sally a big hug too.

'Albie, you're a complete star,' said Molly as she flung her arms around a very red-faced, but happy, Albie. 'Wait till we're home in London this Christmas. We're going to throw you the best party you've ever had!' Albie was now almost purple-faced below his curly red hair.

'Come on, Pippa, and we'll explain the whole thing on the way. You won't believe some of it! It's so good to have you back.' Maria squeezed Pippa's hand affectionately.

'I'd better see you later, girls,' Sally beamed at her new friends. 'The fewer opportunities Lucifette has to bust us together, the better. Pippa, you HAVE to find somewhere to hide and quickly.'

'Wait a minute, Sal – did you just call her Lucifette?' Maria asked. 'Amazing.'

'Loving your work, Sal!' echoed Molly. 'See you at the gala for part deux of the big Lucifette exposé!'

'Mimi, was this really the best place you could come up with?' asked Molly, nearly gagging at the smell of bird poo.

'Well, if you've got any better ideas – I'm all ears!' snapped Maria. 'There's a workbench for a dressing-table, and a plug for your straighteners – what more do you need, FGS?'

When Maria had racked her brains earlier that morning for a safe place to hide Pippa and for them all to get ready for the gala, the lake boathouse had seemed like the obvious place. It was near enough to the Kodak Hall for them to sneak back and forth unseen and had its own outdoor loo, running water and electricity.

Molly was not-so-secretly horrified at the environment she had to work with, but the thought of Lucinda's face when she realised she'd been rumbled was keeping her sane.

As Molly busied herself setting up the makeshift dressing room, Pippa just kept firing questions at the twins, trying to work out how the day's events had unfolded. The biggest shocker for all of them had been the bravery of lovely Sally.

'Oh, Sally was absolutely fabulous,' Molly marvelled.

'If not a little ingenious,' Maria joined in. 'The way she sent me that anonymous email to the *Yours, L'Etoilette* address.'

Pippa was a bit confused. 'What do you mean, sent you the email? If she sent it to *Yours, L'Etoilette*, how did it find its way to you? Actually, if it was anonymous, how did you even find out it was from her?'

Maria looked at Molly and Molly looked back at Maria – both in shock at the ease with which Maria had quite forgotten her anonymity as the mysterious *Yours, L'Etoilette*.

'Oh, Pippa, I reckon it's going to take weeks of midnight feast chats for us to fully explain all this to you. But for starters – and if you tell another living soul, you're dead – I'm *Yours, L'Etoilette!*' Maria said.

Pippa smiled in admiration. 'You're so clever, Maria – although I should have guessed really. Who else in this school would have the know-how and techy expertise to pull off something like that around a jam-packed timetable!'

Maria glowed at Pippa's compliment. 'Oh, it's been soooo difficult keeping it from you, Pips,' Molly cried out in relief. 'The only chance Mimi has to check and update it away from prying eyes is in the mornings before school, so you did us a big favour every time you left the dorm early for your meetings and rehearsals.'

'Moll, I was only leaving early to either rendezvous with stupid Lucifette who kept sneaking me notes to arrange follow-up meetings, or I was just trying to leave early to avoid bumping into her altogether! I felt so awful deceiving you both. All I really wanted was for you two to rumble me by asking too many questions – but now I see you were both too busy with your own sneaky business to notice any weird behaviour!' The trio looked at each other fondly and burst out laughing.

'We've been so stupid, haven't we?' admitted Molly. 'Let's make a pact – no more secrets?'

'No more secrets!' Maria and Pippa sang back in unison and the three girls piled their hands one on top of the other to seal the deal.

'Talking about secrets . . . Come on, Maria, spill the beans on how we're going to expose Lucifette tonight then,' Molly urged, desperate to hear her sister's clever plans.

'Well,' Maria started as she drew the girls close. 'It involves you, Pippa, a spare radio microphone and a well-timed CD swap.'

14

The Calm Before the Storm

*F*ive o'clock approached, and seemed to mark the start of the gala audience arrivals.

As one fabulous car after another rolled up the drive, the spectacle of outfits and hairdos was enough to keep *Hiya!* magazine in print for years to come. The guest list read like a *Who's Who* of the entertainment industry.

Leading the throng of parents and industry folk to the theatre was, of course, Madame Ruby – in all her glory. She was sporting the most dazzling gold sequinned gown and a hairdo to rival Marge Simpson. Parents cooed and aahed as she recounted tales of their daughters' achievements over the course of the term.

Mr and Mrs Marciano, however, were absolutely nowhere to be seen, which was starting to send Madame Ruby into a pink mist.

'Helen,' she squawked. 'Have you phoned Elodie Wyatt?'

Poor Miss Hart, who hadn't even had time to change, what with overseeing the girls all afternoon, was scuttling after the Grand Madame with yet another clipboard stuffed with notes.

'I've just spoken to her, Ruby – for the fourth time since lunch – and she assures me that they are en route.'

'En route . . . en route . . . that could mean anyth—'
Madame Ruby was stopped in her ranting tracks by a very large man in a dinner suit, waddling down the path sporting what could only have been magnifying-glass spectacles.

'Calamity, darling!' Madame exclaimed, displaying every one of her lipstick-coated teeth. 'How are you? Welcome to L'Etoile. Thank you so much for coming. The girls are simply dying to meet you.'

The man in question, Calamity Mossback, was one of America's hottest talent scouts, and had come all the way over from Creative Management Inc. in Los Angeles. He held out a stubby-fingered hand to Madame Ruby.

'The pleasure is all mine, Ruby, dear. Now let me at 'em. What time does this shindig start anyway? I've come straight from the airport and I'm on the red-eye back to LA tonight.'

'Six o'clock sharp,' Madame Ruby stated confidently. 'It'll be worth the wait, dear man. I can assure you I have some real diamond talent in this new crop of starlets. Look out for Lucinda Marciano – she's my hot tip for you – you will know her mother and father, of course.'

Calamity's hairy ears pricked up. 'Marciano, eh? I'd best get the best seat in the house then, hadn't I?' He grabbed a glass of champagne from a passing waiter, and continued down the path to the Kodak Hall – completely oblivious to having toppled the entire tray in his wake.

As the cars continued to empty out their glamorous occupants, the buzz around the dorms was at fever pitch. The only girl who was calm for the first time in three weeks was Faye, who had now successfully dressed each and every starlet to perfection. She was just doing a last-minute costume check and felt really proud of herself.

'We just love them, Faye!' Sofia and Charlotte called out as she whizzed past. 'They're the most beautiful opera costumes we've ever seen.'

Lucinda, one had to admit, looked stunning in a red 'look at me' chiffon number which her mother had indeed sent over from Paris. Having seen rather less of Sally than she would have liked that day, Lucinda was in dire need of some attention and had decided to use the Garland corridor as a catwalk to see how many gasps of admiration she could amass from her classmates at the sight of her in her glorious dress. But apparently everyone had lost their voice! Not a single girl uttered a word to her. *How dare they?* she thought, turning the same colour as her dress. But even Lucinda wouldn't stoop so low as to fish for a compliment. 'SAAAAALLLLLLLY!' she screeched into thin air.

Where was she? She couldn't be still rehearsing that same idiotic poem. Didn't she realise she was going to totally bomb, no matter how much practice she put in? 'SAAAAAAAALLLLLLLLLLLLLLYYYYYYY,' she called so loudly that her voice cracked.

Sally appeared suddenly from the Garland ladies room, where, if the truth be known, she'd been hiding for most of the afternoon. Not that she'd really needed to; it was just that she was terrified Lucinda would see into her soul and discover how she'd betrayed her to Pippa and the twins. It wasn't that she regretted her decision to do the right thing for once – not for one second – it had felt wonderful to do some good for a change and to be on the receiving end of a hug. She just felt she couldn't face Lucinda . . . not yet . . . not until it was almost over.

'Where the heck have you been? I've told you a hundred times, there's no point practising that stupid poem. Let's go – I want to see if Mom and Pop have arrived. I'm quite surprised no one's come to escort us down, to be honest.' Sally, as usual, maintained a submissive silence, but was relieved that Lucinda seemed even more self-obsessed than usual.

'Oh, never mind – come on,' said Lucinda and dragged Sally, still clutching her poem, to the Kodak Hall.

Beep, beep. Maria snatched up her mobile from the makeshift make-up table.

'Yikes, it's Mum and Dad. They're here and want to see us before the show,' she announced to Molly, who was putting the final touches to Pippa's hair and make-up.

'What time is it?' Molly looked up.

'Nearly half-five,' answered Maria. 'Are you almost done?'

'Just give me two secs and I'll be with you.' Molly

grabbed the enormous – now nearly empty – can of hairspray, and released a last fog of spray onto Pippa's beautiful 'up-do'.

'There!' Molly gasped, as Pippa stood up quickly and ran into an area of the boathouse where she could breathe without swallowing a mouthful of hairspray.

The three girls looked at each other in awe.

'We look amazing!' said Molly, ecstatic. In addition to the stunning hair and make-up she'd managed to produce in an hour of madness, Molly had added her own accessories to the gorgeous outfits Faye had provided for all three of them – and had to admit she'd outdone herself. Luckily, Pippa had left her dress in the dorm before she had been forced to pull out of the gala that morning.

'How do you feel, Pippa?' Molly asked, holding up a rather small mirror in her direction. Pippa, desperately trying not to well up and smudge her carefully applied mascara, swirled around, admiring her appearance. She hardly recognised herself.

'Oh, Moll, you're a genius,' she exclaimed. 'I feel a million dollars. Lucifette won't know what to be more angry about – the fact that I'm going to scupper her evil plan, or the fact that I look like a real star!'

'Yes, well done – you've done a fabulous number

on us,' confirmed Maria. 'But we'd best be going. We have to at least say hi to Mum and Dad before we go on or they'll be devastated – and you're up to perform second, Molly, so we need to get a move on!'

'Second? How could I have forgotten? I've got butterflies now!' Molly grabbed her script from the side. 'Please don't let me forget my words, please don't let me forget my words,' she muttered to herself, looking to the sky for help.

Pippa grabbed Molly's hand. 'You'll be wonderful – just wait till they get a load of *Molly Hollywood*!' Molly's blue eyes twinkled back at her.

'You go on, both of you,' Pippa continued. 'My legs are like jelly. I could do with a couple of minutes alone to run through my song anyway and you're both on well before Lucifette – *and me*! I can't believe she managed to get the headline spot as the last act of the evening. She really doesn't miss a trick, does she?'

'Well, all the better for you to be the Grand Finale no one knows they're going to get!' said Maria with a glint in her eye.

'Break a leg.' Maria hugged Pippa. 'And don't you worry about a thing. I'll be ready for you. Remember – when you hear Sofia and Charlotte singing their "Flower Duet" – and you'll definitely hear that –

scoot round to the back of the hall by the sound and lighting desk. There's a big black curtain running from the raised desk platform down to the floor to hide the scaffold, so there will be plenty of space for you to hide there with us until the penultimate act has finished and Lucifette has been introduced.'

'Who is on before Lucifette?' asked Pippa.

'Poor Sally,' announced Maria. 'No doubt she'll be a nervous wreck by then, after everything that's happened today.' Molly and Pippa winced in sympathy.

'Are you sure you'll be able to switch my vocal track that Lucifette is planning to mime to to my purely instrumental track?'

'Don't worry!' Maria said. 'Moll and I will think of something. Have we ever let you down?'

Pippa gave the twins one last squeeze. 'Love you, girls,' she breathed. 'Thank you.'

And with one last sweep of lip gloss, Molly grabbed Maria and crept out of the boathouse, closing the door firmly behind them.

'Please let this work,' pleaded Pippa quietly to herself. 'I promise I'll never screw up again.'

15

A Star-Studded Christmas Gala

The twins entered the main hall just in time to see Madame Ruby link arms with their poor, unsuspecting father and lead him and their mum, who had been left somewhat behind, over to two empty seats.

'There they are, Mimi!' Molly cried, her heart jumping. 'Yeah, and look who old Ruby's putting them next to!' Maria gulped.

'Mr and Mrs Fitzfoster, I'd like you to meet some of my other VVIP guests – Blue and Serafina Marciano.' Madame Ruby snaked around both couples. She couldn't have been more delighted with her introduction and hoped the whole theatre was watching in awe.

Mrs Marciano held out a diamond-laden hand to Mr Fitzfoster.

'Brian, darling – I can hardly believe we've never met before. All of the Marciano diamonds are Fitzfoster diamonds,' she sang, wiggling her fingers in his face to show off her jewels.

'Mrs Marciano, Mr Marciano. I know you by reputation, of course,' Mr Fiztfoster said. He was too polite to allow his face to show anything other than a smile.

'This is my wife, Linda.' The glamorous Mrs Fitzfoster stepped forward to say hello. Even Blue Marciano's breath was taken away by her beauty – which earned him a well-aimed ankle kick from his wife's sharp stiletto heels.

'Mummy! Daddy!' Molly and Maria shrilled as they launched themselves at their parents – who had never been so grateful to be interrupted by their daughters.

'Darlings . . . let me look at you both – gosh, you've grown up so much! Daddy and I have missed your cheeky faces!' Mrs Fitzfoster enveloped both the girls in the biggest cuddle she could muster. 'Don't you both look divine! Good job, Moll!' Linda said proudly.

'Mimi, I'm so proud of you for letting your sister at

you with the curling tongs. Didn't think you had it in you!' mocked Mr Fitzfoster gently, looking at his girls lovingly.

Maria thought at that moment how awful it must be for Pippa to be doing all of this alone tonight without her mother being there. But the diary clash with her own school had meant that Mrs Burrows would never have been able to make it. Maria, however, hadn't let that get in her way and had, of course, come up with a plan.

'Daddy – did you bring the camera like I asked?'

'Would I dare disobey either of my daughters?' Brian Fitzfoster said and flashed her a glimpse of the newest, state-of-the-art video camera.

'Great – be sure to get Moll and me, obviously, but would you also film the last two acts too? They're on the programme. I, er . . . need the footage for a gift.' Mr Fitzfoster looked suspicious but agreed.

'Thanks – wish us luck!' the twins cried out.

'My Lords, Ladies and Gentlemen,' came Madame Ruby's voice over the microphone, a single spotlight picking her out against the rich, red-velvet safety curtain. 'Welcome, one and all, to L'Etoile, School for Stars. I give you this year's Christmas gala . . .'

And as the orchestra struck up the tune 'There's

No Business Like Show Business', the audience erupted into applause.

'Molly, Maria! Are you trying to give me a heart attack?' gasped Miss Hart. 'I've had staff members looking absolutely everywhere for you. Where on earth have you been?' she asked, exasperated. 'Don't answer that!' she continued. 'Molly, stay here as you're on in about seven minutes, and Maria, go to the dressing rooms and stay there until you're called. No wandering off. Am I making myself clear?'

Neither twin dared argue and simply hugged each other for luck. They'd been through enough nannies to recognise a woman on the edge! Molly stood at the side of the stage, trying desperately to run through her lines in her head.

'Five . . . six . . . seven . . . eight!' Molly swung round to see a petrified Heavenly Smith marking out her dance routine in the wings.

'Don't worry!' Molly said in a stage whisper.

'It's too late now! Wish me luck!' Heavenly said as Madame Ruby announced her name.

'Ladies and Gentlemen, I give you Miss Heavenly Smith.'

And with a shove from Miss Hart, Heavenly leapt through the curtain to give the performance of her life.

Molly's words were starting to make her feel nauseous. She could see acts three, four and five (Betsy, Nancy and Elizabeth) lining up by the door waiting to follow her on. Trying to get a grip of her nerves, she thought about Pippa and what she must be going through all alone in that boathouse, dreading what might go wrong with the big plan. 'Oh, it'll be fine,' she scolded herself. 'It'll have to be!'

Explosive applause erupted again and a grinning Heavenly flitted past her. 'Break a leg, Molly! You'll love it out there!!'

Molly could hear Madame Ruby describing her act. 'And our next artist is a divine little actress by the name of Molly Fitzfoster. Molly will be performing a split personality piece for you. See how she jumps from persona to persona as if the previous one never existed. Ladies and Gentlemen . . . I give you Miss Molly Fitzfoster!'

And, with a heaving chest, Molly grabbed her chair and glided out, all smiles and confidence, into the spotlight.

Her effortless performance was met with laughter and booming applause as she took a bow. As she ran off stage, she crashed straight into Maria.

'Oh, Mimi! What are you doing here – I thought you weren't allowed to stay and watch, seeing as you're on nearer the end!'

'Would I miss your big moment?' Maria announced. 'I swapped with Betsy, who was up next, so I could see you. You were amazing! Good job, Moll.'

'Thanks so much. And this means I'll get to watch you too.' Miss Hart shot the girls a warning look to be quiet.

'So next for your delectation, Ladies and Gentlemen, I give you an exquisite pianist by the name of Bets . . .' Madame Ruby frowned as she attempted to read through the crossings-out and new scribble on her script. 'Ah, another Fitzfoster . . . of equal brilliance, we hope . . . Maria Fitzfoster.'

Maria strode confidently over to the huge, black, grand piano, which stood on a built-out part of the staging. As she sat down, she composed herself for a moment and then launched into the most exquisite piano performance you could imagine. The audience were once again on their feet in raptures as Maria took a bow and exited the stage.

'Oh, Mimi – you were divine!' said Molly, who had managed to get Miss Hart to allow her to stay on to hear her sister's act.

'Really? Thanks, Moll – felt a bit of pressure there for a minute having to follow your triumph! Cheers for that, BTW!'

Molly threw her arms around Maria and whispered, 'Right – that's us done and dusted – now on to Pippa! Let's get this show on the road!'

16

Lucifette Gets Her Comeuppance

The dressing room was a war zone. Lucinda was sitting at the main make-up chair with one of the glamsquad, pretending to rehearse her song. Sally was cowering in a corner clenching her fists in an attempt to stop her hands from shaking. Sofia and Charlotte were singing like a couple of canaries in their matching yellow dresses. Alice Parry was at another mirror adjusting the silk flowers in her *My Fair Lady* hat, moaning that she was losing her voice. And between Daisy, desperately trying to tune her bassoon, and Lydia doing the same with her cello, it was like opening night at *The Royal Variety Performance*.

Molly and Maria were hunting through the dressing-room debris like commandos trying their hardest not to be seen. 'Where did you say you put it?' Molly hissed, incredulous that her genius of a sister could mess up something so important at this point.

'It was on the chair by the make-up mirror with the rest of my stuff,' Maria groaned. 'Someone must have moved it all. Oh no – it's sitting under that tissue box by Lucifette! Of all the luck!'

Molly looked at Maria in complete disbelief.

'I couldn't help it!' blurted out Maria. 'I left in such a hurry when I thought I was going to miss your performance that I didn't even think. How was I to know Lucifette would pick that seat?'

Suddenly Molly realised Sally was trying to catch their eye.

'What's up?' Sally mouthed.

'PIP-PA'S C-D!' Molly mouthed back and signalled to where Lucinda was sitting. Sally glanced across and spotted a silver CD poking out from underneath a tissue box.

Sally rolled her eyes, then jumped up and walked over to the mirror.

'L-L-Lucinda?' she stammered. Lucinda flashed her a look that would kill.

'What?' she snapped.

'Er, I just wondered if there was any hairspray I could borrow . . .' And with that, Sally leaned across Lucinda, sending the whole make-up table – including the tissue box – flying.

'SAAAAALLLLLYYYYYYY – you imbecile. Get out of my sight! NOW!' Lucinda screamed at her.

'I'm sorry, so sorry, sorry everyone . . .' As Sally bent to pick up the blusher brushes and lip glosses she caught the CD case under her foot and shot it backwards in the twins' direction. No one noticed a thing. Sally winked at the twins and continued Operation Clear-up. Molly blew her a kiss and they exited.

'That girl deserves a medal!' exclaimed Molly once they were safely out of earshot. 'Imagine the sort of onslaught she's experiencing at the hands of Lucifette now!'

'I know – she's a total honey,' agreed Maria. 'Blimey, Molly, time's getting on – they've probably gone through about ten more acts since we left the stage. We've got to get to the sound desk and get this CD swapped with the one with Pippa's voice on it. This will only work if we can replace it with this clean backing track.'

'You don't have to tell me!' protested Molly. 'I'm in on this already – remember?'

'I'm sorry – just nerves, I guess. There's just so much at stake!' Maria answered.

The angelic voices of Sofia and Charlotte echoed around the theatre. 'There's only this one and then Sally to go! Sound desk – now!'

Molly followed Maria through the foyer and into the back of the theatre. No one noticed them sneak in as everyone was facing the stage, totally mesmerised by the performance. As they climbed the small staircase to the raised platform where Mr Potts was sitting at the sound desk, Molly felt a tug at her dress.

'Pippa!' she exclaimed. Pippa motioned to her to shhhhh and disappeared beneath the curtain below them.

'What are you girls doing here?' Mr Potts fretted as he tried to remain focused on the stage.

'Sorry, Mr Potts,' Maria smiled brightly. 'I'm just so interested to see how this all works. You really are a marvel, the way you've held this whole show together. The sound is just tremendous . . . I don't know anyone who could have done a better job . . . truly!'

'Thank you, Maria,' Mr Potts said. 'I suppose it wouldn't hurt for you to stay for just a moment.'

Ha! Flattery will get you everywhere, Maria thought.

'Could I help you at all? There are only a couple of acts to go and I'd love to be able to tell my parents I'd actually helped with the technical side of the show as well as performing.'

Mr Potts looked at Maria, slightly bemused. This young lady really was quite different from the rest of the starlets. None of them had ever shown any interest in the nuts and bolts of production. Besides, there were only two acts left to go and only one needed technical help – the final act.

'Grab that folder of CDs over there. In the compartment numbered nineteen, there is one entitled Lucinda Marciano, "Life's a Dream". Pass it to me, would you, and give it a wipe on the cloth there.'

Maria couldn't believe her luck. As she grabbed the CD file and fingered through the pages she spotted number nineteen. She reached her hand down to where Molly was crouching, ready and waiting with the replacement CD. In a swift movement, hidden by the polishing cloth, Maria completed the swap and Molly ducked under the curtain to join Pippa, who was sitting there shaking with nerves.

'All done!' Molly whispered excitedly. Pippa was white.

'Oh Pippa, don't be scared – just think about Lucifette's face when you waltz up that centre aisle belting out for real the song she's pretending to sing.' Pippa turned even more ashen. Molly squeezed her hand as they heard Sally being announced on stage, reciting her 'Recipe for Perfect Friendship' poem, which she'd written herself. Sort of written herself . . . she'd taken a famous reading she'd once heard at a wedding, 'Recipe for the Perfect Wedding Cake,' and put her own slant on it.

As the audience applauded her entrance, Pippa grabbed Molly's arm. 'Where's the microphone?' she spluttered in a panic.

'Here it is!' declared Maria as she popped her head through the split in the curtain. 'I even got old Potts to show me how to put a new, full battery in. Not taking any chances now we've come this far!'

Pippa smiled and grabbed it. She suddenly felt so much better with her friends at her side. All three girls stopped to listen to Sally's poetry recital. To their delight, Sally was actually doing rather well. Her poem was simple, beautiful – and clever. She was coming to the end:

> Take 4 tablespoons of love
> A cup of loyalty
> Six grams of fun and laughter,
> A pinch of luck and a kilo of adventure.
> Mix until well blended
> And bake gently forever.

The audience exploded into applause – there were even a few whoops of appreciation.

'Oh, I'm sooooo pleased for her,' Molly hugged her knees to her chest. 'She's such a good writer, isn't she?' Pippa and Maria nodded in agreement.

'Well, my goodness me. Thank you, Sally Sudbury,' said Madame Ruby, slightly surprising herself. 'And now to our final performance of the evening. A singer with whom you are more than familiar, by the name of Lucinda Marciano.' As she mentioned Lucinda's name, she couldn't help throwing Blue Marciano a little wave from the stage. 'Lucinda will be performing "Life's a Dream", which will seem all the more exciting to you all when I tell you that this talented young lady penned this song herself!' The audience gasped.

'What the . . . ?' gasped Pippa. 'How dare she! That evil little . . .'

'Don't, Pippa! Not now – not when you're so close. You need to channel your energy into your performance. She'll get her comeuppance and it's moments away.'

Pippa lowered her eyes and, as she did so, Molly whipped out her lip gloss and held Pippa's chin up. With one swift stroke, Pippa was transformed into a goddess again. 'Go get 'em, tiger!' Molly said, and Pippa stepped into the shadows at the back of the hall.

As she heard the melody of her song, her very first song, float out across the theatre, all her fears fell away. She watched Lucinda walk onto the stage in the distance and raise the microphone to her mouth to begin. Pippa, unknown to anyone, least of all Lucinda, began to sing too. She sang out of the darkness at the back of the hall; Lucinda's lips synched to her voice in perfect unison.

Molly and Maria, who had also emerged from their hiding place, were in awe of what they were witnessing. It couldn't have been more perfectly executed.

Pippa's incredible vocal range and tone filled every nook, every cranny and every heart in the theatre as she slowly began to glide from the shadows. Her silver gown shimmered like a minnow darting through a stream as the lights picked her out. Only those in the back row of the auditorium had started to murmur, unsure whether this was part of the show or not.

If you look into my eyes
You'll see a shining light

More and more of the audience turned round but Lucinda was too engrossed in her own performance and her own shining light to notice.

Pippa continued to glide through the central aisle, looking like a mermaid emerging from the depths of the sea.

Of everything within I hid from sight
Nothing is what it seems

Suddenly Lucinda, still miming away, was aware of whispering below her. At first, and unable to see clearly into the theatre beyond her parents in the front row, she presumed the gasps and whispers were due to her captivating the audience. She continued to mouth the words . . .

So use the love and keep the faith,
And you'll find that life's a dream

. . . but before she reached the end of the final lyric, her mouth fell open in utter surprise. Pippa had reached the stage and was making her way up the steps towards her, like a silver goddess riding the crest of a wave.

Now, Story-seeker, at the risk of annoying you by interrupting at such a crucial moment, we're going to give you a couple of guesses as to what happened next. Can you guess? No? Then we'll continue.

As Pippa belted out the final few notes of her beautiful song, turning to face the delighted audience, Lucinda ran off the stage like the little coward we all knew she was.

Pippa stood tall and proud, bathing in the spotlight and applause. People were stamping their feet on the floor, whooping, whistling, clapping . . . and that was just the parents! The rest of her year had all been standing at the back of the theatre to watch Lucinda's 'performance of the night' and so had all been there, watching open-mouthed.

Madame Ruby was aghast and furious at what had just occurred on her stage, but couldn't do anything other than congratulate Pippa and draw the gala to a close.

'Hey, Ruby!' Calamity Mossback rasped as Madame Ruby made her way down to her guests. 'Who was the girl in the silver? She's got it! Send me her details in the morning. Oh, and the blonde actress. What a looker and what a talent! I wanna talk to them both.'

Madame Ruby, somewhat defeated by the realisation that Lucinda Marciano had been a complete wash-out in front of the critics and scouts, nodded solemnly in his direction and, with that, Calamity disappeared to catch his flight.

Blue and Serafina Marciano weren't far behind him, disgraced by what had unfolded. *What a disaster!*

17

A Star is Born

*P*ippa was in a whirl as she finally exited the stage into a throng of chattering girls. Molly and Maria pushed through the mass and launched themselves at her.

'Oh Pippa – you were breathtaking!' Molly cried, literally sobbing with joy.

'And what a song! Bloomin' marvellous!' echoed Maria, jumping up and down with excitement.

Pippa was unable to speak. It was more than she could have ever hoped for. She just wished her mum and Uncle Harry could have seen it – they'd have been so proud.

'We'd better get out of here quick – I've a feeling

this is going to get a bit ugly on the Lucifette front. Come and meet Mum and Dad, Pips . . . none of the Marciano clan will dare come near us so long as we're with Daddy. They're waiting for us to say goodbye in the car to avoid having to make any more small talk with Madame Ruby!'

The girls ran off up the path to where all the cars were waiting. It wasn't difficult to spot the Fitzfoster Bentley, together with the ever-obliging Eddie running around opening doors for their parents.

'Mummy . . . Daddy . . . what did you think?' Molly called.

Mrs Fitzfoster swung round, delighted to see her girls bounding towards her like puppies. 'Oh, girls. You were exquisite. Daddy and I are so proud of you. I think Madame Ruby was a little overwhelmed by the unexpected ending to the gala though. What a finale!'

'I know! Wasn't she amazing?' Molly said. 'Mum, Dad, this is Pippa Burrows.' The Fitzfosters turned their attention to the raven-haired beauty who sang like an angel.

'It's a pleasure to meet you finally, Pippa, darling. The twins have told us so much about you. And, my goodness, congratulations on your performance. What a voice!' As Mrs Fitzfoster swept Pippa up, Pippa

♥ 166 ♥

imagined she was in the arms of her own mother.

'Oh thank you soooo much. I'm so happy to meet you and Mr Fitzfoster. The girls never stop talking about you both.' Pippa was beaming with pride and admiration.

'Is that right?' Mr Fitzfoster asked. 'Well, perhaps you ought to come and stay with us at home in the Christmas holidays. I'm pretty sure you girls won't be able to last four whole weeks without seeing each other!'

'That's a wonderful idea, darling,' said Mrs Fitzfoster. 'I'll give your mother a call to fix it. Bye-bye, my darlings. I know it's the end of term and I've only to wait until tomorrow but I can't wait to have you home again. Eddie will be back to collect you at noon tomorrow – make sure you're all packed and ready. Have a lovely last night together. I'm sure you've tons to talk about.'

'Yes, and when you get home, you can tell us exactly what went on behind the scenes at tonight's show,' Mr Fitzfoster said. 'I'd bet my biggest diamond on the fact that you two twizzles were up to your necks in the plot to expose that little Marciano fraudster!' He winked at his girls, secretly proud of their high jinks. After all, how could he ever scold them – it wasn't their fault they'd inherited the infamous Fitzfoster mischief gene. He chuckled to himself as the old Bentley bounced away up the drive.

Molly, Maria and Pippa stood together in the night air as they had done that first evening of term when they'd met in their dorm, like three perfect corners that made up the triangle of friendship.

'What a night!' giggled Maria, hugging the girls in turn.

'Truly amazing!' Molly agreed.

Pippa was overcome with all the emotions of the day. From start to finish it had been a whirlwind, and now it was over, she found herself missing the adventure already.

'Don't cry, Pippa. There's plenty more fun where that came from – and just think, anyone who's anyone in showbiz got to hear your beautiful melody and lyrics tonight. You were a triumph!'

As Pippa opened her mouth to answer, Miss Hart's voice interrupted them from the path behind. 'Finally . . . there you are, girls,' she called out in relief. 'I honestly feel as though I've spent the entire evening tracking you Fitzfosters down – and as for you, Miss Burrows, there are definitely conversations to be had following today's most irregular events!'

Pippa winced and looked at Maria, but Maria, for once, had nothing to say. None of them had thought about how they'd explain Pippa's miraculous reappearance to Miss Hart!

'But all of that can wait for the moment,' Miss Hart continued, and as she stepped into the light on the gravel, the terrified trio saw that she was not alone. A tall, handsome man joined them.

'Pippa Burrows,' Miss Hart gestured to her companion. 'I would like you to meet your first *mega-fan*.' The man took Pippa's hand and shook it firmly.

'Great to meet you, Miss Burrows. I'm Emmett Fuller, Director of Universal Music,' he stated. The girls gasped in astonishment.

'I watched your performance this evening with keen interest and, with your permission, would very much like to follow your development here at L'Etoile, with a view to signing you to my record label in the future.'

'Oh my goodness . . .' Pippa stammered. 'M . . . M . . . Mr Fuller – I don't know what to say. Oh my goodness.'

Emmett Fuller grinned. He loved this bit of the job – seeing the hope twinkle in a young artist's eyes for the first time. 'Just say you're interested and that'll be it for the moment. We'll keep in touch via my dear friend Miss Hart here, who'll make sure I receive all your latest material.'

Helen Hart, who, if Molly wasn't mistaken, while nodding in agreement, also seemed to be gazing at Mr Fuller. Something's definitely going on there, she thought with glee. And what's more, the admiration seemed to be mutual. Emmett Fuller continued his conversation with Pippa, but all the while he barely took his eyes off Miss Hart.

'Thanks for everything Miss Hart, Mr Fuller,' Pippa said as she shook his hand.

'Yes, thank you!' Molly piped up. 'I'm Molly Fitzfoster, BTW. And this is my sister, Maria. We haven't been introduced. Great to meet you, Mr Fuller. Hope to again very soon. I sing too. Perhaps you'll come again to another performance?'

Maria smiled at her sister – ever graceful, but ever the opportunist for her own piece of the action.

The girls ran off back to Garland in silence, each saving their own explosion of excitement for the minute they were alone in their room. So much to discuss, and only one evening in which to do it before the Christmas holidays.

Two hours later, totally stuffed from the midnight feast to rival all midnight feasts, Maria, Molly and Pippa had exhausted every avenue of the day's events.

'Fancy Mr Fuller being there anyway!' Maria marvelled.

'If that's not fate, I don't know what is!' Molly exclaimed, attempting to brush a carpet of biscuit crumbs from her duvet.

'I know. Can't wait to hear the feedback from your performances too, though, girls. I overheard some great big American wearing massive spectacles praising "the fabulous diamond twins" as I left the theatre.'

'Are you kidding?! Big black-framed specs with ten-centimetre-thick lenses?' Pippa nodded, oblivious to the significance of what she'd just said.

'That's Calamity Mossback!' Molly exploded.

Pippa looked blank.

'THE Calamity Mossback! He's only the BIGGEST talent scout in Hollywood . . . and I don't just mean he's eaten too many doughnuts!'

Maria and Pippa collapsed into giggles. 'I can go to sleep a happy girl now,' Molly continued, stifling a yawn.

'Yes, let's all turn in, shall we?' agreed Maria. 'I don't think I can take much more excitement today. And we need to get up super-early to pack – we haven't done a thing tonight and Miss Coates'll be on the warpath first thing if she sees this mess. Looks like a bomb's gone off in a cake factory in here.'

"Night, sisters, well done on a great end to a great term. I've got enough material to keep the blog busy for the entire Christmas period! Roll on January's adventures!' Maria mused.

'I'm not sure I'll even be allowed back next term! Won't know until I've had a dressing down from Miss Hart tomorrow morning. I've got some real explaining to do – I'll be lucky not to be expelled for the stunt I've pulled today.'

'Don't worry, Pips – the Fuller Factor will smooth things over there . . . didn't you see the way they looked at each other? If he's as interested in you as he made out, it'll be in L'Etoile's interest to nurture every aspect of you – you know Madame Ruby'll never turn down an opportunity like that!' Maria grinned.

'And anyway – no matter how bad it is for you – just take comfort in the fact that Lucifette's probably been grounded for the rest of her life for embarrassing the Marcianos like that. Look, just tell Miss Hart the truth, the whole truth and nothing but the truth. She'll understand your succumbing to the temptation Lucifette laid at your feet. But for the record – 'scuse the pun – no more sneaking off for imaginary deals – got it? There aren't any shortcuts to success, just a whole lot of hard work, I'm afraid – but while we're working hard we can have some serious fun!'

Molly's eyes flashed with delight. "Night, darlings, . . . 'night, lovelies . . . 'night, dudettes . . . 'night, starlets . . .'

'M O O O O O L L L L L L L L L Y Y Y Y Y Y ! ! ! ! SHHHHHHHHHHHHH! And with that Maria launched a well-aimed slipper at her sister's head.

"Night, L'Etoilettes,' Molly whispered.

Second Term at L'Etoile

School for Stars

Holly & Kelly Willoughby

Orion
Children's Books

For girls who make the best of friends;
for girls who are inspired to achieve their dreams;
for girls who then go on to inspire others;
for girls who go on to become mothers.

Contents

Welcome back, dear Story-seeker, to this second term at L'Etoile.

We're so happy to have you with us once again, to share in the life and times of Maria, Molly, Pippa and their friends. There's so much gossip to catch up on from the Christmas holidays, and so many adventures ahead.

Are you ready? I know we are.

Love,
Holly and Kelly Willoughby x

1

L'Etoile, Sweet L'Etoile

'Molllly!' Maria shouted to her sister. 'Would you please shut that window – it's like an iceberg in here.'

Reluctantly, Molly tumbled backwards onto her bed, slamming the window shut as she fell.

'Where on earth can she be?' Molly groaned. 'I can't believe it's been nearly a whole month since we've seen our lovely Pippa. Barbados was *amazebells* and all that, but a bit last minute and I would far rather have had some fun at home with her.'

'Don't be so ungrateful, Moll,' Maria snapped. 'Do you know how many girls dream of having a holiday like the one we've just had?'

'I know, I know – I just miss her, that's all. Plus, I can't wait to give her her Christmas present.' Molly undid the bow on the little red box for about the tenth time since they'd arrived back at L'Etoile that morning, to admire the little gold star necklace engraved with a 'P'. 'She's going to absolutely love it!'

'I have to agree there, Moll. Mum really does have the best taste ever and the fact that all three of us have one, the same little L'Etoile star – each with our initial on – makes it all the more special.'

'I know! M, M and P. BFFs! It was such a shame Pips couldn't come and stay with us over Christmas but, like Mum said, hopefully this necklace will make up for us doing a disappearing act for the whole break.'

'Yo! Anyone ho-ome?' came an excited voice from the corridor. All at once, the door burst open and Pippa appeared, loaded with bags and sporting her best attempt at a posh 'hair up' do to impress Miss Molly.

'Pips!' Molly shrieked, launching herself at Pippa, knocking her backwards into the corridor. 'And you've done your hair! Very sophisticated.'

'What a welcome,' Pippa giggled, delighted her efforts hadn't gone unnoticed. 'Oh, girls. I've missed you so much! Can't wait to hear all your news.'

'What took you so long?' asked Molly. 'It's typical. I've been watching for you out of the window for the last hour – and then the second my back is turned, you show up!'

'It's like I told you, Molly – what is that saying about a watched pot never boiling?' said Maria with a grin.

Pippa and Molly both gave her their very best 'put-a-sock-in-it' look.

'So come on then, tell me . . . what's the goss?' Pippa asked, as she dragged her case onto the bed and started to unpack.

'I don't know where to begin,' Maria answered. 'Have you been keeping up with the *Yours, L'Etoilette* blog while we've been on hols?'

'Yes. I loved all your backstage blogs about the Christmas gala, but all of that was mainly school stuff – what's new with you two? I want to hear about all the latest Fitzfoster twin shenanigans since we said goodbye,' said Pippa.

'Ha! OK. But first things first – is it present time, Mimi?' Molly asked Maria desperately.

'I can't believe you've waited this long!' Maria said and then turned to Pippa. 'It's just a little something from Mum . . . erm . . . and us, to say happy Christmas and so sorry you couldn't come and stay with us. Mum felt so guilty for having to cancel our sleepover, she bought us all matching presents!'

Molly dragged Pippa over to sit on her bed and handed her the little red box with the bow, now frayed and untidy from too much tying and untying. 'Mum said it's so we can always feel close to one another, even when we are apart.'

Pippa was intrigued. 'Oh, but I haven't bought you girls anything. You shouldn't have . . .' Pippa was speechless when she saw the beautiful gold star necklace glittering up at her, with the letter 'P' inscribed in the centre. 'Oh my goodness, I love it!' she exclaimed. 'I don't think I've ever had anything so gorgeous! Thank you soooo much, girls. Quick, Molly, will you put it on for me?'

Molly was on cloud nine. In some way, getting the right gift for someone who loved it was far more fun than receiving one.

'Look, Pips – we all match now.' The twins held out their stars, both inscribed with the letter 'M', for her to see.

'I just don't know what to say. Really, thanks a million, girls. This means the world to me,' Pippa said, clutching it tightly.

'And I have a little something for you too, Pips,'

Maria said, handing over a silver DVD. 'I would have posted it to you over Christmas but didn't get a chance to download it before we went away.'

'What is it?' Pippa asked.

'It's a recording of your performance at the Christmas gala . . . so you can show your mum and Uncle Harry. Maybe it'll go some way to make up for them not being there for your big moment.'

'You're kidding me! I can't believe it. Is there anything you girlies haven't thought of?' Pippa said, turning the disc over and over in her hands. She couldn't wait to show her family – and to watch it back herself. 'Ooooh, I love you girls! What a welcome! Right, now it's my turn,' she said, rummaging around in her music bag.

'What have you lost?' Molly asked, excitedly.

'Ah ha! Here it is. Actually, this can be my Christmas present to you two,' Pippa said, sliding a CD into the player. 'While you were sunning yourselves in the Caribbean, I spent pretty much every day of the holidays in the studio with Uncle Harry, working on some new songs. And here's one I wrote for you both. It's called "Friends Forever".' She pressed play and the song burst out of the speakers.

Ooooh . . . just little old me,
Ooooh . . . then we were three.

I can't explain the feeling,
The one that leaves me reeling.

I never thought that friends could be
A second kind of family,

Ooooh . . . this ain't no short-term endeavour
Oooooh . . . you know we're friends forever . . .

The L'Etoilette trio sat bobbing their heads to the beat, grinning from ear to ear as the track continued to play.

'It's BRILLIANT!' exclaimed Maria and Molly in unison as it finished.

'I just don't know how you do it. And I love the lyrics . . .' Molly began singing at the top of her voice:

Ooooh . . . just little old me,
Ooooh . . . then we were three.

'Well, if you've picked it up that quickly – at least we know it's catchy,' Pippa beamed, loving the twins' response to all her hard work.

Knock, knock.

'Who is it?' Maria called out.

A voice boomed through the door, making them jump. 'L'ETOILETTES, WOULD YOU PLEASE KEEP THE NOISE DOWN!'

Who on earth was that? All of a sudden, Sally Sudbury thrust open the bedroom door, which hit the wall with a crash.

'SALLY!' Molly cried with delight. 'Sally, Sally – so good to see you. You look great. I love your boots – so this season! How are you?'

'Really, Molly? Thanks!' Sally said as she hugged the girls, delighted her Christmas-present footwear was a hit with the queen of fashion. 'I'm good, thanks . . . really good, as a matter of fact. Guess what?' she almost burst with excitement, 'Lucifette's not coming back to L'Etoile this term!'

'WHAT?' Maria, Molly and Pippa gasped with glee.

'Now *that* is what I call a Christmas present!' Maria joked.

'Oh, Sally – that's wonderful news. Quick – grab a fairy cake,' Molly pointed to a box of half-eaten homemade cakes on the bed. 'And tell us everything!'

Sally sat down and took a deep breath. 'You should have seen her after the gala. Boy, was I ever in the wrong place at the wrong time. Stupidly, I stayed backstage after I'd done my poem because I wanted to witness her get busted – but I didn't think far enough ahead to realise I would be the first person she'd run into as she came off stage! Honestly, she was in that much of a rage, I thought she was going to knock me out!'

'Oh, Sally, you poor thing. But by the way, your poem was simply wonderful. I didn't get a chance to say after the show. You're so clever,' Pippa said, and then realised she was changing the subject too soon. 'Sorry – do carry on – then what happened?'

'Oh, thanks so much! I'd quite forgotten that went so well with everything that's happened since,' Sally said. 'Anyway, as you can imagine, she was furious and mortified about being caught out like that in front of everyone. She was ranting and raving at such a pitch all the way to the car, I couldn't even understand what she was saying. I thought she was going to bust a vocal chord!'

'Hoped she would, you mean,' chuckled Maria.

'No such luck. It wasn't a pretty sight. As you know we didn't even go back to the dorm to get our bags. Miss Coates had to pack them and give them to the courier the next day. Mr and Mrs Marciano wouldn't hear of us going back to Garland. They couldn't bear the humiliation of having to see anyone after the show – for Lucifette – or themselves! So we were whisked straight off to London. From what I gather, the Marcianos sent a fairly large cheque for the L'Etoile Founder's Fund – to try and smooth over the embarrassment.'

'Well, they do say money talks,' said Pippa.

'Yes and Lucifette's walked!' said Maria, excitedly. 'So, is she gone for good, Sal? And, more to the point, how did you manage to get them to let you come back to L'Etoile by yourself? I should have thought Lucifette would have needed to bully you more than ever after what happened.'

'Well, that's the funniest part!' Sally said. 'That family is so arrogant, Mrs Marciano actually said as part of my punishment – for not somehow preventing the situation – I was to come back to L'Etoile on my own rather than having the honour of being by her daughter's side!'

'How lucky is that!? You're going to have the time of your life this term, Sally. You'll feel free for the first time in years I should think,' Molly said. 'And judging by the fact you're still breathing, I'm guessing they don't know you helped expose Lucifette then?'

'Oh, don't. In actual fact, for a minute I thought she might have realised that I was the only other person who knew the whole story to betray her. But luckily she thinks I'm too stupid to think for myself. She's put the whole thing down to Pippa chickening out of the fake Universal Music audition.'

'Oh, great!' said Pippa. 'So I am public enemy *numero uno*. Just tell me she's not coming back – ever!'

'Sadly, we're not that lucky. She managed to talk the Marcianos into letting her spend a term at a special acting school in LA. She's aiming to be back next term so she can sit the end-of-year exams and pass with flying colours.'

'Well, that's something to look forward to then,' said Maria sarcastically.

'What? Lucifette coming back – or end-of-year exams?' groaned Molly. 'Just listen to us!' she continued. 'Let's focus on the positives and be happy for now that we've got a whole term without her. Think how deliciously uneventful it's going to be.'

But as we know, Story-seeker, those are famous last words. Life is never quite what you expect it to be!

2

One Hundred Years of L'Etoile

'Welcome back, L'Etoilettes, to this, our first assembly of the spring term. I trust you have all had a good rest over the Christmas period and that you haven't eaten too many mince pies.' Madame Ruby raised an eyebrow at the students. Only Sally winced at the mention of mince pies. Her mum really was the best cook on the planet.

'The aim this term is for you all to build upon the strong foundations you laid before Christmas, so that you will excel in the third-term examinations.'

A muffled groan rippled round the Kodak Hall. Madame Ruby flashed a red lipstick smile at the students. Why did teachers always seem to relish the pain of exams?

'I do, however, have one piece of news, which will be exciting for you to hear. As some of you may know, Friday 28th February will mark our 100th Founder's Day and, to celebrate, I have arranged something so special, I can hardly believe it myself.'

As she looked around the hall, she noted how she had the complete attention of everyone present – just the way she liked it.

'This year we will not only have the usual key entertainment industry figure as Founder's Day speaker, but we will be honoured to have a member of the Royal Family in attendance, to present a select few students with some special Centenary Celebration Awards.'

A gasp went up from the girls, followed by excited chatter and speculation as to which royal member Madame Ruby might be talking about.

'Ladies, please, I require your attention a moment longer. I know you will all be desperate to know *who* it is, however, I have been sworn to secrecy by Buckingham Palace officials, as a matter of national security. It is essential, for the safety of the royal in question, that his or her visit be kept under wraps until the very last moment. My only assurance to you is that he, or she, is one of the high-ranking, younger members of the Royal Family.'

That was enough to send the assembled audience into orbit. There were two young princes – one, the newly married heir to the throne, and then his handsome, single, younger brother. Could L'Etoile be any more wonderful?

'After His, or Her, Royal Highness has presented the Achievement Awards to the selected students, I would like us to show our appreciation in the form of some outstanding entertainment. After all, that is our forte, L'Etoilettes! In order to decide who will perform, I would like each year to prepare and select three solo or group pieces, to present to me at the end of the month. I will then choose one winning entry from each year group, so that we may display something worthy of a royal audience.'

As the girls began to clap and cheer, Madame Ruby put up her hand for silence and continued, 'Weather permitting, our L'Etoile Centenary Founder's Day celebrations will be brought to a close with fireworks at sundown by the lake.'

And with a triumphant nod, Madame Ruby swooshed off the stage leaving her audience applauding as if they were under some kind of spell.

'I just can't believe it,' said Molly as they filed out of the hall. 'It's just TGTBT!'

'TGTBT, Molly?' asked a dumbfounded Pippa. She'd quite forgotten about Molly's habit of abbreviating words.

'Too good to be true, Pips,' Molly grinned. 'I mean, a real live, up close and personal, introduction to one of the royal princes. This truly is what dreams are made of.'

'Wouldn't be so sure it is one of the princes,' Maria pointed out. 'The Queen does have other grandchildren you know. It could easily be one of the young cousins.' But Molly wouldn't hear of it. She had every faith that Madame Ruby, for all her faults, wouldn't settle for second best. 'Well, you think what you want to think Mimi, but my money's on it being handsome Prince Henry. You just wait and see!'

'Oooh, do you really think so, Molly?' Belle Brown asked, overhearing the twins. 'Wouldn't that just be the best thing ever to happen in the history of the whole world?'

As Form 1 Alpha readied themselves for their first history class of the term, everyone was talking about Founder's Day.

'Doesn't your mum work at the palace, Amanda?' Daisy, the bassoonist, asked the dancer.

'Not any more,' Amanda answered. 'She has a new job working for the Prime Minister at Number 10, but she might still be able to find out some insider info. I'll phone her as soon as I can tonight.'

'Well so long as there's an HRH in front of their name, I'd be 'appy to meet any member of the Royal Family!' Alice, the cockney car-park-heiress joined in. 'I fink I might faint though if I actually had to speak to one.' The class giggled, all picturing lovely, but clumsy Alice attempting a wobbly courtsey.

Maria was busy scribbling down notes for her first *Yours, L'Etoilette* blog of the term. She'd made two columns – the first listed the points Madame Ruby had made that morning and the second was a to-do list of all the things she needed to research. Things like some background on the history of L'Etoile and its founder. The only thing she knew about it was that it had been founded by Madame Ruby's great-grandmother, Lola Rose D'Arcy, and that there was a huge oil portrait of her hanging above the fireplace in the entrance hall of L'Etoile.

'Good morning, girls,' said Mrs Butter – or 'old Butter-boots' as the girls had nicknamed her, as she insisted on wearing the same yellow wellies, day in day out, come rain or shine.

'Good morning, Mrs Butter(*-boots*),' the class sang sweetly back to her.

 The boots part, of course, said under their breath. Story-seeker.

'So lovely to see you all looking so refreshed after the holidays. And I see you've bought this term's study books – very well done indeed. But for our first few lessons together Madame Ruby has instructed me to teach you a short history of L'Etoile, in preparation for the Founder's Day Centenary festivities.'

Bless old Butter-boots, Pippa thought. She didn't think she'd ever met anyone so enthusiastic about life.

Maria was, of course, delighted. It was as if her mind had been read. This would save her valuable, swotting-up-in-the-library time and probably mean that she could upload her first blog of the term before lights out that night.

In fact all the girls were more attentive than usual. They were keen to know more about the event that would lead to an audience with a prince.

Old Butter-boots finished rummaging around in

her bag and pulled out some slightly dog-eared fact sheets, which she handed to Lydia, the cellist, to pass around.

'L'Etoile School for Stars, was the brainchild of Lola Rose D'Arcy,' she began, pushing her spectacles down the bridge of her nose, so that she could peer over them at her class.

'Lola Rose was a beautiful, creative, wealthy widow and mother to one little girl, Eliza Rose. After her husband passed away, she bought the L'Etoile estate from Lord Wilton in the early 1900s, with the intention of transforming it from the huge family home it had been since it was built in 1800, to the fabulous, functional school building you see today.'

Molly gazed around the room, with its high ceilings and towering sash windows, and let her imagination run wild, picturing the Wilton family going about their daily life.

'Once the proud owner of the estate, it took Lola Rose another seven years to research and find the perfect architect to take on the project of transforming it into her vision. Eventually, she learned of a man by the name of Frank Hart, who was at that time working on an important commission for the Royal Family of Monaco at one of their palaces. You might think that Lola Rose was being a bit too fussy, but from the minute she met Frank Hart and discussed her hopes and dreams for the school with him, she felt he was so in tune with her vision, it just had to be him. Sadly, this meant waiting another two years for him to finish the project in Monaco.'

'Oh, Miss. Do you think she fancied him, Miss?' asked Alice.

Mrs Butter smiled sweetly. 'It's funny you should pick up on that, Alice, dear. In actual fact, there were rumours of a romance between Frank and Lola, but nothing was ever known for sure.'

As the class continued to listen to the history of the school, how the buildings were extended and new parts like the Kodak Hall added one by one, Maria had become obsessed by the mention of a potential *love affair* between their founder and her architect. *This was it!* she thought. This was the interesting route her research could take for the blog. She, Maria wannabe-hot-journalist Fitzfoster, would uncover the truth about this couple and *Yours, L'Etoilette* would report back with the facts!

3

The Legend of the Lost Rose

'Here, listen to this, Moll,' Maria whispered from under her duvet.

'Oh, what now?' Molly grumbled, sleepily. 'Can't you put that laptop away, Mimi, it's gone ten o'clock. I'll never get up in the morning.'

Maria had been up very late finishing her first blog, entitled, *Will The Prince be Charming?* but still thought she'd do a little extra research of her own.

'I know it's late, and I'm sorry, but you know I can't sleep when I get a bee in my bonnet! I've been trawling the internet for hours now trying to find something on Frank and Lola Rose, and hadn't found a single scrap of info . . . until this,' she whispered excitedly.

'Go on then – but bring it over here. You always skip bits if you're tired. I need to read it myself,' Molly said, throwing back the covers to make space for her sister.

As Maria got up, Pippa flicked the lamp on. 'What are you two up to? Don't you dare go leaving me out of this,' she said, leaping over to Molly's bed too. 'I've been desperate for a bit of adventure all holidays!'

'Sure!' Maria said. 'The power of three is a whole lot better than the power of one. Budge up, Moll.'

The happy trio huddled together for warmth and began reading an article Maria had uncovered, by hacking into the *London Gazette* newspaper archives. The piece was written by a journalist hilariously named Luscious Tangerella and, for some reason, had been removed from normal public access.

'I'm going to have to think up a fake journalist name for myself. Maria Fitzfoster seems so dreary compared to the exotic Miss Tangerella!'

'Shush, Mimi – how can we possibly concentrate if you keep talking!' Molly snapped.

Maria smiled at her sister, and mimed fixing an imaginary padlock to her lips and throwing away the key.

'Give it here, I'll read it out.' Pippa grabbed the laptop from the squabbling twins.

THE LONDON GAZETTE

THURSDAY 10TH FEBRUARY 2000

The Lost Rose of L'Etoile, School for Stars

One could hardly deny the force of attraction between the wealthy widow, Lola Rose D'Arcy and her architect, Frank Hart. It was undeniably love at first sight, but out of respect for their departed spouses, it was a love which was always to be observed from afar. There was a mutual respect and adoration for each other, which was never to be anything more than friendship.

'How heartbreaking,' sighed Molly. 'Just like Romeo and Juliet.'

Pippa continued:

If that wasn't enough sadness for one couple, true tragedy struck when Lola Rose died unexpectedly of influenza a mere two weeks before work on her beloved L'Etoile was finished, and the school was due to open. It was no secret that Frank Hart was unable to hide the depth of his despair. It was rumoured that he had been on the verge of proposing to Lola Rose, but alas, they were never to have that their happy-ever-after ending. The story goes that Frank cleared

the estate of workers on the day of her memorial service, so that he could be alone with the memory of his lost love, and that while there, he hid one of his most precious possessions somewhere on the L'Etoile estate, as a gift to her. That night, he died in his sleep, apparently from a broken heart. The secret location of his hidden treasure has never been revealed.

As years have gone by, the story has become a legend. The Legend of the Lost Rose of L'Etoile remains, to this day, one of the most intriguing, unsolved, local mysteries. I guess the question you have to ask yourself is, do you believe in fairytales?

Molly had tears running down her cheeks. 'I can't bear it. How much sadness can one family take?'

'Two families you mean!' Maria exclaimed.

'Shhhhh!' Molly and Pippa both warned.

'Sorry,' Maria whispered. 'It's just too exciting for words. You see, there's more. I found another website, which pieces together family trees, and look what else I've discovered.'

She clicked open another article and the trio scanned Lola Rose D'Arcy's family tree and Frank Hart's family tree. As they read the names of each generation, they couldn't believe their eyes.

'It turns out,' Maria went on, 'that there was some covenant in Lola Rose's will, that should anything happen to her, the D'Arcy family would always do right by the Hart family, giving them a roof over their heads and gainful employment, for as long as L'Etoile still stood.'

'So let me get this right,' Molly breathed, incredulous. 'Frank Hart had a son called Freddie Hart who became the first in a line of 'Hart' caretakers at L'Etoile. Freddie then had a son called David Hart who had a daughter called . . .'

THE D'ARCY LINE

Lola Rose D'Arcy
m. Benjamin D'Arcy (widowed)

|

Eliza Rose D'Arcy
m. Calum Yarwood

|

Amber Rose Yarwood
m. Nicholas Rees

|

Ruby Rose Rees
(never married, but chose to keep the
D'Arcy name of her great-grandmother)

THE HART LINE

Frank Hart (widowed)
m. Sophie Brooks

|

Freddie Hart
m. Olivia Buch

|

David Hart (widowed)
m. Alexandra Battle

|

Helen Hart

(Helen's mother died in childbirth. Helen was a
good ten years or so younger than Madame Ruby.
Madame Ruby's mother, Amber Rose D'Arcy,
doted on Helen as though she was her own.)

'Helen Hart!' Pippa exclaimed, with a gasp.

'Sshhhhhh!' the twins grinned at Pippa.

'Sorry . . . Helen Hart,' she repeated in a whisper.
'Oh my goodness, it all makes sense now. So Miss
Hart literally grew up at L'Etoile, as kind of a kid
sister to Madame Ruby, with her father, David Hart,
the caretaker. Wow – no wonder Madame Ruby is
so overfamiliar with Miss Hart and treats her like a

little sister – the adopted little sister she never wanted and was forced to share her life with. And we already know Miss Hart attended L'Etoile as a student – I can't imagine how resentful Madame Ruby must have been about the caretaker's daughter getting the same education she did. As much as she goes on about the importance of scholarships, and everyone having equal opportunities to develop their talents regardless of their financial background, there is a part of her which seems to resent it. Take me, for instance; she could hardly look me in the eye at the Christmas gala, when everyone else was so kind and positive about my performance. I think she would have much preferred the Hollywood princess, Lucinda, to steal the show over little old me! In a way, I probably remind her a bit of Miss Hart.'

'And you probably remind Miss Hart of Miss Hart!' said Maria, fondly. 'I know who I'd rather have fighting my corner. She adores you, Pips.'

'Well done, Mimi! You've uncovered more facts in the last few hours than a lifetime of old Butter-boots' history lessons.'

'Ah thanks, girlies,' said Maria, blushing. 'But you're right Moll, it's really late now. We really should get some sleep or we'll never get up in the morning.'

'Totes agree!' whispered Molly. 'Our minds need to be razor sharp to solve this little mystery!'

The exhausted trio clambered back into their own beds, each hoping their dreams would be filled with ancient maps and lost treasure.

4

A Very Happy Distraction

'You know, I was thinking, Mimi, it's a good job you had to hack into the *London Gazette* archives to access that report. Can you imagine the competition we'd have trying to solve this mystery if the rest of the school could access that info easily and knew about *The Legend of the Lost Rose*?' Molly said to her sister, after almost a whole week without any new clues.

Maria was barely listening. The frustration of hitting dead end, after dead end, was killing her. She couldn't even be bothered to blog – which was creating havoc with the school rumour-mill. There were all sorts of stories going around about the student behind *Yours,*

L'Etoilette having been discovered by the teachers and expelled. But that was the least of Maria's worries. She simply had to get some answers – or at least another lead to follow up on soon.

As luck would have it, Story-seeker, a happy distraction arrived courtesy of Molly's weekly fashion delivery driver, Albie Good.

'Pips – do you want to come with me to meet Albie this afternoon?' Molly asked one Friday, not daring to ask miserable Maria.

'Love to – when's he coming?' Pippa answered.

'He's just sent me a text saying he's running a bit late – mentioned having to see a man about a dog or something. Goodness only knows what goes on in that boy's life. Anyway, he should be here just after individual music study. I'll meet you in the usual place behind the caretaker's shed halfway up the drive.'

'Perfect!' said Pippa, running off to class.

Albie Good was one of the girls' favourite people. He'd been instrumental in the rescue operation which had brought poor Pippa back from that disastrous trip to London, before Christmas.

Today was Friday, or 'Albieday' as it was now known and Albie was making his way to L'Etoile with Molly's latest fashion delivery and any odds and ends her parents wanted to send down for their daughters – usually the latest gadget or gismo Maria had begged for to assist her with her journalistic work. Molly had put in such a huge order in the January sales on *www.looklikeastar.com*, she'd been literally marking the days off her calendar waiting for Friday to arrive. It would be like Christmas all over again. She was particularly proud of the three fluffy white dressing-gowns she'd ordered for herself, Maria and Pippa, each embroidered with their names on the back so they didn't get muddled up. They'd come in so handy during those cold midnight chats when there were important issues to be discussed! She was a bit worried that Albie wouldn't be able to fit everything on the back of his bike and that he might have to save some of the stuff to bring down later. *Pleeeease don't let it be the dressing-gowns and those new Hollywood Curl hair tongs* she thought. She couldn't wait to get her paws on Pippa's crazy locks again.

Albie always looked forward to this part of the week – but today he was distracted. When he'd said he had to see a man about a dog, he hadn't been joking. He honestly had been to see a man about a dog. Or to be more specific – a beautiful, black, Labrador puppy.

As Albie waved to Molly and Pippa, and started to slow his bike, the girls spotted a little black ball of fur jump out of the sidecar and come hurtling towards them.

'Moll . . . did you see . . . what on earth . . .' Pippa almost got her question out, before Molly was leapt on by an adorable, panting pooch.

'Oh puppy dog! Hello puppy, hello!' she cried, burying her head in the soft black fur as the puppy licked her face all over. 'Oh, Albie, it's so cute!'

Albie, also panting, had thrown down his bike, ignoring the fact that his precious parcels were getting soggy on the wet lawn as he ran towards the girls.

'Sorry, Miss Moll. I just don't know what to do with her. She's so naughty!' Albie stammered, clearly furious with the little dog.

Molly covered the puppy's ears. 'Oh puppy! Don't you listen to that mean Albie Good. *Albie Bad* more like! How can you be naughty when you're so sweet?'

'Come on, Albie – spill the beans. What's with the dog?' Pippa teased.

'There's nothing dodgy about her, Miss Pippa, honest,' Albie said. 'I rescued her. One of the boys at the warehouse came in with a box full of stray puppies on Monday, saying they'd have to be put down if he couldn't find homes for them by the end of the day. I asked Dad if I could keep one at the flat, but he said no. You know I've always wanted a dog, so I was gutted. But when the end of the day came, and I saw that there were no takers for this last little pup – the runt they called her – what could I do? I couldn't very well leave her, could I?'

'No, you most certainly could not!' answered Molly.

'Not sure it was such a good idea now though,' Albie admitted, wiping his nose on his sleeve. 'Every time I stop the bike to deliver something, she slips her collar and runs into the middle of the road. And the biggest thing is that I have to hide her in the warehouse at night or Dad'll hear her barking and take her down to the RSPCA himself. The poor little thing – she must be terrified in that big, drafty building alone every night. I love her, but it's no life for her. I haven't even given her a name yet – just can't bear to get too attached.'

'Twinkle!' cried Molly.

'What?' Albie and Pippa said together . . . both horrified!

'Her name is Twinkle!' said Molly. 'And she's coming home with us, aren't you, Twinkle?' and she smothered the puppy's head in kisses again.

'Molly, we couldn't possibly. How would we keep her hidden in the dorm . . . where would we get food to feed her? It would never work. And don't even get me started on the name. No self-respecting dog wants to be called *Twinkle*!' Pippa was very nervous about the prospect of taking the puppy back to Garland.

'Don't be such a *worrying-Wilma*, Pippa. Everything you've just said is easily sorted – all except the name change, of course. Didn't you see the twinkle in her eye when she came running up to us? I'm not budging on that. She couldn't possibly be called anything else.'

'Woof!' barked Twinkle on cue, as if in complete agreement with her beautiful new mummy.

♥ 214 ♥

Molly looked at Pippa. Pippa looked at Molly. Then both girls looked at Albie.

'Are you sure?' Albie asked, secretly totally relieved to hand over puppy responsibility, after the last twenty-four hours he'd had with her.

'NWCC!' Molly exclaimed. Albie looked at Pippa for a translation.

'No worries chicken curries!' Pippa said, relieved she knew that one.

'Now what else have you got for us in that bike box – or should I say, what's soaking up all the rain from the grass?' Molly asked, oblivious to her Mollyism confusion.

And with that, the deal was done. Pippa was absolutely dreading what Maria would have to say about it, but Molly couldn't have been happier with their new little friend. What fun!

As it happened, Pippa had completely misjudged Maria's reaction. Having managed to smuggle one snuffling, excited puppy and half a dozen Albie parcels past Miss Coates into Garland, Pippa couldn't believe Maria, when they finally reached their room and told her the whole story.

'Told you, Pips,' said Molly with a cheeky grin. 'Mimi only has one weakness in life, which causes her to act with uncharacteristic abandon – animals. Dogs, cats, even mice! I honestly think she'd give her own life before she let someone kill a spider.'

She wasn't wrong, Pippa thought, watching Maria dote on Twinkle.

'Right, Molly. The first thing to accept is that we are going to need help with Twinkle,' Maria said decisively. Molly looked immediately panicked.

'I just mean, we're going to have to get some of the other Garland girls in on this little furry secret of ours. It's going to take too much sneaking about for us three to be able to do it alone.'

'She's right, Molly.' Pippa had now given up worrying and was a fully functioning member of the *Twinkle Rescue Society*. 'Shall I try and catch some of the others now before homework starts? From what I could hear when we came down the corridor earlier, Sally and Belle are definitely back in their rooms.'

'Perfect, Pips. The main thing is that everyone needs to start sneaking food out of the Ivy Room – just until we can get Albie to bring some proper dog food over next week. I just hope Mackle the Jackal isn't back to her itchy, twitchy self today. It's been bliss with her off sick with a bad back these past few weeks. I'd even go so far as to say I've started to enjoy the school food, without her beady eye all over my dining experience.'

Pippa made a face as if she was going to throw up, and ran off to tell the others the exciting news.

'I'm so pleased you agree with me, Mimi. Isn't she just the best, most beautiful dog you've ever seen?'

Twinkle looked up at the twins with huge, brown eyes and, as if she knew making a noise would get her into trouble, she gave the quietest little bark of approval and buried herself under Molly's duvet.

5

Twinkle Twinkle Little Star . . .
How I Wonder Where You Are!

Things with Twinkle went surprisingly smoothly over the next week or so. As you can imagine, the Garland girls, without Lucinda there to upset everyone, had all become very close since returning from the Christmas holidays, and with a secret like Twinkle to knit them together, it was one very happy house.

The only tricky part was taking the puppy for her last toilet trip before lights out. The girls would go in pairs, so that one could keep an eye on Twinkle, and one could keep watch. Only the night before last, Belle and Alice had so nearly been caught by Mr Potts, who was having an evening stroll, that they'd asked the twins for a week off TTD . . .

. . . to get their nerve back. The twins and Pippa tended to cover every other evening between them so it wasn't a problem. Tonight however, when it was Molly and Maria's turn on TTD, Molly, Pippa and the rest of Garland it seemed, had got caught up at some after-dinner question and answer session, with a famous British actress, which Maria had no desire to attend. As the clock struck eight-thirty, poor Twinkle was so desperate that Maria decided that just this once, she'd have to take her out alone. Better that than poor Twinkle having an accident. She was such a sensitive little thing. She might never recover from it! Maria grabbed her new fluffy dressing-gown Molly had given her, threw it over them both, and crept into the quad garden, which separated Garland from the main school.

Moments later, a very relieved Twinkle was scurrying around in the bushes while Maria anxiously hid in the shadows. Time's up, Maria thought, but as she called softly to the puppy, she realised she suddenly couldn't hear any dog sounds at all.

'Twin-kle!' she repeated more loudly, venturing

slightly further into the moonlit garden. Suddenly, naughty Twinkle popped her head out from behind the sundial in the middle of the quad. What should Maria do now? The sundial wasn't in the shadows. It was brightly lit, not only by the moon, but also by the lights of the windows on all four sides of the garden. Maria couldn't risk losing her again, so quickly, she ran over to the puppy, and scooped her up under the folds of her dressing-gown.

'So is this the kind of mischief you girls get up to when you think no one's watching?' boomed a deep voice. Both Maria and Twinkle nearly jumped out of their skins, as they swung around to see David Hart, the caretaker, behind them . . .

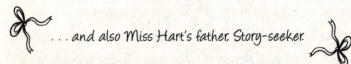

. . . and also Miss Hart's father. Story-seeker.

Maria was so shocked that she couldn't think of a single lie to tell. She was also terrified that if she spoke suddenly, the shivering, soggy dog, cosying up for warmth under her dressing-gown, might start barking and give the game away altogether.

'Who does that dog belong to?' Mr Hart asked sternly. Oh no, he's already seen her, Maria realised.

He ignored her silence and continued, 'Don't you

know it's against the school rules to keep pets on the school premises? Hand the dog over immediately – I will have to confiscate it until your parents can come to collect it. And as for your punishment, Miss . . . ?' he paused for Maria to give him her name.

'Maria Fitzfoster,' she said, slightly more in control. 'But please Mr Hart . . . please don't phone my parents. You see, the puppy isn't really even mine. We rescued her.'

Mr Hart's expression softened to a look, which Maria knew only too well, as that of a fellow animal lover, the look of unconditional, adoring love for something you've never met before, but just want to help. Twinkle's little black nose was clearly visible now. Defeated, Maria had no choice and held her up to Mr Hart whose heart melted as he smiled at the puppy licking his chin. Maria looked at Twinkle, proudly thinking *clever dog*.

'Miss Fitzfoster, while I appreciate that you seem to have the best of intentions towards this little dog, you will appreciate that now I know of its existence, you can hardly expect me to let you carry on behind the school's back and take it back to your room.'

Maria was beside herself with worry about what Molly and the rest of the girls might say if she came home without Twinkle. At the same time, everything she knew about Miss Hart, and her own instincts, were telling her that Mr Hart was a nice man. She'd already seen from his reaction to Twinkle that he wasn't going to hurt her, so she listened in silence.

'Equally, I think if we go bothering Madame Ruby at this hour, I fear she will have a total melt-down and send me straight to Animal Rescue. So what I suggest is this . . .' he paused. 'I think that I will have to take the puppy home tonight and speak to Helen . . . erm . . . Miss Hart, about what's happened . . .'

Maria's jaw dropped. How could she have got herself into this much trouble so early on in the term – and for doing something so selfless too. Life just wasn't fair.

'Don't worry, Miss Fitzfoster,' Mr Hart said, seeing Maria's expression. 'I'll try and think of something which doesn't give the game away too much about how long you've been hiding this puppy! How long exactly have you been hiding it?' he asked.

'Erm, about two weeks,' Maria answered honestly. It was too late to start making anything up now. 'What will you tell Miss Hart, sir? Please don't say we've been smuggling her into Garland. She'll go crazy at us. We don't have the best track record for not breaking the school rules. But it's always for a good reason, to help someone or other. I'm not sure we wouldn't be expelled for this one. Wouldn't you have done the same when you were our age, sir?' she asked, her big green eyes staring up at him, hopefully.

Mr Hart smiled, trying to remember what it was like to be Maria's age again. 'Yes, I probably would,' he said with a smile. 'Don't worry, I'll think of something which doesn't incriminate you too much when I speak to Miss Hart. I'll say you spotted a stray dog on school property and reported it to me. Then in the morning you can ask Miss Hart's permission to pop into the Support Staff Room to discuss what happens next – whether we advertise in the local community to see whether anyone has lost a puppy, or whether we take it to the local rescue shelter to find a new family, or whether perhaps you would like to speak to your parents about adopting it. Is that a sensible plan, Miss Fitzfoster?' Mr Hart asked, breathing out condensation like a dragon, as he spoke. It really was freezing!

'Oh thank you, Mr Hart. That's so kind of you. Yes please, that would work perfectly. Just one thing though, she didn't come from the local community, so we won't need to do that.'

Mr Hart raised an eyebrow, confused. 'I don't think I want to know any more . . .'

'No, it's nothing bad,' Maria jumped in. 'We didn't steal her or anything. A friend rescued her from certain death, but they couldn't look after her, so we said we would, but if I'm really honest . . . and my sister would kill me for saying this . . . it is all getting a bit too much for us,' she paused for a second. 'Wouldn't you like to keep her yourself, sir? She seems to like you.'

Mr Hart looked down at two more big, beseeching eyes – this time they were brown. 'Well, you are rather adorable aren't you, whatsitsname . . . what is her name anyway?' he asked.

'Twinkle,' Maria said quickly. 'Twinkle, meet Mr Hart, Mr Hart, meet Twinkle. You're going to be the best of friends I can tell!'

'Twinkle?' Mr Hart said. 'Twinkle?' he said again, incredulous at such a silly name. 'Do you think she knows her name yet, or could I change it?'

'Not a chance, sir! She loves it! Thanks so much, . . . see you in the morning, Mr Hart!' Maria cried and ran off back to Garland before he could respond, giggling all the way at the thought of such a big, burly man, calling out to a little dog named *Twinkle*.

Phew, she thought, as she approached their room.

That was a close shave. Thank goodness Mr Hart was a fellow animal lover. She didn't even want to think about what might have happened if he had wanted to report her straight to Miss Hart, or worse, Madame Ruby. Just two more obstacles to overcome, the first to comfort Molly and the rest of the girls for their loss, and the second, to talk Mr Hart into keeping Twinkle. That way everyone won and the girls would get to see her all the time.

Molly woke next morning, red-eyed from a whole night's dramatic grief at losing her little Twinkle.

'I can't bear to see you like this, Moll,' Maria said. 'I promise, promise, promise to convince Mr Hart to keep her and bring her into school. He looked as if he'd like a companion. I just hope Miss Hart believed his story last night.'

'Let's all just focus on how lucky we are that Mr Hart is on our side about this. He could have got us into a world of trouble!' Pippa said, secretly glad not to have to sneak about any more. In fact, all the Garland girls who had been in on Operation Twinkle were sad but relieved someone else was now taking care of the nightly TTD.

'But what if you can't, Mimi – what if she's already on her way to some horrible place with no children and no cuddles?' Molly cried.

'Over my dead body!' Maria answered confidently. 'Look, I'm going to go now to see Miss Hart and ask if she'd mind me speaking to Mr Hart about Twinkle's future ... I won't tell her we know her name's Twinkle though, obviously! I mustn't forget that we aren't supposed to know her at all. With any luck she'll be impressed that I want to follow up on her welfare.' Maria was interrupted by a note being pushed under the door.

Dear Maria,
 My father has brought me up to speed on the events of yesterday evening. What a good eye you must have, spotting a black dog running through the grounds in the pitch-black darkness, from your bedroom window.

'Ha, she's not silly, is she!' Pippa laughed. 'Sorry, carry on ...'

I am delighted that you followed the correct procedure in reporting the animal's existence, although it would have been easier for you to tell Miss Coates rather than venturing outside to investigate for yourself. I am only pleased Mr Hart found you when he did.

Maria winced, but if that was the only telling-off she was going to get, she'd take it!

I understand that you would like to be involved in the decision as to what happens next to the stray, so would you be kind enough to pop over to the Support Staff Room before class to discuss it with Mr Hart at 8:30 a.m. I'm not sure if you've been before – it's located next to Sister Payne's office on the ground floor.
Please ensure that you are not late for your first class of the day.
Regards,
Miss Hart

Maria breathed a sigh of relief.

'Oh that's easy – I'll take you, Mimi. I spent ages there last term after we staged our sprout-choking performance to save Betsy from Mackle the Jackal,' Molly answered.

'Ha!' Pippa exploded, remembering. 'That was so brilliant, you two. I'd forgotten that. I don't think that witch Mackle has ever been able to work out what happened that day.'

'Come on then, Molly – we've only got half an hour if we're going to make it to class for nine. Pips, are you OK to go ahead and cover for us if needs be? We'll try our best to get this sorted out in time though.'

Pippa nodded and the twins disappeared off to meet Mr Hart.

Secretly, Story-seeker, Maria had a few extra topics of conversation for Mr Hart, and hoped half an hour would give them enough time!

6

A Very Productive Meeting

The girls heard Twinkle bark as they knocked on the staff-room door, and both immediately felt relieved that she hadn't been given away overnight.

Mr Hart's kind, weathered face appeared at the door; he started as he looked at Maria and then at Molly – the almost identical girls who stood in front of him.

'Twinkle!' Molly exclaimed as the puppy leapt into her arms.

'Sorry, Mr Hart. This is Molly, my twin sister. Hope you don't mind me bringing her along. We've both invested quite a bit of time in Twinkle and Molly's been pretty devastated at the thought of losing her.'

'Of course, it's fine,' Mr Hart answered and signalled to the girls to sit down wherever they could. The office was a bit of a mess with books and paperwork all over the place.

Moments later, Maria had told the whole story of how Twinkle had come to be a refugee at L'Etoile with Molly filling in anything she missed out. Rightly or wrongly, Mr Hart couldn't help but be impressed by the way the girls had rallied round to try and provide a home for her.

'Regardless of any rules that have been broken, what is clear, and I agree with you on this front, is that Twinkle needs a proper place to live, where she isn't permanently at risk of being discovered and sent away. I've no doubt that you and the Garland girls have given her all the love in the world, but a puppy needs freedom to explore and grow into a happy, well-rounded dog. I have to admit, I'd love to give her a home in the caretaker's lodge myself . . .'

Maria, not being one to miss an opportunity, seized her moment. 'Then do it, sir,' she said.

'Yes pleeease, Mr Hart,' Molly said, at which point, Twinkle jumped from her lap to Mr Hart's. She really was a very, very, clever puppy!

'What I mean is . . .' she continued at a pace,

'Twinkle could stay with you. That would work out for everyone, wouldn't it? You get a companion – I can see you love her already, Twinkle gets a wonderful life in the countryside, and the girls and I can see her whenever we like. There isn't really any other option, Mr Hart. I can't bear the thought of her being sent to the rescue home where she'll have to fight for food, fight for a warm place to sleep and, more importantly, fight for a family to notice her and take her home. And who knows what kind of family may come along . . . you never really know what—'

'OK, OK!' David Hart exclaimed. 'I get the picture. But are you sure she doesn't already belong to anyone? Are you really sure?'

'Absolutely positive!' cried Maria, knowing she'd cracked him. 'She's all yours, Mr Hart – aren't you, Twinkle?'

'Woof!' Twinkle barked in agreement.

'Twinkle Hart,' said Molly. 'Has a lovely ring to it, don't you think?'

Maria could have kissed her sister. Molly had no idea that she had just given her the perfect opening for a conversation about the Hart family.

'You're right, Molly – she's definitely a wonderful addition to the Hart family.' She turned to Mr Hart.

'Funnily enough, we've been doing some research on the history of the school and I came across your family tree. You and Miss Hart must be so proud to be related to the great L'Etoile architect, Frank Hart.'

David Hart was completely stunned now. This little girl was so much more mature than her years. It had been a lifetime since he had discussed his ancestry with anyone and it felt good to be asked about the past.

'Why yes, I suppose we are. I thought all that had been long forgotten. My father, Freddie Hart, was also caretaker here at L'Etoile, you know, so you see the Harts have been involved with the school for generations.'

'Did your father ever mention anything to you about *The Legend of the Lost Rose of L'Etoile*?' she asked, innocently.

'Well, now Miss Fitzfoster, how the blazes do you know anything about that? I thought Madame Amber Rose – that was Madame Ruby's mother – had squashed any talk of that, as she didn't want any treasure hunters turning up here, distracting the students from their studies.'

Maria smiled at him. 'Let's just say I can be pretty resourceful when I need to be.'

'Indeed. And it seems I am already a victim of that,' he replied, looking fondly at Twinkle. 'In answer to your question, I know about the legend, of course, but I have absolutely no idea *what* the reported lost treasure is, or *where* it is. My grandfather, Frank, passed away shortly after he is said to have hidden his memorial gift to Lola Rose and, as far as I know, there's no such thing as a treasure map or anything which points to its location.'

'Did Frank leave anything – anything at all – to be passed down through the Hart generations?' Maria pushed, feeling as if she was about at the limit of what she might get away with.

Mr Hart looked thoughtful. 'There is one thing – the only thing, in fact – but it's just an old book about growing roses.'

Maria jumped up, knocking over a tower of books and an empty coffee mug as she did so. 'May we see it?' she asked, scrambling to save the mug before it hit the floor.

'I don't see why not!' he laughed. 'It's somewhere among that lot.' He nodded at the even bigger mess of books and old newspapers strewn all over the floor. Maria turned and caught sight of a large, red leather-bound book sticking out from the pile with the word 'Rose' just visible. She tugged it free.

'*How To Grow The Perfect Rose*,' she read out loud.

Molly had quite forgotten her grief at losing Twinkle as she gleefully watched her sister work her genius.

Trying to maintain a poker face to mask her excitement, Maria said, 'At the risk of pushing our luck, I don't suppose we could borrow this for a couple of days, could we? Might help with a school history project.'

'Be my guest,' said Mr Hart. 'But you won't find anything interesting in there. Just a load of gardening tips – and you don't strike me as particularly green-fingered, Miss Fitzfoster.'

'DING!' The bell sounded to signal the start of school.

'Wow, is it that time already? We'd best get going. Thanks so much for everything, Mr Hart. I know you and Twinkle are going to be very happy together.'

And with that, Maria, followed closely by Molly, planted a huge kiss on the top of Twinkle's head and ran off to class, both confident that there *must* be some kind of clue within the pages of this Hart family heirloom. It just couldn't be a coincidence – *Lola Rose, Legend of the Lost Rose, How To Grow The Perfect Rose*. There simply had to be some meaning hidden within it.

7

How to Grow the Perfect Rose

'Close the door, Moll,' said Maria after they returned from their evening homework session in the library. 'Tonight's the night that we crack this mystery wide open! Pippa, we've got something we need your help with.'

'It's not a kitten, is it?' joked Pippa. 'I'm a bit animal-rescued-out if I'm honest.'

The trio laughed. 'No, Missy P – this has most definitely got nothing to do with the living!' answered clever Maria.

'Grab those chocolate chip cookies and come see,' Molly said, having decided that she could eat junk food, solve a mystery and plait every strand of hair on her head before lights out so she'd have corkscrew curls for the morning.

'Well,' Maria paused. 'There was one more thing to come out of the re-homing Twinkle saga,' she said as she pulled the red, leather-bound book from under her pillow and passed it to Pippa – who thankfully wasn't in hair-braiding mode and had both hands free.

'A book on growing roses?' Pippa asked, confused. 'Great! Like we've got time to start another hobby. Perhaps I'll take up chess too while I'm at it.'

'CO, Pips – it's nothing like that. I thought that at first until I cottoned on to what Maria was thinking,' said Molly.

'OK, OK, I'm *chilling out*. Tell me more,' Pippa answered.

'It's the Hart family heirloom – the only thing to be passed down from generation to generation apparently. I'm convinced it holds a clue to the location of *The Lost Rose of L'Etoile*.'

'Ooooh. Have you found anything?' asked Pippa, turning the pages one by one.

'That's just it, Pips,' said Maria. 'I can't find anything mysterious about it all. I've been looking at it all week now and as far as I can tell, it does exactly what it says on the cover! I can't believe it. I was so sure it was going to be a treasure map of some kind.'

Maria was close to tears. Closer, in fact, than Pippa had ever seen her, and enough to make Molly give up on her braids. She took the book from Pippa.

'And you've been through the whole thing?' she asked.

'Every word – at least five times! I've tried looking for codes within the chapter titles, patterns with the first letter of each line, the last letter of each line, scanning for secret messages, but have come up with precisely nothing!'

Molly turned the pages – starting from the back. 'It even smells old,' she commented, wrinkling her nose and causing Maria to nearly lose her temper, both for stating the obvious, and for reading from back to front!

'And aren't the pages thick? It's like old parchment. It has to be way older than L'Etoile is. There are antique books in the library written around the time L'Etoile was built and even they are not written on paper this thick.'

Pippa felt the pages for herself. 'But wait a minute,' she said quickly. 'You're absolutely right, Molly. These back few pages are much thicker than the ones at the front of the book. Here, Maria, have a feel!'

Maria grabbed the book in astonishment. 'So they are, Pippa, so they are!' she agreed. 'How could I have missed that? I was so obsessed with looking at the words for hidden meanings, I totally didn't notice anything odd about the pages themselves.'

'What if Frank Hart stuck two pages together and the clue is on the inside?' Molly joined in, excited.

'Yes! Well done, girls! That has to be it!' cried Maria. 'An iron, we need an iron!'

'*Fashion Faye Summers*!' they shouted together and Molly ran off to Faye's room to beg, borrow or steal one, if she had to.

'Dah-dah!' she called out, as she arrived back in the doorway, moments later.

'Blimey, that was quick!' said Pippa, plugging it in.

'I know. Luckily, she was on the phone so I didn't get caught up in a conversation.'

By Maria's reckoning, the last six pages were stuck together to make three thick pages. Now that she examined the page numbers more closely, she could see that they had also been tampered with, so that they didn't appear to be incorrectly numbered.

Molly had cleared a space on the end of the bed, and was armed ready with a hot iron and a pillowcase.

'What's the pillowcase for?' asked Pippa.

'We don't want to burn the pages, do we? I say we fold the book open and slide each page into the pillowcase before ironing it – as if we were photocopying it on both sides. The material will soak up some of the steam too and prevent whatever is on the inside from smudging.'

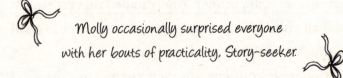

Molly occasionally surprised everyone with her bouts of practicality, Story-seeker.

The girls held their breath as she finished steaming the first page to melt the glue. As she removed the book and picked gently at the corner, the page began to split into two. Amazing! They read what was on the inner pages. Alas, nothing out of the ordinary there, just more tedious rose-growing advice.

'Maybe he had a practice run first?' Pippa suggested. The twins looked blank. 'Quickly, Molly – steam the next one.'

But as she peeled apart the next pair of pages, they were faced with the same, uninteresting print. Maria's face fell. Even Molly looked totally deflated.

'Third time lucky and all that. Don't give up now, Molly,' Pippa said.

As Molly steamed the final pages and stood the

book up to peel them apart, a single sheet of paper fluttered onto the bed.

The girls gasped. Now this was more like it!

As Pippa went to pick it up, Maria grabbed her hand. 'No, Pips. Don't touch it yet. I don't think this piece has anything to do with the rest of the book – which means there's a chance that whatever is on it could be handwritten. Let's let it dry a bit. The steam may have loosened the ink.'

'Good thinking, bat-mite,' agreed Pippa.

With the iron safely switched off, the excited trio stared at the paper on the bed for what seemed like an age.

'Now?' asked Molly desperately. Maria and Pippa both nodded.

As Molly turned the sheet over, they first noticed the crest in the corner with a heart in the centre, and immediately recognised it from the Hart family tree website. It was Frank Hart's family crest.

Remember the crest on the Hart's family tree, Story-seeker?

Maria read the words out loud:

To Whom It May Concern,

If you are reading this, I accept that the time has come for the beauty of my rose to share itself with you and perhaps with the rest of the world. In return, I ask that you make one vow: that, upon discovery of my rose, you do not keep it for yourself, but you ensure that it is returned to the last lady of my line. If you choose to ignore my wishes, you will be cursed to lead a life without love and, believe me, there is no worse punishment.

Yours,

Frank Hart

'W.O.W.,' Molly spelled out.

'Double wow!' said Pippa.

'How cool is that?' said Maria excitedly. 'And there's more. Although goodness only knows what it all means. It's just a load of numbers and symbols.'

The girls looked again at what followed Frank Hart's handwritten note and sat back in dazed confusion.

⇧ ↓ ■ 7 ⇨ □ 4 ⇧ ■ 9 ⇦ ■ 5 ⇧ ■ 2 ⇨ □ ⇧ ☄ ⊙

'I can't possibly take in any more right now. My brain just won't compute a load of gobbledygook like that – not right now anyway,' Pippa said, scratching her head. 'But if I don't try and think about it tonight I'll never get those symbols out of my mind before bed!'

'This just gets more and more unbelievable!' Molly cried as she carefully laid the note back where it had been hiding for over a century. 'Let's talk about it tomorrow. I feel a bit overwhelmed too, if I'm honest.'

Maria laughed, happy in the knowledge that this decoding challenge was right up her street and definitely something she might have some luck with solving alone. She'd already put two and two together and knew that the last lady in Frank's line had to be Miss Hart. So whatever it was he had hidden all those years ago would now belong to her. That should throw the cat among Madame Ruby's pigeons! Now all she had to do was figure out the rest.

8

Back to the Day Job

At the risk of too much talk of adventure, Story-seeker,
we would like you to cast your mind back to the main
focus of the term. Despite our heroines' obsession with
the discovery of the lost rose, we must not forget about
the looming Founder's Day Centenary celebrations.
One must not forget how much preparation a programme
of entertainment worthy of royalty requires!

While Maria's brain worked around the clock
trying to decode Frank Hart's message, the
rest of the school had their knickers in a complete
twist about the forthcoming royal visit.

The first years had asked Miss Hart if they could

take their own music session that afternoon, in order to discuss among themselves which three acts best represented their year group for Madame Ruby's auditions on Friday. Miss Hart was intrigued by the girls' team attitude. Never before had she been faced with such a close-knit year group. Usually there were several fame-hungry students in any year, ready and willing to trample on another girl to get to the top. It seemed that ever since Lucinda Marciano had decided not to return for the spring term, the first-year girls had united in their delight. Miss Hart thought what a lovely change it made, and she was happy to grant their wish.

'Right then, we've only got an hour to come up with something that will knock the other years out of the park!' exclaimed singer, Alice.

'Why don't we start by writing a list of everyone who thinks they've prepared something really special – then we'll know what we've got to choose from,' suggested the dancer, Elizabeth Jinks.

'Good idea, Jinksie,' ballet dancer Heavenly answered. 'Bags do the writing,' she continued, as she pirouetted over to the whiteboard at the front of Mozart Room 1.

'Great. Who's up first?' Elizabeth asked, looking

round the room. 'OK, I'll start us off shall I? Amanda, Heavenly and I have been working on this *Swan Lake* ballet routine since we got back. Can't get it out of my head since I saw it on Christmas Eve. We're pretty pleased with ourselves and it's just about ready, so we'd like to throw that into the mix if that's all right with the rest of you?'

'Ooooh, that sounds lovely,' said Faye. 'I can see the beautiful costumes now – we'd need a lorry-load of feathers from somewhere, though.'

Charlotte and Sofia nudged each other and both put their hands up. 'Not sure if it's what you're looking for,' Charlotte addressed the group, 'but Sofia and I have been trying to write our own opera number. We've got the melody and lyrics – we're just not convinced it sounds right sung in English.'

'Exactly!' Sofia joined her. 'I'm waiting for my father to email me the correct Italian translation so that we can try that. I think it'll be a million times better, to be honest. Everything sounds so much more dreamy in Italian.'

'Sounds lovely!' Pippa said. 'That's definitely in the mix. How clever of you both.'

Molly, who had been going out of her mind trying to think of something she'd performed before, was suddenly struck with a brainwave. 'Talking of clever, Pippa, I've just had the best idea!'

'What?' said at least ten of the girls, in unison.

'Well,' started Molly, 'when we came back after Christmas, Pippa played us a song she's written about friendship. It's fantastic! It's current, punchy, great lyrics, and has a wicked beat too.'

Pippa blushed crimson.

'What I was thinking was, that we're at our best when we come together as a group and combine all our talents. What if we only submit one piece – an orchestral/choral version of Pippa's song? It would be so strong and I bet no one's ever done it before.'

'Brilliant!' cried Sally. 'I haven't even heard it and I love it already. Beats performing a solo any day! Don't think I'm ready for that again just yet.'

Molly looked around the room to check that everyone was happy. The girls' reaction was even better than she'd hoped for. Everyone was beaming. The atmosphere had turned from glum to glee in one hit. Molly loved it when a plan came together!

'Why don't you go and get the track, Pippa, so we can get cracking. I can't wait to hear it,' said Daisy. 'What a brilliant idea!'

While Pippa scooted back to Garland to collect

her iPod, cellist Lydia started to work out whether they had a full house of instruments and players between them for the orchestra. They'd have Maria, Autumn and Betsy on keys; herself on strings, Daisy on woodwind, Lara on percussion. That left a choir of eleven: the singers, Pippa, Molly, Sofia, Charlotte, Corine and Alice – plus the dancers, Amanda, Belle and Heavenly, who all had beautiful voices too. The actresses Sally and Nancy would also join the choir and of course there'd be Faye on wardrobe! It just might work, Lydia thought excitedly.

As Pippa docked her iPod and played her song 'Friends Forever', the girls fell silent. By the first chorus, every single head in the room was bobbing to the beat and Belle was twirling around.

'What do you think?' asked Pippa, terrified, when the track ended.

'BRILLIANT!!' the girls shouted back. 'Marvellous . . . you're so clever . . . what a song!'

Pippa glowed with pride. 'Well, if you're all sure?'

'Sure?' cried Alice. 'It'll blow their socks off!'

'Pippa, I think you and Molly should take this idea to Miss Hart after class,' Lydia said. 'Tell her it's what we've all decided we really want to do, in a we-won't-take-no-for-an-answer kind of way.'

'Sure thing, jelly bean,' Molly said. 'I'm so pleased you're all on board with this idea. A good afternoon's work, girls. Pippa – will you start working with Maria, Lydia and the girls on the musical parts, and I'll figure out some harmonies with the singers. Then I think we should get together again on Thursday afternoon for a proper full group rehearsal so we're ready to perform it to Madame Ruby in the auditions on Friday.'

'Blimey, we've left ourselves quite a challenge time-wise,' Pippa said, feeling worried.

'This isn't a challenge, Pips. You know all about a challenge!' Molly whispered, reminding her about Frank Hart's coded message. She turned to the group. 'I'll burn off a load of CDs with the track on and bring them to supper, so you can each have a copy. Let's give old Mackle something else to moan about!'

The group went back to their rooms, feeling excited and proud about their decision to enter as one act. They just hoped Miss Hart and Madame Ruby would agree with them!

9

A Revealing Rehearsal

The meeting with Miss Hart went very well indeed. She seemed overjoyed that the first years had been so generous to one another, having found a way that they could all shine in a single performance. Molly and Pippa left her on the phone to Madame Ruby explaining why there would only be one first-year act performing for her on Friday.

'Rather her than me!' giggled Molly, scrabbling about in her bag for her new *Glimmerglass* lipgloss.

'Ha! I know. Knowing what we do now about Miss Hart always having lived in Madame Ruby's shadow at the school, I admire her being brave enough to try new things,' Pippa said.

After supper, the whole year took their CDs back to their dorms to listen and learn every note and lyric of 'Friends Forever' so that they'd be ready for the next day's rehearsal. Unfortunately, the Mozart Music Rooms and the Kodak Hall had already been booked by other year groups, but Miss Hart had come up with the idea of using the main L'Etoile entrance hall. It was big enough to accommodate them all – and in actual fact, if the choir stood on the steps of the grand spiral staircase with the mini-orchestra below, they'd all be able to see their conductor – which, of course, would be the lovely Pippa.

'I just don't know how I'm going to write up all the parts for the orchestra in time for tomorrow,' Pippa said, as she got into bed with a pencil and a wadge of music paper.

'I just might be the answer to all your problems!' said Maria, looking up from her laptop. 'I figured we'd be under pressure, and I've had a reply from Miss Hart agreeing to excuse us both from tomorrow morning's lessons.'

'You're joking!' Pippa exclaimed, a look of pure relief crossing her face. 'Oh, Maria, I don't know why I don't think of these things. That makes the world of difference. Thank you sooooooo much!'

'Listen, you're the artist! I'm the practical one. Together, we're dynamite!' Maria answered.

'What am I? Pedigree Chum?' said Molly, hurt at being left out.

'You, sister dear, are the icing on the cake of our little operation,' Maria answered. 'Where would we be without your belief and your beauty – not to mention your harmonies in that choir tomorrow?'

Molly smiled and the happy trio sat up working on their parts for 'Friends Forever' until the early hours.

'I truly think that this might be my favourite room at L'Etoile,' Molly exclaimed, as she helped Maria fix up the keyboard in the entrance hall.

'Just look at that sweeping staircase . . . and that big old fireplace . . . and wasn't Lola Rose beautiful,' she continued, gazing up at the portrait that hung above the fireplace. The artist had captured Lola Rose's face so perfectly. Her skin was like porcelain, warmed by the glow of the fire below. And her eyes seemed to watch over the entire room, taking in every student, teacher and guest who passed through the L'Etoile doors.

All at once, the rest of the first years filed in noisily from various different directions.

Pippa was setting up a music stand in the centre of the hall, to ensure she was perfectly positioned for both the choir snaking round the staircase, and the mini-orchestra below. Maria began handing out scores to the musicians, sincerely hoping the girls could read her and Pippa's rushed efforts.

'What, you've written all these parts since yesterday?' Betsy said, looking impressed.

'Yep! Maria and I have been up all night!' said Pippa, whose wild raven hair was even more crazy as a result.

'The only part we couldn't do, Lara, is your drums. We figured you're the best person to work that bit out,' said Maria, somewhat hopefully.

'I've already nailed it!' answered Lara, triumphantly. 'I set my alarm for five o'clock this morning, so I could get into one of the Mozart percussion rooms before they were booked. Can you believe it – the third years had filled every available rehearsal space by seven o'clock. What a bunch of saddos!'

'You won't be saying that if their contribution puts ours to shame tomorrow,' muttered Daisy, as she looked through a very complicated woodwind part, which meant her changing from the bassoon to the clarinet, and back again, halfway through the song.

'Daisy, chill out. You'll breeze through this!' said Pippa, giving her arm an affectionate squeeze. 'Do you think Maria would have written you something you couldn't do with your eyes shut?' Daisy blushed and started to practise.

Molly had arranged the singers on the stairs – tallest (Alice) at the bottom, to shortest (Belle) at the top, so that they looked more on one level.

This had given Faye the chance to see them all together and think what might work best for costumes. Should they go for a classical choir-type uniform, which would clash with the modern song they were singing? Or should they go as themselves, but with some sort of theme attached? Yes, that was it. They'd go in their own clothes, to be as up-to-date as Pippa's song, but dress head-to-toe in white – to make them look like angels on this special occasion.

'I don't know why it matters where we stand today, Moll,' said the pianist, Autumn, as Molly moved her around in the choir line for the third time. Autumn had decided to join the choir, as Maria and Betsy had the piano parts covered. Singing would make a lovely change for her. 'We'll be performing on one level on the Kodak stage for the real thing.'

'I know, I know. I just think we'll rehearse better if

we look good,' Molly answered, feeling a bit silly.

'Erm, Molly, I see what you're trying to do,' Heavenly added, 'but surely we should be standing in our vocal groups – say, altos at the bottom, and sopranos at the top?'

'Oh my goodness, how stupid do I feel now!' cried Molly. She couldn't believe she'd forgotten that bit. Well, this was her first choir. 'OK girls – just stand in your vocal groups like we did last night.'

'Right everyone,' Pippa suddenly announced. 'How do you feel about doing a quick run-through of the whole song – just to see what we're dealing with here?'

'Yep . . . yes . . . sure . . . ready . . .' came a multitude of replies.

As Pippa raised her conductor's baton – or in this case, one of Faye's knitting needles – to signify the start, Lara brought the beat down on one of two drums she was improvising with, not having been able to bring a full kit.

The singers sang their hearts out – filling the entrance hall with their beautiful, flawless harmonies. And the orchestra managed to muddle through the song, most of the girls sight-reading their parts for the first time.

By the time Pippa brought the needle down for the last beat, she and at least half a dozen other girls were shaking with excitement.

'Blimey, we're a bit good, ain't we!' Alice Parry summed it up in the only way she could.

Faye, the only spectator, was jumping up and down on the big leather armchair by the front door, whooping. 'Girls, that was flippin' amazing!' she cried, confirming what they all felt.

Maria tried to put on her best serious face. 'Calm down, girls; after all, we're a whole afternoon's worth of rehearsals away from feeling one hundred per cent about this performance – but I will say this,' and her face cracked into the biggest, cheekiest grin she could muster, 'Good luck to the rest of the school – they're gonna need it!'

Everyone exploded into claps and cheers and the rehearsals continued until the bell sounded for supper.

'Can you believe how well this afternoon went, Mimi?' Molly asked as she collected the rest of the lyric sheets. 'Everyone's worked so well together to make this happen. Pippa must be delighted with the result.'

'Yes, it's going to be fantastic. I can't wait for

Miss Hart to see it tomorrow. I reckon she'll be the proudest person in the room.' Maria paused for a moment, watching her crazy sister scurry around like a lunatic, picking things up and dropping them at the same time.

'Molly, how is it that, for someone so immaculately presented, you really are the most disorganised person at L'Etoile? Hurry up, will you – the others left ages ago and I'm starving!'

'Hang on . . . two more seconds. OK, I'm done. I just want to make sure we've left everything exactly as we found it. You might call it being slow, I call it being thorough!' Molly answered. 'If you're in that much of a hurry, why don't we go out of the front door and run round the outside to the Ivy Room. It'll be so much quicker than going through the school.'

'Good thinking,' said Maria as she unlatched the huge double doors to L'Etoile.

Just a couple of footsteps behind Maria, Molly managed to trip over the doormat, falling with a thud – closely followed by her satchel, spilling papers and various make-up brushes all over the steps.

Maria turned in alarm to see her twin lying spread-eagled, halfway out of the entrance to their grand school. Thank goodness they were alone, she thought.

'Moll,' she cried out in alarm. 'Are you all right?'

Molly started to giggle. 'I'm fine . . . it's just my ego that's bruised. Don't worry, Mimi, you're unbearable when you're hungry. You go on and I'll catch you up.'

Maria couldn't help feeling irritated by Molly's clumsiness on this occasion, and felt an eye-rolling moment was appropriate. As she raised her eyes, she noticed the huge gold L'Etoile star door knocker, glinting in the light directly above where Molly was scrabbling around. All at once, something in her mind clicked and she was reminded of Frank Hart's letter. She whipped it out from her sleeve – which was where she'd decided was the safest place to hide it. She looked again at the symbols and then up at the star. A huge, smug grin spread across her face. Thank goodness for clumsy, clever, Molly, she thought and ran off to supper.

But, Story-seeker, further investigations would have to wait.

10

One Step Closer

*M*aria decided not to distract the others with her latest discovery – not until she was absolutely sure her suspicions were correct. She decided to wait until the Friday audition performance to Madame Ruby was out of the way. Everyone was in such a panic about it, despite how wonderfully the rehearsal had gone.

As the first years sat in The Kodak Hall watching the other year groups' entries, they felt sick with nerves.

'Imagine what we're going to be like next Friday when we do this for real in front of the prince!' whispered Betsy.

'Oh, don't even say the "P" word,' groaned Lara. 'I've no idea how I'm going to keep the drum beat straight when my heart is pounding to a different one in my chest!'

Pippa was quietly taking it all in, watching the audition pieces from other year groups. She felt so proud that her friends had chosen her song as their only entry. It was at that moment that she suddenly realised she'd never felt this complete before. As an only child, she'd never known what it felt like to have such closeness with people her own age. She was, of course, immensely close to her mother and Uncle Harry, but having all these wonderful girls around her made her feel special in a different way – a way that made her want to do anything for them.

'Earth to Pippa Burrows,' said Molly.

'Eh? Sorry? Oh, Molly, I was miles away,' Pippa answered.

'I could see that, Pips. Is everything all right?' Molly asked, always concerned when anyone fell silent for more than two seconds.

'Couldn't be better!' exclaimed Pippa, giving her best friend an unexpected hug.

'And now, L'Etoilettes,' Madame Ruby's voice sounded through the speaker system. 'To our last audition piece. Can we have the one and only first-year entry . . . I must say, girls, it's quite a risk you've taken, putting all your eggs in one basket like this. I just hope it's good enough.'

'Come on, girls. Let's get this show on the road!' said Lydia, ponytail swinging as she led the way.

The first years ran over to the stage and got themselves ready. As Pippa stepped onto the conductor's podium and raised her knitting needle, she gave the group a huge grin, which they immediately returned and began to play and sing their hearts out.

Even before Maria had finished playing the last few notes, the Kodak Hall audience, including Miss Hart, were on their feet applauding. Molly was sure she'd even seen Madame Ruby make a move to stand up at one point, before she checked herself and resumed her usual poker-faced expression.

'Thank you, first years,' said Miss Hart as she collected the microphone. 'I know Madame Ruby would agree that that was a truly inspiring and cutting-edge performance, girls.'

The whole room looked immediately to Madame Ruby for her reaction. After an agonising pause, she gave the slightest nod of approval, but that was enough for a few squeals of delight from the likes of Betsy and Belle.

Madame Ruby's only addition to Miss Hart's commentary was, 'I would like to make one request – that Miss Burrows exchanges that ridiculous knitting needle for a proper conductor's baton from Mr Potts at her earliest convenience. It wouldn't do for us to be seen without the correct equipment now, would it?'

Maria could have screamed. That old bat! She just couldn't let the performance go without throwing in a negative, could she!

Miss Hart took to the microphone again. 'Thank you for all of your efforts. The final running order for the show will go up on the board outside the Ivy Room by the time you've finished supper this evening, so that you can all enjoy your weekend. You are now dismissed, girls.'

'To us!' said Pippa, standing and raising her glass of water to all the first-year girls at supper. 'We totally rock!'

'Cheers!' they all shouted back, clinking glasses and slopping water everywhere.

'Wait until you're all wearing white for the real

thing next week,' Faye said. 'It'll push the whole performance up another notch – if that's even possible. Well done, everyone. You really did leave the rest of the school standing. There wasn't anything new or exciting about any of their performances. I can see why they all played it so safe and chose classical pieces, but could they have been any more yawn-boring?'

'Thanks, Faye!' said Autumn. 'Now that's what I call a critique. Next time, why don't you do the feedback for Madame Ruby?' The girls all fell into a fit of giggles.

'GIRLS! WE'RE IN!' Charlotte and Sofia shrieked, as they came hurtling through the Ivy Room towards their classmates.

'Oh thank goodness!' cried Pippa.

'Yes, and that's not all, we're going to close the show!' Sofia explained. 'We're late as we got caught up helping Mr Potts tidy, but as a result we made it here just in time to see Miss Hart pinning the running order up outside the Ivy Room. Can you believe it? We – the first years – are the headline act! Isn't that just amazing?'

Pippa thought she might burst with happiness.

The celebrations continued until lights out. None of the girls could believe they'd beaten off competition from the senior years to get the top slot in the Founder's

Day Centenary entertainment programme. What an honour! As an extra special sneaky treat, Pippa had spread the word among their year that there would be a secret jelly-sweet midnight feast in their room, at the slightly earlier time of ten-thirty. No one would be able to stay up as late as midnight for gossip and wine gums after the euphoric day they'd had.

'You two still awake?' Maria asked Molly and Pippa when everyone had left. 'Can you believe the Monroe girls had the guts to sneak over to us tonight. It's so cool!'

'I know Pips. WATC.' said Molly.

What are the chances, Story-seeker!
Do let us know when you no longer need
Mollyism translations won't you?

'Totes well done for organising – it was an inspired idea. No idea how we managed to fit everyone in here though. It looks like a bomb has gone off. I swear there are strawberry shoelaces stuck in between the floorboards!' Pippa giggled.

'I might have something else a little inspiring for you too,' said Maria suddenly.

'Ooooh I just love a Maria late-night revelation!'

whispered Pippa excitedly, grabbing her new 'Pippa' white fluffy dressing-gown from the back of the bedroom door. 'Do tell!'

'You know our little treasure hunt? Let's just say I might have had a bit of a breakthrough with decoding Frank's message,' Maria answered triumphantly.

'How can you possibly have had time to think about that these past couple of days, with everything else that's been going on?' asked Pippa, aware that Maria had been dutifully at her side helping with the musical arrangements, ever since they'd made the decision to perform her song.

Maria smiled. 'It was thanks to Molly really,' she said.

'What?' Molly asked, confused. 'What did I do?'

Maria explained how Molly's clumsy fall after their rehearsal the other night, had led to her noticing the big gold L'Etoile star door knocker, which had in turn, reminded her of the first symbol:

'I'm ninety-nine per cent sure that the first arrow pointing up, followed by a star, is our starting point to crack this mystery. We need to get back into the entrance hall with the code, and look for other things there that might relate to the symbols.'

Pippa and Molly were shocked at Maria's discovery. She was a genius even when she wasn't trying to be!

'I keep trying to picture the hall, but just can't in enough detail to solve this without physically being there. And now that whole area is annoyingly out of bounds while the security teams move in to prepare for the royal visit . . .' Maria went on.

'Oh no!' exclaimed Molly. 'Do you mean we're going to have to wait until after Founder's Day before we can get in to have a proper look? Knowing what we know now, I don't think I can bear it.'

'My sentiments exactly,' Maria whispered. 'I've been looking online for any photos of the entrance hall, to see if we can work through the line of code but, would you believe, there isn't a single shot anywhere of the whole room. There are lots of close-ups of Lola Rose's portrait and the staircase – even the black entrance doors, with the star knocker – but not as a complete room.'

'I don't know what to say. Could this be any more frustrating?' said Pippa, exasperated.

'I know!' Molly said suddenly. 'What about asking Mr Hart if he's got any old pictures lying around?

Surely the Hart family have taken loads of pictures of the school over the years.'

'Of course!' Maria cried. 'Why didn't I think of that? I'm so stupid!'

'Don't be daft,' Pippa said. 'Sometimes you just need a fresh mind on a situation – even you, brain-box!'

'Oh girls, what would I do without you?' Maria exclaimed, as she jumped out of bed to give them both a hug.

'That's settled, then. I'm bound to see Mr Hart working in the gardens in the morning. I can ask him about it.'

'We'll come too,' said Molly. 'I'm desperate for cuddles with Twinkle-pooch!'

'What, are my cuddles not good enough for you any more, Moll?' Maria joked.

At that, Pippa launched a well-aimed pillow at the pair of them and flicked the lamp off.

11

A Weekend of Disappointment

'Where can he and Twinkle have gone to? Mr Hart never leaves L'Etoile!' Maria groaned, when there was no sign of him working anywhere in the grounds.

'I hope it's not something serious,' Molly answered. 'Don't forget, it is Saturday. Generally, people have stuff to do on Saturday.'

'Yes, me! I have something of the utmost importance to do today,' Maria said, jumping up and down on the spot.

'Calm down, Maria,' said Pippa. 'Look, let's come back later. The bus leaves to take us swimming in half an hour anyway. Mr Hart will probably be home by the time we get back. Let's try and forget about this for a couple of hours.'

But much to the girls' annoyance, Mr Hart didn't come back that evening. And he still wasn't home on Sunday afternoon.

'I just can't believe our luck,' said Maria. 'Usually I see that man pottering about the school seven days a week, fixing something or other. Isn't it just typical that the one time we actually need him, he's decided to do a disappearing act!'

'Why don't you write him a note saying you were hoping to catch him to see if he has any old photos of the school for your history project, and pop it through the lodge front door. That way you'll be sure to get his attention as soon as he's back, and he might have a look straight away,' Pippa suggested.

'Pippa's right, Mimi. Do it now, so we can go down and watch the Sunday night movie with the others. It'll do us all good to switch off for a bit. All we've done is rehearse and look for Mr Hart and Twinkle this weekend. I'm pooped!'

'All right,' Maria said, beaten. 'I'll do it now.' And no sooner had she sat down to write to Mr Hart with her request for photos, than she was out of the door, posting the envelope through the letterbox before hot-footing it back to the TV room to join the others.

Maria was absolutely exhausted as she filed out of assembly on Monday morning. It seemed that having a little knowledge about something but not being able to do anything with it was far worse than having no knowledge at all. Her imagination had kept her awake half the night – to the point where she couldn't remember which of her theories about the Lost Rose was based on reality and which she'd dreamed up. And to top it off, Madame Ruby had announced that everyone was to follow her to the lake straight after assembly, for some boring Founder's Day tree-planting ceremony, so she'd have to wait even longer!

'Come on, Mimi!' Molly said, linking her sister's arm. 'You're really not with it today, are you? Mr Hart will come and find you soon – I'm sure of it!'

Maria grunted back at her as they reached the clearing, named Founder's Copse, on the other side of the lake. Madame Ruby stood in the centre, sporting black wellington boots and armed with an enormous spade. At her feet was a pre-dug hole, with a young silver birch tree standing in it, and an enormous pile of earth, ready to be scooped and scattered onto the tree's roots.

'L'Etoilettes,' she said, 'it is with an enormous amount of pleasure that I give root to this silver birch, to commemorate one hundred years of our beloved L'Etoile. May it grow in strength like the ninety-nine other Founder's Day ceremony trees you see around you, and encourage the same growth in the success of L'Etoile for many more centuries to come.'

As the audience of staff and students clapped and watched, she moved a tiny pile of soil into the hole and then laid the spade back down on the ground.

'Is that it?' Alice whispered to the twins. She'd been looking forward to seeing Madame Ruby break a sweat, filling that big hole up with earth.

'I'm amazed she managed to lift one shovelful,' Molly giggled, 'with those matchstick arms. I reckon even Betsy's got more muscles!'

'I heard that, Moll,' Betsy whispered. 'But you're absolutely right. I reckon I'd beat old Ruby in an arm wrestle any day.'

The girls doubled up laughing. The mental image of Madame Ruby, sitting with her sleeves rolled up, face to face with little Betsy, was too funny for words.

Maria however, was, as usual, distracted by her own thoughts. As soon as they'd arrived at the lake and she'd seen the immaculate tree-planting preparations, she knew Mr Hart must be back. Who else could have set up the tree-planting ceremony so beautifully?

Suddenly, almost magically, Maria spotted Twinkle bounding through the trees around the circle of onlookers. Amazingly, no one else had seemed to notice her yet. And what was that she was carrying in her mouth?

By the time she had reached Maria, some of the other girls had spied her and were pointing and calling out. Molly, who had also just spotted her, was patting her thighs and calling, 'Come on Twinkle, here girl,' over and over again.

Twinkle, however, was a puppy on a mission and dutifully ignored everyone, including Molly! Instead, she stopped right in front of Maria, dropped a small cellophane-wrapped envelope at Maria's feet, gave a quick bark to say 'There you go, Little Miss Impatient,' and scampered back off into the bushes, as though she'd never been there.

Maria, seeing a furious-looking Miss Hart making a beeline for them, quickly stuffed the puppy-slobbered envelope under her jumper, hoping no one had noticed it, and tried to appear as confused as the rest of the girls by what had just taken place.

'Girls, was that a dog I just saw running loose around the copse?' Miss Hart asked, expectantly. 'Thank goodness Madame Ruby didn't witness that. She'd have had a heart attack.'

'Erm, Miss Hart,' Pippa said quietly. 'I think it was actually Mr Hart's new puppy, Twinkle.'

Miss Hart suddenly went very red, having quite forgotten about her father's newly acquired pet.

'Well, if you see her again, would you kindly come and find me or Mr Hart and return her? I don't want to think what will happen if she runs amok in Madame Ruby's precious rose garden!'

'We will, Miss, don't worry,' said Molly. 'Although I'm sure she's back in her bed as we speak.'

Miss Hart raised an eyebrow. There was something else afoot here. These ladies seemed just too sure of their answers about something they shouldn't really know anything about. She must remember to pay her father a visit later to see what he had to say for himself and the puppy!

'OK, ladies. Thank you for your . . . your . . . input. Off to class with you now. We all have a very big day ahead of us tomorrow. After all, it's not every day you meet a member of the Royal Family is it?'

The girls nodded and ran off to what was left of their history lesson, desperate to sneak a peek at whatever was in Twinkle's surprise delivery!

12

Founder's Eve

$\mathcal{M}$aria took a detour via the Ladies on her way to history class. She couldn't wait a second longer to see if there was anything useful in Twinkle's envelope. Even before she'd slammed the cubicle door shut and flipped down the loo seat, she'd torn the envelope open.

> *Dear Maria,*
>
> *I'm very sorry to have missed you this weekend. Twinkle and I took a wonderful trip up to the Lake District to a special forestry estate to collect Madame Ruby's silver birch, ahead of this morning's centenary planting ceremony. Madame is very specific, as you well know, but we didn't mind, as it gave Twinkle an opportunity to chase rabbits*

for a whole day!

I've had a good hunt around for any old pics of L'Etoile but, to be honest, there aren't all that many. Have you tried the Founder's book in the library? Of course you will have, silly question. Anyway, I've enclosed what I have — hope Twinkle hasn't dribbled over everything!

Keep them safe for me and I'll collect them from you when all of this royal visit madness is over.

Best wishes,

David Hart

Ps. Twinkle misses you girls!

Maria's first thought, as she opened the envelope within the envelope, was how uncannily like his grandfather's Mr Hart's handwriting was. She held her breath as she pulled out several photographs of the school. The first three were incredibly old, brown and white sepia shots of the Kodak Hall and the Mozart Rooms while they were being built. The fourth was a picture of a handsome man standing at the entrance to L'Etoile. Frank Hart, Maria whispered to herself, feeling as though this dream world where she'd tried to imagine Frank's final days, searching for a place to hide his treasure, had finally come to life. The last picture would, to most people, have appeared to be the least interesting, showing the chessboard-type black and white floor tiles being laid in the entrance hall. But to Maria, this was the jackpot! As she stared at the photograph, and then back at Frank's coded message, which she'd laid on her lap, it was as though the symbols were all jumping out at her, revealing their secret meaning.

⇑ ↓ ■ 7 ⇨ ☐ 4 ⇑ ■ 9 ⇐ ■ 5 ⇑ ■ 2 ⇨ ☐ ⇑ 🔥 ☉

Using a mixture of her memory of the room, the photograph of the floor and a little bit of her genius, Maria smiled the biggest smile you've ever seen. She, Maria Fitzfoster, in that moment, was pretty convinced she had solved *The Legend of the Lost Rose*. And tomorrow night, under the cover of darkness, she would take the girls on a real-life treasure hunt!

'Mimi – we totally lost you! I bet you sneaked off to take a look at what Mr Hart sent for us,' Molly said as Maria sat down at the desk next to her.

Maria grinned at her sister. She could never tell her a lie, but equally, there was absolutely nothing they could do about the *Lost Rose* until Founder's Day was over and all the extra bodies had gone back to London.

So Maria decided that she would keep quiet and hope the others would be too wrapped up in the imminent arrival of *Prince Charming* to notice.

'Nothing much, Moll. No obvious "X" marks the spot or anything. But never mind that now. What have I missed? Can't believe I've managed to make it here before old Butter-boots! And I thought I was late.'

'No, she was here, but she's popped out to collect some print-outs of the Founder's Day running order for us. At last I think we might be about to find out what exactly is happening tomorrow. With any luck, they might even spill the beans on our royal visitor.'

The noise level in the history room was deafening, due to the excited chatter of half a dozen very giddy girls. In fact, there wasn't a soul at L'Etoile, students, teachers or facilities staff, who wouldn't have been lying if they said they weren't just a teeny bit excited about tomorrow.

'Here you are, girls,' announced Mrs Butter as she returned to the classroom, her arms flailing with a wadge of schedules. 'Lara, dear, would you do the honours? I'm quite breathless from running up to the staff room and back. I really must remember to go back to my aerobics class,' she muttered.

As Lara handed the sheets out, Pippa began to read out loud:

ONE HUNDRED YEARS OF L'ETOILE, SCHOOL FOR THE PERFORMING ARTS

✳   ✳   ✳

9 a.m.–12 p.m. Final dress rehearsal for performances in the Kodak Hall with Miss Hart

12:30 p.m. Hot buffet lunch in the Founder's Day marquee to the rear of the Ivy Room

1:30 p.m. Seats to be taken in the Kodak Hall

2 p.m. A royal arrival marks the start of the Founder's Day ceremony

2:05 p.m. Special Founder's Day speech by Emmett Fuller, President, Universal Music

2:20 p.m. Special awards ceremony presented by HRH TBC

2:45 p.m. Special student entertainment performances:

YEAR 6 – Orchestral Arrangement of 'Clair de lune'

YEAR 5 – A Soprano Trio

YEAR 3 – A Percussion Extravaganza

YEAR 2 – A Modern Twist on a Shakespeare Classic

YEAR 4 – A Royal Dance Medley

YEAR 1 – The First-Year Choir and Orchestra Perform 'Friends Forever'

3:30 p.m. A royal send-off – students and staff to line the drive and wave off HRH TBC

4 p.m. Memory box contributions with form tutors

7 p.m. Fireworks by the lake (weather permitting)

'HRH! HIS ROYAL HIGHNESS!!!' Molly squealed with delight. 'They've slipped up there, girls. It's just got to be Prince Henry. It's got to! Oh but what can I do with my hair . . . it's got to be something he'll never have seen before!'

Maria couldn't bring herself to burst Molly's bubble and say that HRH could also mean *Her* Royal Highness.

'I hope so. I'm keeping my fingers crossed, my toes crossed and my eyes crossed!' Alice joked. 'My dad nearly fainted when I told him a prince might be paying me a visit this week!'

'And I see Mr Fuller's coming too,' Pippa said, feeling more proud than ever now that he would see the girls performing one of her songs. 'This whole thing just couldn't have worked out any better.'

'I think he's kind of handsome for an older chap,' Sofia commented, having also met Mr Fuller after the Christmas gala.

'So does Miss Hart!' giggled Maria.

'Maria! You can't say that!' Molly snapped. 'You'd be hit with the biggest legal case for slander if you were a real journalist. You have to have proof of the facts before you start spreading gossip like that.'

'Oh Molly, it's just a bit of harmless fun,' Maria

insisted. 'Anyway, you saw the way those two looked at each other at Christmas. Can you honestly say, in your heart of hearts, there's nothing going on there?'

'Really? How lovely!' Sofia said dreamily. All the girls loved Miss Hart. And it was nice for them to think of her happy and in love with such a successful man – if it was true, of course.

'Well, I just don't think we ought to be spreading rumours at the moment. Don't want to jinx it for them, do we?'

The truth is, Story-seeker, that Emmett Fuller and Helen Hart were hopelessly in love. They'd met many years ago, when Miss Hart was in her twenties, trying to make it as a singer, and Mr Fuller was a young record company talent scout. He had been besotted with her since the first time he'd heard her sing. Miss Hart had had such a promising career as a singer with Mr Fuller behind her, but when Madame Ruby's mother – Amber Rose D'Arcy, the headmistress of L'Etoile, the lady who had treated Miss Hart like a daughter, giving her all the opportunities she afforded her own daughter – fell desperately ill, Miss Hart gave up her dreams of stardom, to nurse Amber Rose until she died some years later. It is indeed a tragic tale

*of sacrifice, Story-seeker, but one that must be told if
you are to understand the love and attraction between
two people whose circumstances kept them apart when
they were young, and then reunited them later in life
in love. The Christmas gala was the first time
Miss Hart and Mr Fuller had seen each other in
over a decade. And they'd barely been out of
each other's company and thoughts since.*

'I'll soon let you know if there's anything magical going on between them,' Belle joined in. 'I'm a bit witchy about these sorts of things. I can always tell, you know.'

'Don't be daft, Belle Brown!' Amanda said. 'Next you'll be telling me Mr Potts is about to propose to old Butter-boots!'

The girls fell about laughing.

13

The Big Day Arrives

'I officially hate anyone who managed to get a good night's sleep last night,' Molly groaned, as she saw how dull her tired eyes looked in the mirror. 'Honestly, it was as if everyone was up, pacing corridors and clunking about. They should have called this place L'Etoile, School for Over-Excited Insomniacs!'

'Nothing a bit of expertly-applied make-up can't fix, I hope,' Pippa mumbled, feeling exactly the same way, as she climbed out of bed. 'Do you think it's like this the night before your wedding day?'

'Goodness, I hope not. I couldn't bear that. Remind me of this, will you, when the time comes? I'll need to hire a hypnotist or something to send me off to sleep,' Molly replied.

'Are you two girls seriously having this conversation?' Maria looked up, laughing at her daft room-mates. 'Here, what do you think of this? Just read the last bit before I upload it,' she said, reading out her Founder's Day *Yours, L'Etoilette* blog.

TO BE OR NOT TO BE: A RIGHT ROYAL SUCCESS?

. . . and so, L'Etoilettes, we go once more into the Kodak Hall with knotted stomachs and high expectations.

Will our royal visitor be the prince of our dreams? Will Madame Ruby manage to contain herself in the presence of royalty? Will the prince be over the moon with year six's 'Clair de lune'? Will year four dance their way to a knighthood? Will year three drum up a royal storm? Will the year five sopranos reach such dizzying heights that only the royal corgis can hear them? Will the year one students rock L'Etoile to the rafters with their chart-worthy pop song? Which students will be awarded the special Founder's Day prizes and get to shake the Royal Hand? All will be revealed.

Good luck girls!

Yours, L'Etoilette

'Brilliant, Mimi,' Molly said, impressed. 'You're so good with words.'

'Right, I'm going on ahead,' Maria said, closing her laptop after uploading her article. 'I want to catch Mr Potts about a conductor's baton for you, Pippa, before he gets all flustered this morning.'

'Thanks so much!' Pippa said, now rushing about to get ready and go. 'I'd forgotten about that. Mind you, if I had my way, I'd stick with Faye's knitting needle. Call me superstitious, but it seems to have brought us luck so far!'

The dress rehearsal went as smoothly as could be expected considering it was being both run and attended by a bunch of headless chickens.

Fashion Faye had sensibly banned the girls from wearing their white stage outfits to the marquee lunch. And looking back, she had been wise. *Italian Tomato Soup*, followed by *Chicken Fajita Wraps* and *Chocolate Melting Middle Puddings* weren't the easiest foods to eat without leaving a trail of something down your front. But it did mean that they had to rush their food in order to nip back and change in time to be in their seats for 1:30 p.m. No student was willing to incur the wrath of Madame Ruby — or indeed any of the tetchy staff — for being late. It would mean immediate expulsion — or, in keeping with today's royal theme, 'Off with their heads'!

'Oh no!' Sally exclaimed, as the zip broke on her only pair of white jeans. It was at times like this when she wished she had a room-mate. Not Lucinda, of course, but just someone to share the jokes and the nightmares with. And this was definitely a nightmare! She grabbed her bag and bolted over to the girls' room to see if anyone could help.

'Molly!' Sally called, seeing Pippa and the twins in the corridor, looking angelic in their outfits.

'What's up, Sal?' Molly came running towards her. 'Oh no! What terrible timing — we've got about four minutes before we're thrown in the tower for being late. Let me think.'

'Think quickly!' Maria said. She had even bigger issues with being late than Madame Ruby did.

'I've got it!' Molly said and she dragged Sally back into the bedroom. 'We'll be one minute — don't you dare go without us!' she yelled through the door.

As Maria and Pippa shifted about nervously in the corridor, Sally re-emerged, looking like a Greek goddess.

'And you did all that in a minute?!' Pippa said, astounded.

'That had better not be my bed sheet you're wearing, Sally Sudbury!' Maria raised an eyebrow.

'No time for that,' Molly giggled. 'Anyway, she'll buy you a new one. That'll teach you for being so OCD and keeping an extra one, ready-ironed!'

But Maria was already halfway to the Kodak Hall, arriving with seconds to spare.

The Hall looked and smelled beautiful. There were garlands of flowers draped from the edges of the room up to a centre display, forming a kind of summer canopy. It felt magical. Suddenly, a fanfare sounded. Ripples of excitement spread around the room. It was the royal fanfare everyone had been dying to hear, marking the arrival of HRH.

As two big security guards opened the double doors at the back of the hall, Madame Ruby entered unaccompanied and made her way down the aisle – pausing slightly when she saw poor Sally dressed in what could only be described as an ancient Greek toga.

The fanfare sounded again. More footsteps were heard. Finally, the mystery royal made an entrance. As predicted and dreamed of by the vast majority in the room, it was indeed Prince Henry, second in line to the British throne.

The girls had been so determined not to react as if they were at a concert seeing one of their favourite boy bands for the first time, but alas, the sight of this young *Prince Charming* was too much for them to control their delight.

The room erupted into applause, with whoops and foot-stamping coming from all around, as Prince Henry made his way down the red-carpeted aisle to a velvet seat next to Madame Ruby, which she'd had ordered especially for his royal bottom alone.

Next to arrive was poor Mr Fuller and half a dozen more security guards. He wasn't the most extrovert of men at the best of times, so this pomp and ceremony made him want to die with embarrassment. Thankfully, Miss Hart was waiting on the stage to welcome him as guest speaker and had saved him a seat next to her.

The girls were in heaven. In those few moments, all their hopes and dreams had come true. They were not only in the presence of royalty, but a real live prince. It was truly going to be a day to remember.

'Your Royal Highness, L'Etoilettes, Ladies, Gentlemen,' Madame Ruby began, 'I am delighted to welcome you all to this very special Centenary Founder's Day service at L'Etoile, School for Stars. I think I speak for all of us, Your Royal Highness,' she turned and courtsied to Prince Henry, 'when I say how truly humbled and honoured we are, by your kindly agreeing to be with us today to share in the wonderful memories which will doubtless be with us for another one hundred years.' Everyone clapped and cheered again.

'And to you, Mr Fuller,' Madame Ruby turned to face him. 'We are entirely grateful to you too for the time you have taken out of your busy schedule to be with us today. I know the girls will each take away some precious advice about the industry from your speech and we are all very much looking forward to hearing your stories.' As she handed him the microphone and the rest of the school applauded, the Garland girls caught a look between Mr Fuller and Miss Hart, who was blushing with pride.

The next fifteen minutes while Emmett Fuller spoke were a blur to most of his audience. His tales, advice and anecdotes were both invaluable and entertaining, but he was well aware that he was far from the main attraction. But he didn't mind being the warm-up act. It was lovely for him to have been asked by Miss Hart, and for him to be part of something that was so important to her. He ended his speech by telling the girls to work hard and, most importantly, to believe in themselves and never to give up on their dreams. This struck a chord with everyone in the room – after all, the subject of most of their dreams was sitting before them on a velvet cushion – and they once again exploded with applause. Emmett Fuller took his seat, amused that he'd managed to connect with the girls in one way at least.

'Thank you for those wonderful words of wisdom, Mr Fuller,' Madame Ruby said. 'If any of our girls ever get the opportunity to work with you and your staff at Universal Music, they will indeed be in the best hands in the industry.'

Maria and Molly both nudged Pippa so hard at the same time, she nearly leapt out of her chair.

'And now to a part of the proceedings which is special to this particular Founder's Day Celebration. His Royal Highness, Prince Henry, has kindly agreed to present a select group of students with some awards, which my staff and I feel are most deserved.'

Another ripple of excitement travelled around the room. The atmosphere was electric with anticipation.

'Your Royal Highness, would you be so kind as to do the honours?'

14

A Royal Dream Comes True

As Prince Henry stood up to take the microphone, in his beautifully tailored navy-blue suit, crisp white shirt and tie, the girls gasped. He was even more wonderful in real life – and, standing there before them on that great stage, he looked more handsome and more regal than ever.

'Ladies,' he began.

'Ladies, he called us ladies . . .' Whispers echoed around the hall.

'It is my great pleasure to be with you on such a momentous day in the history of L'Etoile, School for Stars. And may I begin by saying how simply ravishing you all look?' More gasps.

'Ooooh, if he smiles in this direction one more time, I think I might faint,' squealed Molly as quietly as she could manage.

'And so to the business of the afternoon . . . the awards. I have here five awards for five very talented ladies. I believe Miss Hart is going to assist me and ensure I give the correct lady the correct award.' Miss Hart was blushing a shade of crimson now as she stood, ready and waiting to oblige.

'He said her name, the lucky thing!' Belle whispered. 'What I'd give to hear him say mine.'

'The first award is the *Most Inspiring All-Rounder Award* and goes, I believe, to a young lady in the fifth year who has continuously delivered the best performances in dance, singing and acting since joining L'Etoile.' Prince Henry looked up. 'Would Julia Knight please come and accept this award?'

The entire school turned to where the beautiful Julia was making her way to the stage.

'Ouch, that's like a knife in my beating heart,' exclaimed Molly again.

'Molly, will you pull yourself together,' said Maria. 'You're out of control. Of course all the prizes are going to go to the older girls. They've so much more experience than us first years. Now CO – or Mr Potts will throw you out. He's already looked over this way about four times for everyone to calm down.'

Molly did as she was told. Maria was pretty scary when she needed to be.

Julia courtsied, secretly thanking her lucky stars for all the ballet training that had made this moment so perfect. As she returned to her seat, amazingly unflustered and poised, the prince was already on to the next award.

Everyone held their breath again. It was like opening a chocolate wrapper to see if you had one of five golden tickets, knowing that there were now only four left to be claimed.

'Next to the *Critic's Choice Award*. This goes to a young lady who I'm told has received the most acclaim for her work and is already on the path to fame and fortune.'

'Oh, this has to go to Cissy Love!' Pippa whispered to Sally. 'She's just had her second play picked up by the Royal Theatre Company. Bet you any money it's her.'

'Would Cissy Love please come to the stage and accept her award?' Prince Henry announced.

'Told you!' Pippa cried, as the applause went up.

'Another fifth-year girl,' Molly groaned.

Cissy was slightly less poised than Julia had been, but who could blame her, as she bounded up to the stage and shook the Prince's hand. She blushed a shade of fuchsia pink as she made her way back to her seat, her face clashing with her red curly hair. Still, very well deserved, was the general consensus on her award.

The third award, the *Royal Philharmonic Award*, went to a third-year pianist called Jessica Ivory.

'Isn't Miss Ivory just the most wonderful name for a pianist?' Betsy cooed. 'And I have to say, she's absolutely mind-blowing to watch,' she continued, as Jessica thanked His Royal Highness and attempted a rather awkward courtsey.

Oh don't be too hard on her, Story-seeker.
Courtseying doesn't come as naturally to pianists
as it does to ballet dancers.

'The second to last award,' Prince Henry announced, 'is the *Composition Award*, and I'm told it goes to a student who has an extraordinary gift for songwriting.'

The room fell silent once again. There were a number of brilliant candidates for this award, most obviously, sixth-year student, Lucy Anthony, who had just had one of her compositions selected for the latest Walt Disney movie.

After a short pause, where he had deliberately allowed the room time to guess the winner, Prince Henry continued, 'And the award goes to a young lady who holds all the promise of being one of the greatest songwriters of our time. I believe we may even be hearing one of her compositions shortly.' The first years gasped in delight.

'Would Pippa Burrows please come and collect her award?'

Pippa was frozen to her seat. Molly threw her arms around her, genuinely over the moon for her friend. 'Pippa, it's you – he's talking about you!' And she shook her friend into consciousness. 'Up you get, Pips. Go and collect your award!'

Pippa started towards the stage, her face as white as her outfit. She couldn't believe it. First, her triumph at the Christmas gala, and now this. She must be dreaming. By the time she shook the Prince's hand and tried to courtsey, she was shaking like a leaf – all the time trying to make sure she didn't forget a single detail of what was happening. As she made her way back to her seat, she was grinning from ear to ear.

'Oh girls – she's so adorable,' Sally said to the twins.

'She has no idea how good she is, does she?'

'Such a lovely quality,' Maria agreed.

Pippa sat down to all of her friends patting her on the back and shoulders. She felt as though she'd truly won the lottery.

The prince waited for the happy reaction to die down a little before continuing.

'And so, ladies, to the final award of the day. This award is dedicated to the art of theatre, and its recipient, I'm told, is one of L'Etoile's most promising actresses. To make this award seem all the more deserved, it is accompanied by an invitation from Hollywood's top talent manager, Mr Calamity Mossback, for this young lady to attend an audition to star in the next Warner Brothers film.'

The whole school gasped again, knowing what an achievement it was to even be called up for that kind of casting.

'And the award goes to . . .' – the prince held his breath for what seemed like a lifetime – . '. . . Miss Molly Fitzfoster!' he announced.

Molly, who had been gossiping with Pippa and admiring her award, heard her name and gasped so loudly she nearly choked.

Maria jumped up, pulling her sister to her feet, and

gave her the biggest cuddle. 'Molly you've done it! Did you hear that?!'

'I . . . I . . .' Molly stammered in shock.

'Never mind that now – just get your little bottom up those steps and meet your prince!' Maria giggled, ecstatically happy for her sister.

Unlike Pippa, Molly didn't need to be told twice, and skipped over to the stage to claps and cheers. Older girls she didn't even know grabbed her arm as she went, congratulating her on the Warner Brothers audition. *What audition?* she thought, wishing she hadn't been so busy chatting. But she'd been so caught up in Pippa's happiness, she never dreamed she would be dealt the same wonderful luck.

As she climbed the stairs, to her utter horror, she caught her foot on the top step, but before she could tumble forward, a strong hand reached out and caught her arm, helping her up the rest of the way. Molly looked up and glowed with delight as she saw that it was the prince himself.

'Are you quite all right, Miss Fitzfoster?' he asked, gently. 'Congratulations on this wonderful achievement. And you must be so excited about your audition. I believe the appropriate term is *break a leg* – but not before you've even accepted the award, eh?'

The audience giggled and cooed. 'He just made a joke!' 'Did you hear that? Isn't he hilarious? Who'd have thought the prince would have such a sense of humour!'

'Oh thank you, Your Royal Highness,' Molly glowed, practically doing the splits as she performed the lowest courtsey she could. 'I am overwhelmed with pride and joy to have met you and to receive this award from you.'

As she walked back to her seat in a dreamlike trance, Molly Fitzfoster was sure she had just experienced the happiest moment of her life – past, present and future. How would she ever be able to top that?

'Mollyyyyyy!' Maria shook her dumbstruck sister. 'You've got to snap out of this – or at least put this daydream on hold until after we've performed "Friends Forever". Have you forgotten you're leading the choir? The girls are relying on you!'

Something about the end of that speech jolted Molly back to reality. 'Oh, my goodness. I'd quite forgotten about our performance! I'm all of a dither!'

'You don't say,' Lydia laughed, as the first-year students stood huddled together backstage waiting for the fourth years' 'Royal Dance Medley' to finish.

'You can hardly blame her,' Belle whispered. 'I'm not sure I'd have made it to the stage if the prince had called my name out. In fact I'd probably be in the sick bay with Nurse Payne prodding me for signs of life!' The girls were relieved to laugh to release some of their nerves.

'Pippa are you all right – you look a bit traumatised too!' Sally asked.

'Don't say that. Do I? I'm fine – just feeling a bit of pressure having just won a songwriting award – and as soon as we sing "Friends Forever", everyone will be able to judge for themselves whether I deserve it or not!'

'You're a genius songwriter, Pippa! Would you do me a favour and start believing in yourself? We're going to smash it!' Maria winked.

And on that note, Madame Ruby announced the first years on stage.

'And finally, Your Royal Highness, a performance which encapsulates the very spirit of L'Etoile. The first years asked to appear as a single group choir and orchestra. They have chosen to perform a song written and composed by their own special *Composition Award* winner, Pippa Burrows. I give you "Friends Forever".'

The school fell silent as Pippa stepped on to the conductor's podium and raised her hand.

'Wait a minute . . . is that a knitting needle Pippa's conducting with, Helen?' Emmett Fuller whispered to Miss Hart.

Helen smiled and nodded. Funny, superstitious Pippa. She must have kept the knitting needle for luck, rather than exchange it for a proper baton.

The first years sang and played their hearts out for the prince, as though he was the only person in the room.

Ooooh . . . just little old me,
Ooooh . . . then we were three.

I can't explain the feeling,
The one that leaves me reeling.

I never thought that friends could be
A second kind of family,

Ooooh . . . this ain't no short-term endeavour
Oooooh . . . you know we're friends forever . . .

As Lara brought down her drumstick with a

final crash of the cymbal, the whole school – staff, students, security and prince alike, were on their feet in rapturous applause.

The girls took their bows and hugged each other, each squealing with delight at the audience reaction. What a wonderful end to a wonderful ceremony!

They watched from the stage as the prince made his way out of the Kodak Hall to where his transport was waiting.

As soon as he was out of earshot, Miss Hart grabbed the microphone. 'Quickly everyone, would you please take up your positions along the driveway to wave His Royal Highness off. Safely though, please . . . try not to run each other down!'

But the girls were beyond listening and bolted out of the hall, desperate to catch one last glimpse of their Prince Charming before he disappeared from L'Etoile – and their lives – altogether.

'Have I missed him?' Betsy asked urgently, as she squirreled her way to the front for a better view.

'Not yet,' Molly answered, applying some smuggled blusher to her cheeks. 'But I think I can see the cars starting to move away now.'

The fanfares sounded for the last time as the first, second and third security cars drove past. It was easy to make out which car the prince was in, as his hand was waving from the window.

'He's coming, he's coming,' Sofia shouted.

The girls could no longer contain their emotion as the whole driveway exploded into a tunnel of whoops and cheers as they saluted the prince in their own way.

'Goodbye, Prince Henry. See you again in my dreams,' Molly said under her breath.

15

Calling Special Agents Fitzfoster and Burrows

Sadly, the Founder's Day fireworks were later cancelled, due to the fact that, after the prince's departure, the heavens had opened and it hadn't stopped raining for a second.

Frustratingly for the girls, this meant more time in class, writing up their memories from the day. Goodness only knows how the L'Etoile teaching staff managed to bring the girls back down to earth enough to get them to focus, but they did, and every classroom was buzzing with excited chatter.

Form 1 Alpha, with two recipients of the prince's special Founder's Day awards, was on an all-time high. The girls, including form tutor Mrs Spittleforth, crowded around Molly and Pippa, as they gave blow-by-blow accounts of their individual experiences with His Royal Highness.

While Maria outwardly appeared to be involved in the gossip of the day, her mind was a million miles away. As soon as the royal motorcade had disappeared from sight, Maria had bolted back to Garland to gather the Hart letter and photographs, neither of which she'd been able to hide under her white costume. She'd almost managed a full fifteen minutes thinking time to herself, before the rest of the house invaded to change back into their uniforms. The more she looked at Frank Hart's symbols alongside the photo of the L'Etoile main entrance hall, the more convinced she was that she knew exactly where to find the treasure. The only thing still a mystery to her was what the treasure would be. She decided in that moment that she couldn't possibly wait another day to find out the truth.

Maria Fitzfoster, and her team of investigators, would solve the mysterious *Legend of the Lost Rose* that very night.

'Molly . . . Molly . . . wake up,' Maria whispered, as she gently shook her sister at midnight.

Molly snuffled in her sleep and pulled the duvet over her head.

'Molly!' Maria repeated, poking her a little more forcefully this time.

'Wha . . . whatsssup?' Molly mumbled.

'It's time to solve a mystery!' Maria answered, excitedly. 'Pleeeease, Molly. Wake up!'

'Did someone call for a secret agent?' Pippa asked, giggling.

She leapt out of bed and stood posing like an assassin, dressed from head to toe in black lycra.

'Pippa, what are you wearing?!' Molly could hardly believe her eyes.

'And how did you know to be ready?' Maria said, aghast.

'I think I know you better than you know yourself, Agent Fitzfoster!' Pippa said, with a wink. 'I noticed you twitching all afternoon and sneaking looks at those old photos and knew it was only a matter of time before you'd have to investigate properly. So I went to bed prepared!'

'Didn't you just!' Maria said, laughing at Pippa. 'And you look like a proper spy, Agent Burrows.'

'And you will too by the time I've finished with us,'

said Molly, now wide awake with the excitement of getting to dress up. She flung a pair of black leggings and matching top over to Maria.

'You two are even crazier than I thought you were. Why has everything got to be such a drama?!' Maria said, exasperated. 'Oh all right then, but let's be quick about it.'

Four minutes later, the secret trio were creeping along the corridors of Garland, making their way to the entrance hall.

'What makes you so sure you've got this right?' Molly asked Maria after they successfully sneaked past Miss Coates' bedroom door without creaking a single floorboard.

'You'll see,' Maria answered. 'Now keep quiet until we get there, and follow my torch. I've deliberately put an almost dead battery in it so the glow isn't too bright. Thought it might show up under the bedroom doors as we go past. Last thing we need is for anyone to wake up. It's hard enough keeping three of us from being discovered, let alone if we have to take any of the others with us!'

Molly and Pippa obediently followed Maria. This was no time to get into a discussion.

As the girls approached the Garland door to the

quadrant which separated them from the main school, Pippa suddenly gasped.

'Oh girls, I've just thought . . . it's easy for us to get out of Garland, we can just wedge this door slightly so we can get back in later, but won't the back doors to L'Etoile be locked?'

'Oh no, she's right, Maria. Tell me you've already thought of that?' Molly asked, hopefully.

Maria shone the torch up under her chin so the girls could see her face. 'What do you take me for, an amateur?' she answered, insulted. 'Do you honestly think I haven't thought through every step of this route? Now chill out, the pair of you, or I'll go and solve this by myself. Just think of the glory headlines in the newspapers . . . *Maria Fitzfoster, Journalist and Super-Sleuth, Solves Legend of the Lost Rose – ALONE!*'

'I was only saying!' Pippa said, a little hurt. 'Maybe you need to CO!'

Molly giggled.

Maria realised she'd got a bit carried away with herself. 'OK, I hear you. I'm sorry. I think the adrenalin is starting to flow now. You know I can't do this without you . . . either of you. I'm blinking terrified of the dark if the truth be known, but please, would you just trust me? And no more questions; we're wasting valuable mystery-solving time.'

'Agreed,' Pippa nodded. 'Lead the way, Agent F1.'

'F1?' Molly asked, confused.

'Yes – there's two of you aren't there? Maria's Agent Fitzfoster 1 and you're . . .'

'Will you come on!' said Maria, agitated, from halfway across the quad.

'Is that doorstop firmly fixed, Pips?' Molly said before they left the safety of Garland. 'I'd die if we couldn't get back in.'

Pippa gave it a good wiggle. 'Yep!' she whispered back. 'Come on, before your sister bursts a blood vessel.'

As Agent B and Agent F2 approached L'Etoile, they made out the dimly-lit silhouette of Agent F1 scrabbling around in the bushes by the doors.

'Mimi, what are you doing?' Molly asked and then shivered. 'Oh my goodness, it's absolutely freeeeezing out here!'

'It should be just over . . . ah, here we are.' Maria produced a plastic box from behind one of the tall holly bushes. Pulling a hairpin from her bun, as she'd seen in so many movies, she wiggled it in the lock and, to her relief, the lid popped open and a silver key dropped out onto the earth below.

'One back-door key!' Maria announced.

'But how did you know . . .' Pippa said, her teeth chattering as she spoke.

'Probably best not to ask, Pips. What you don't know can't hurt you! I'm not sure breaking and entering is something you want to add to your list of achievements,' Maria answered.

The truth, in fact, wasn't as exciting as the mystery . . . more a stroke of luck, Story-seeker. Back in the days of TTD, Maria had seen Mr Hart lock the back door and hide the emergency key. She just knew that little discovery would come in useful one day! The only risky bit was whether the hairpin trick would actually work in real life. She didn't mention she'd been practising on the lock on Molly's diary!

By the time the trio entered the main L'Etoile building, their hearts were beating out of their chests. Fear and excitement now consumed them as they suddenly realised the seriousness of what they were up to.

'Come on, girls,' Maria said, seeing how pale Molly and Pippa looked. 'We're so nearly there. Just one more hurdle to get past before we reach the entrance hall.'

Pippa looked alarmed.

'Oh no, I forgot about Madame Ruby!' Molly groaned.

As bad luck would have it, Madame Ruby's living quarters were located directly above the main entrance hall, in a corridor off the staircase.

'We'll just have to be quiet as mice and only talk if it's absolutely necessary,' Maria said. Molly and Pippa nodded in silence.

The girls made their way along the main corridor, passing all the empty classrooms as they went. Molly wondered how somewhere so wonderful could be so unbelievably creepy in the dark.

'As we're getting near the hall, try to follow in my footsteps,' Maria said. 'I've planned this route carefully, I know where all the creaky floorboards are. The slightest sound will echo like mad and we don't want to wake you-know-who!'

At that moment, the faint sound of music drifted down the corridor.

'I think you-know-who might still be awake!' Pippa whispered in alarm.

Maria hadn't seen that one coming! It was nearly one o'clock in the morning, for goodness' sake. What was Madame Ruby still doing up?

'Right, the way I see it, we have two choices. Either we turn back now and try again tomorrow. Or we carry on as planned, and I for one say we go for it. We've come too far to waste this chance. Come on, you two, what do you say?'

Pippa couldn't remember ever having felt so terrified. But as she looked at Molly for support, she saw she was on her own.

'Nothing ventured, nothing gained and all that,' she said as cheerfully as she could. 'I just hope Madame Ruby's not in the habit of walking the corridors at night!'

'Don't, Pippa! Oh, Mimi, she wouldn't . . . I mean, why would she?' Molly stammered, but Maria was already making her way by torchlight along the corridor towards the entrance hall.

As the girls reached the little door under the staircase, they could hear Madame Ruby's music system, clear as a bell, belting out Michael Bublé.

'You two stay here for a sec while I check the coast

is clear,' Maria ordered. She switched off her torch, as there was plenty of light flooding the hall from the corridor above.

'Is she crazy?' Pippa said, watching Maria make her way up the staircase above them. 'I thought we were avoiding that area like the plague!'

'She's got to make sure Madame Ruby's actually in her apartment, before we start creeping about. That's our only hope of making sure we don't get caught,' Molly said.

'That sister of yours must have nerves of steel!' Pippa whispered. 'My heart can beat louder than Michael Bublé can sing, that's for sure.'

'Me too, Pips! But you have to admit . . . it's exciting too. Just think what a story we'll have to tell our grandchildren. We're about to make the history books if we solve this mystery, like Maria says we're going to.'

Pippa managed a smile but, really and truthfully, she wished Agent Burrows was still safely tucked up in bed!

16

A Night to Remember

Maria had never felt so alive. As she mounted the staircase, careful to avoid every creaky patch on the way, she felt the adrenalin rush through her body. Tiptoeing down the corridor, she could see clearly that one of the apartment doors was ajar, which was why they could hear the music. Maria wondered if she dare pop her head inside to check whether Madame Ruby was there.

She took a deep breath and gently eased the door open enough to see through it. What a beautiful room, decorated wall to wall with mirrors. Suddenly, she saw the reflection of Madame Ruby, in a long cream silk dressing-gown, dancing around, with a champagne glass in one hand and a fan in the other. Maria had to smile, but didn't hang around. She'd checked what she needed to check. Now just one query remained: should she silently close the door on the way out? At least, that way, the girls might hear or see a glow if Madame Ruby re-opened it. Yes, she'd close it. And with the utmost care, Maria scurried back to the entrance hall to rejoin Molly and Pippa.

'Oh, thank goodness!' Molly squeezed Maria. 'We were starting to get a bit worried.'

'What happened? Was she up there?' Pippa asked.

'Yes, dancing around without a care in the world. I think she may have had one too many glasses of champagne! One of the doors to the corridor was open, which is where the music and light were coming from – but I've closed it now. At least we'll know if she opens the door again if we suddenly hear the music and see the lights.'

'Well done, Mimi! Now let's find this blinkin' treasure!'

Maria turned the torch back on, as they'd lost the light from upstairs when she'd closed the door.

'Let's start with our backs to the front door as if we'd just come in under the star in the porch, seeing as that's where the clues begin.'

Maria shone a light on Frank's symbols.

⇑ ⬇ ■ 7 ⇨ □ 4 ⇑ ■ 9 ⇦ ■ 5 ⇑ ■ 2 ⇨ □ ⇑ 🔥 ☉

'Right, so the first two we've done – the look up at the star part. Then I reckon the arrow down is telling us to look down.'

The girls looked down at the floor. It was just like the photo, a huge chessboard of black and white tiles.

'Are you thinking what I'm thinking?' Molly asked. 'The next symbol, the black square, is this centre black tile as you come in the L'Etoile doors under the star knocker.'

'Exactly,' Maria grinned with glee.

'So what you're saying is, using this black tile as number one, we need to count seven tiles to our right and we should reach a white tile like the next three symbols show,' Pippa said, starting to enjoy herself a little.

'Exactly,' Maria said again, loving every minute of sharing her discovery.

The girls counted seven tiles to the right and came to a white tile. Looking at the symbols again, they counted four tiles forward and stopped on a black tile.

'I can't believe this is happening!' Molly whispered.

'Don't stop now, Moll,' Maria said.

They followed the next couple of symbol instructions . . . nine tiles to the left to black. Stop. Five tiles forward to black. Stop. Two tiles to the right to white. Stop.

'Now what?' Molly asked.

'There's a forward arrow but no number to say how many – just a flame symbol – it must be the fire!' Pippa whispered back, confused.

Even Maria was quiet. She'd expected the answer to be so obvious once they'd got this far. The three girls looked at the enormous fireplace in front of them, following the beam of Maria's torch as it hovered over every inch, desperately searching for treasure. She came to rest upon Lola Rose's lovely face in the oil painting, which hung above it.

'We must be so close!' Maria whispered, puzzled. 'What is it that we're not seeing?'

Pippa and Molly had nothing to offer. They were all stumped.

'Let's go back to the symbols. We must have missed something vital and made a wrong move somewhere.'

Molly was looking back to the front entrance, counting the tiles again to check they'd counted correctly.

'One thing's for certain, we're in the right place. It's just when we got to the next forward arrow and the flame symbol that it seems to have gone wrong.'

Pippa was looking around and suddenly grabbed Frank's letter to check something. 'What if it's not a forward arrow at all . . . and what if the flame isn't the fireplace?'

'I don't follow you, Pips,' Molly said, even more confused.

'She's right!' Maria struggled to keep her delight to a whisper. 'Go on, Pippa . . . go on!'

'What if it's an arrow *up*, not *forward* – like the first arrow was to look up at the star. And the flame is for *candlelight*, not *firelight*!'

The trio stared up to the ceiling from where they were standing and there, hanging in all its glory, was the enormous crystal chandelier.

'No way. Of course . . . the chandelier! That would have been lit by candlelight at the turn of the century,' Molly answered, scanning the huge crystal light fitting above. 'What's it made of – diamonds or something?'

'Not quite, Moll,' Maria answered. 'But you're not far off. Look again.' And this time, Maria shone her torch up at the central ball, which hung slightly lower than the rest of the chandelier.

Pippa and Molly gasped.

There, twinkling inside the crystal ball, as the symbol of the dot within a circle showed, was the biggest, reddest ruby you have ever seen or imagined.

'The lost rose!' Molly whispered. 'Of course, it had to be a ruby! It's the most precious interpretation of a rose you could possibly find.'

'How romantic!' Pippa added.

'And how clever. Until now, it's been for Lola Rose's eyes only, under the gaze of her portrait,' said Maria as she held up her camera phone to take a photo of it.

CREEEAAAAK!

The girls jumped out of their skin. They hadn't realised how silent it had been until there was a sudden noise.

Without uttering a word, Maria took charge and whisked them all through the door under the staircase, along the classroom corridor, still being careful to avoid any creaky boards, and out of the back door into the courtyard. Their silence continued as Maria locked up and replaced the key. They sneaked back into the safety of their room at Garland, as quietly as they'd left it all those hours ago, still not knowing whether it was safe to speak.

'Can I breathe yet?' Molly said, breaking the silence.

'What was that noise?!' Pippa puffed. 'Do you think someone was watching us? Oh my gosh, I so hope not. That just would be the worst ending to the best day of my life.'

'I've been thinking about that all the way back and I really don't think there can have been. I think it might have been one of the floorboards re-releasing from where I trod it down earlier,' Maria answered. 'If there was someone there, I'm sure we'd have heard more than just that one little creak. There can't possibly be anyone else at L'Etoile who knows more about the location of those creaky boards than me!'

'Are you absolutely sure, Mimi?'

'What else can I say, Moll?' Maria answered. 'I can't be a hundred per cent sure, but I'm ninety-nine per cent convinced there's nothing to worry about. Anyway, never mind things that go bump in the night. Can we talk about what just happened?'

'It's like a dream,' Pippa answered.

'Are you kidding, Pips? The size of that ruby was no dream, let me tell you. It was blinding, even in the nearly-dead light of my little torch.'

'I just can't believe no one's spotted it before now,' said Molly. 'It's extraordinary. I mean, does no one ever clean that chandelier, for goodness' sake? They couldn't miss it!'

'Probably, but without Frank's letter and clues, you'd never in a million years believe that was a real ruby suspended in that crystal ball. You'd just think it was a beautiful piece of glass.'

'Well, I think it's the most beautiful thing I've ever seen. A heart at the heart of L'Etoile; joining her mistress in watching over all who pass under her.'

Maria giggled softly. 'You are sweet, Molly. But when you've finished being soppy, have a think about what we should do with this discovery. Don't forget the last part of Frank Hart's letter about returning the lost rose to its rightful owner. That's something we really need to think about.'

'OK, Mimi, but not tonight, eh? I'm practically sleep-talking right now. Let's get some kip and look at it with fresh eyes in the morning. Night, Agent Fitzfoster 1. Night, Agent Burrows,' Molly said yawning.

The trio didn't even make it out of their secret agent outfits before passing out under their duvets.

What a night of adventure, Story-seeker!

17

Making the Right Decision

The excitement of Founder's Day itself and the sleepless night of anticipation which had preceded it had left the entire school badly in need of a lie-in the following morning – and there wasn't a student at L'Etoile who needed an extra few hours in bed that morning more than our midnight-mystery-solving trio.

As the morning bell sounded at 9 a.m., Maria sat bolt upright.

'We have to tell Miss Hart!' she announced.

'Eh? What time is it?' Pippa said, scrabbling around for her watch.

'Nine o'clock. We've got an hour before classes start

this morning. I say we go via Miss Hart's office. I've been dreaming about what to do and we simply have to tell her that we've found her inheritance.'

'Oh, Mimi, are you absolutely sure that's the right way to play this? I mean, there will be a media storm around L'Etoile *and* poor Miss Hart, once this gets out,' Molly said.

'I'm with Maria on this, Moll,' said Pippa, reaching for her toothbrush. 'Besides, what if we are already not the only people who know about the existence and the location of the *Lost Rose*? I still can't shake the terrible feeling that we weren't alone last night. It would be a total nightmare for someone else to let the cat out of the bag before we've had the chance to . . . or worse, steal the jewel for themselves.'

'Maybe you're right. What have we got first this morning?' Molly asked.

'We're back in our form classes until lunchtime to finish writing up our Founder's Day memory reports,' answered Maria.

'I tell you what then, why don't I go straight to class and explain to Miss Spittleforth that you two have a meeting with Miss Hart this morning. Don't want to raise any suspicions by all three of us not turning up without any explanation,' Pippa offered.

'I think that's a very sensible and unselfish idea, Pips – if you don't mind not being there at the meeting.'

'Not at all. This is your mystery and your big moment anyway, Maria. You've done all the legwork on this one. Go for it, Fitzfosters!'

'Come in!' Miss Hart called, as the twins knocked on her office door shortly before 10 o'clock.

'Good morning, ladies,' she said as Molly and Maria trotted in. 'And many congratulations, Molly, on your wonderful award yesterday. You must be simply beside yourself with excitement for your film audition.'

Molly had to think back for a second. With everything that had gone on since Prince Henry had left L'Etoile, she'd quite forgotten about her forthcoming audition for Warner Brothers.

'Thank you so much, Miss. Yes, I'm absolutely over the moon, as you say.' Miss Hart motioned to the girls to take a seat. 'But actually, Maria and I have come to see you for an entirely different reason this morning.'

'Oh yes?' Miss Hart looked suspiciously at the girls. *What could they possibly be up to now? There simply hadn't been time for mischief around the royal visit. Or had there?*

'Mimi, you start and I'll fill in anything you miss out. You're so much better with the facts than I am. I'll just turn the whole story into a melodrama.'

Sensing that the girls had something serious to tell her, Miss Hart came round from her side of the desk and sat down on the sofa opposite them to relax the atmosphere.

No sooner had Maria taken a breath, than the whole story came tumbling out. She left nothing out, starting from her hacking into Luscious Tangerella's online article for the *London Gazette* about Frank and Lola's relationship and *The Legend of the Lost Rose*; to Twinkle's arrival at L'Etoile as Garland's secret housemate; to getting caught by Miss Hart's father and him agreeing to look after Twinkle; to their discovery of Frank Hart's letter concealed within the pages of her father's book; to their decoding of the clues; to their ultimate discovery of the location of Frank's hidden treasure.

By the end, Miss Hart was completely speechless. What alarmed her most about the whole story was that she clearly had no idea what these girls were capable of. There was a part of her that was secretly very impressed, but she remained in turmoil about how to handle the situation, given that some fairly fundamental L'Etoile rules had been broken. She was the deputy head after all, and had a duty to maintain some sort of discipline at the school. But then, how could she scold them when they'd been so unbelievably clever? Particularly, as the whole adventure was so personal to her and the Hart family. This was going to be a tough one.

As Miss Hart went to speak, Maria jumped in quickly. 'And the last thing we need to tell you – sorry for interrupting, Miss – which is in fact our whole reason for coming to you this morning, is that it's all yours, Miss Hart,' Maria said, a look of relief spreading across her face.

This stopped Miss Hart in her tracks, and whatever she had apparently been about to say went quite out of her mind. 'I'm sorry,' she said, confused. 'I don't follow you. What could this all possibly have to do with me?' she asked, innocently as a child.

'Mimi, why don't you show her Frank's letter so Miss Hart can see for herself?' Molly suggested.

Maria pulled the letter out from her sleeve for the last time, and held it out for Miss Hart. As she read, everything became clear.

To Whom It May Concern,

If you are reading this, I accept that the time has come for the beauty of my rose to share itself with you and perhaps with the rest of the world. In return, I ask that you make one vow: that, upon discovery of my rose, you do not keep it for yourself, but you ensure that it is returned to the last lady of my line. If you choose to ignore my wishes, you will be cursed to lead a life without love and, believe me, there is no worse punishment.

Yours,

Frank Hart

'Well, my goodness me,' Miss Hart muttered, turning the single page over in her hands. 'I see now what you mean.'

Then her attention was drawn to the symbols the girls had spoken of:-

⇪ ⬇ ■ 7 ⇨ ☐ 4 ⇪ ■ 9 ⇦ ■ 5 ⇪ ■ 2 ⇨ ☐ ⇪ 🔥 ☉

'However did you know where to begin with solving these clues?' she asked, more dumbfounded than ever.

Molly and Maria grinned at each other.

'Let's just say that without Molly's natural talent for

tripping up wherever she goes, we wouldn't have had the foggiest idea where to start,' Maria said, as Molly first looked horrified and then saw the funny side of that comment, picturing herself lying spread-eagled across the threshold to L'Etoile.

'It all starts below the L'Etoile star knocker on the main entrance doors,' said Maria. 'Actually, Miss Hart,' she continued in earnest. 'If you have time now, it really would be better to show you, clue by clue. It's so exciting. May we?'

Moments later, the twins were walking Miss Hart through each symbol in the main entrance hall. While Maria had spilled the beans on just about everything that had led the girls to solving the *Legend of the Lost Rose*, she'd not actually given the exact location of the stone away – nor had she said it was a ruby. They'd just said they'd found Frank Hart's precious hidden treasure for Lola Rose and that it now rightfully belonged to Miss Hart. She was in for the surprise of her life!

'And this is the only point we got wrong to begin with,' Maria explained as they came to a halt beneath the chandelier.

'Yes,' Molly jumped in. 'We presumed that this

arrow, followed by a flame,   ⇑ 🔥 ⊙   meant move or look *forwards* like the previous arrows did – the flame symbol representing the fireplace . . .'

'. . . but what it actually meant,' Maria jumped back in, determined to finish the story, '. . . was to look *upwards*, not *forwards* . . . at the chandelier. Luckily we realised there would have been real candles providing the lighting when Frank wrote these clues, not electric bulbs as there are now.'

'Yes, I see. How very clever of you,' said Miss Hart in admiration.

'Now, are you ready?' Maria asked Miss Hart and Molly. They both nodded.

'3-2-1 – look up!' she commanded, triumphantly. At which point both she and Molly gasped in horror.

'I-i-i-i-it's gone, Mimi!' Molly stammered.

Maria was stunned into silence.

'Oh, Miss Hart, it was there, we absolutely promise. We haven't led you on a wild-goose chase, honest!' Molly cried in desperation.

'There must have been someone here watching last night, just as we feared,' Maria said. 'But how could they have stolen it?'

'Now slow down, girls. What exactly is it that's missing?' Miss Hart asked.

But Molly was beside herself. 'Oh, Mimi, I feel awful. Lola Rose's treasure has been there for over a century, keeping watch over L'Etoile, and now it's been taken, all because of our stupid curiosity!'

'Maria, are you absolutely sure about all this?' Miss Hart asked. 'I mean, you say you only discovered all of this by torchlight last night. You said yourself the battery was nearly dead. The mind can play tricks as you well know – and never more so than in the dark.'

Maria was mortified that Miss Hart might doubt their story. How could this have happened – and so quickly too? It was only a few hours ago that they had stood there in very different circumstances, basking in the light of the glittering red stone.

'But we all saw it!' she cried. 'All three of our minds couldn't have played the same trick. It's just impossible.'

Molly suddenly came back to life. 'Mimi, your phone! You took a picture on your phone . . . just before we were scared away by that noise on the stairs . . . remember?!'

Maria grinned. She'd totally forgotten she'd done that. Quickly, she pulled out her mobile – ignoring a faint frown from Miss Hart for having a phone in her possession during school hours.

'Thank goodness! Here!' she announced and thrust the phone into Miss Hart's hand.

And sure enough, Miss Hart saw a red glow coming from the central crystal ball, a central ball that was no longer hanging from the chandelier.

'A ruby?' she gasped, looking at the twins in astonishment.

'The biggest ruby you've ever seen Miss Hart. Red as the reddest rose, from Frank to his Lola Rose,' Molly confirmed, dreamily.

'How unbelievably beautiful,' Miss Hart muttered, her eyes darting between the photograph and then the empty space directly above.

'UNDENIABLY BEAUTIFUL INDEED,' came a voice from the shadows. Miss Hart and the girls swung round so fast that the phone clattered to the floor.

'Madame Ruby . . .' Miss Hart began, feeling like a naughty student herself. 'Maria and Molly Fitzfoster have just been telling me the most unbelievable . . .'

'Silence!' Madame Ruby snapped. And the trio shuddered.

'I am well aware what these thieving little monsters

have been up to – creeping around in the dead of night, attempting to steal my property. I just didn't expect the third criminal to be you, Helen, dear.'

'But—' Maria tried to explain.

'I said, silence!' Madame Ruby snapped again.

'Now that's quite enough!' Helen Hart exploded, much to the twins' surprise. She had always been so timid around the dominant headmistress. Even Madame Ruby looked as if she had been physically punched by Miss Hart's unexpected response.

'I beg your pardon, Miss Hart?' the headmistress said, in a controlled voice.

'I . . . I said that's enough,' Miss Hart continued slightly less confidently. 'That is, it would be far preferable to continue this discussion in your office, without the girls being present, if you don't mind, Madame Ruby. I'm not sure what you are suggesting with regard to my being here with these ladies but, I can assure you, I heard this incredible tale for the first time this morning.'

'It's true . . .' Molly said, plucking up the courage to defend Miss Hart, but she was shot down with a glare.

'Miss Hart had nothing to do with us being here last night,' Maria said suddenly. Nothing made her angrier than seeing Molly upset.

'I'm not going to say who the third person with us last night was, but I can assure you it wasn't Miss Hart. It's all happened exactly as she said. We had no intention of stealing anything . . . and the proof of that is our reporting our findings to Miss Hart as soon as we were able to this morning.'

Helen Hart was shocked and touched by the courage of the girls.

'I can see that perhaps I have been hasty,' Madame Ruby answered, a little more softly. 'But please do not underestimate the stress I have been subjected to, being disturbed in the dead of night and discovering my school being burgled by torchlight. I would have confronted you on the spot if I had realised you were students, but I couldn't be sure of my own safety. You could have been armed gunmen for all I knew.'

Molly and Maria felt awful. As much as Madame Ruby wasn't in their list of top ten favourite people, they did feel bad at the thought of having frightened her silly. They hadn't considered how their actions might affect someone discovering them in the middle of the night.

'We are sorry, Madame Ruby. We never meant to cause you any distress. I guess we were so focused on solving the mystery of the *Lost Rose*, that we didn't really consider anything else,' Maria said.

'None of it matters anyway,' Molly said, glumly. 'The rose really has been stolen now – and goodness knows by who. We'll never get it back.'

'I presume that this is what you are referring to?' Madame Ruby said as she pulled out a glistening crystal ball from her pocket.

Miss Hart and the twins gasped as the ball flashed ruby red as the light caught the stone within.

'Of course!' Maria explained, kicking herself for not realising there wasn't some mysterious third-party burglar, just the Grand Madame herself.

'Oh my!' gasped Miss Hart, as she caught her first glimpse of the lost treasure.

Madame Ruby continued to explain.

'My curiosity was drawn when I noticed that the door to my apartment had been closed at some point during the evening. I'd left it open deliberately, you see, to air some paint fumes which were lingering following Mr Hart's repair work to the hall stand. As soon as I spotted torchlight darting around the L'Etoile entrance hall and heard muffled whispers, I immediately sought a hiding place from where I could observe what I thought was my school being burgled. I'd be lying if I didn't say I was completely petrified of being discovered. Unfortunately for me, I hit a creaky floorboard, which was thankfully enough to frighten the intruders off, but before I'd got a good look at them.

'Finally, I plucked up the courage to go downstairs and see what had been taken. I knew the focal point had been around the chandelier so stood below it trying to work out what had been taken. Then suddenly I spotted the red stone, glittering inside the central ball of the chandelier and put two and two together about the legend surrounding my great-grandmother. I couldn't believe I hadn't spotted it before now, having spent my whole life in these corridors.'

Molly and Maria and Miss Hart were enthralled by Madame Ruby's version of events as she continued her story.

'I wasn't even sure if the jewel was real but thought I should fetch Mr Hart's ladder and unhook the central ball for safekeeping. After all, the school had already been broken into once. Who was to say there wouldn't be another attempt before the morning? But tell me, L'Etoilettes, I am very interested to know how you came to be so very well informed about the *Legend of the Lost Rose* and its location.'

Maria grinned with pride, while Molly looked terrified.

'Madame Ruby,' Miss Hart interrupted, her turn to defend her girls. 'I think that perhaps we ought to retire to your office and I will explain the whole story, while the girls go back to class. It's been quite a morning, and Miss Spittleforth will think they've been abducted!'

'Heaven forbid,' Madame Ruby said. 'Off you go, girls. And thank you . . . I think.'

As Molly and Maria ran off to class, they didn't know how to feel. None of this had played out quite like they'd thought it would.

'I just can't wait to see the look on old Ruby's face when Miss Hart shows her the letter where Frank writes that the treasure is hers. Can you imagine?'

Molly's eyes widened with excitement. Oh, to be a fly on that office wall.

18

A Heart to Hart

Upstairs in the headmistress's office, Miss Hart retold the girls' story, just as they'd told it to her earlier that morning. She, loyally, left out a couple of details which might get both the girls and her father into trouble, mainly the story of how Twinkle came to be at L'Etoile!

'My sincere apologies, Helen, for jumping to inappropriate conclusions in front of the girls,' Madame Ruby said, as she poured Miss Hart a fresh coffee.

'I just don't know what came over me. I can only claim that the lack of sleep, shock and adrenalin at what happened overnight has left me quite out of sorts this morning.'

Helen Hart couldn't believe her ears. Never mind the fact that she had actually apologised for something, Madame Ruby had never been this civil and honest with her in her life. All those years she had spent growing up at L'Etoile, under the care of her father and Madame Ruby's mother, Amber Rose, she'd been like the annoying younger sister Madame Ruby had never asked for, and that resentment had continued well into adulthood.

'It's forgotten, Ruby,' Miss Hart said, warmed by this new level of communication they were sharing. 'What is important now, is to discuss what we should do with the *Lost Rose*.'

'Of course it is,' Madame Ruby snapped, sounding more like her usual self. Her face had been a picture when Miss Hart showed her the letter that said that she was the rightful owner of the jewel.

'I'm presuming you'll want to sell the ruby and disappear off round the world with Emmett,' she continued, grumpily. 'And I can't say I would blame you. A jewel of that size with such a history attached to it would most certainly be priceless at auction. You'd be wealthy beyond your wildest dreams.'

'Yes, that option has crossed my mind,' Miss Hart answered. 'But . . .'

'Yes?' Madame Ruby said quickly, looking desperately hopeful.

'But . . .' Miss Hart continued, 'as much as the ruby appears to be mine on paper, I can't help but believe it truly belongs where it was so lovingly laid to rest all those years ago . . . at the heart of L'Etoile.'

'Oh yes, Helen, yes,' Madame Ruby was uncharacteristically animated. 'I quite agree with you.'

Helen Hart was stunned to experience this side to Ruby after years of getting the cold shoulder. But she had a plan to share.

'I don't know what you would feel about this, but I think that the wonderful story of my great-grandfather Frank Hart and your great-grandmother, Lola Rose D'Arcy, and the *Legend of the Lost Rose* should be shared with the whole world.' She took a breath.

'I was thinking that perhaps we could allow Molly and Maria to grant Luscious Tangerella, the *London Gazette* journalist, an interview, which we would closely control, of course. We could use that interview as a fantastic advertisement for the school, where we also announce that starting this summer holidays, the school's doors would be opened for six weeks for visitors – paying ones, of course – to come and learn about our history. As part of their experience they would all be given the clues from Frank's letter and be guided to making their own discovery of the *Lost Rose*, which will be put back in its usual place for all to see. What do you think?'

'I think that's a marvellous idea, Helen. A most unselfish approach and very generous of you. I would like to think I would have done the same thing in your situation. The revenue from these summer tours will help us to make L'Etoile even bigger and better than it already is.'

'To L'Etoile, then.' Miss Hart held out her coffee cup to toast the school.

'To L'Etoile,' Madame Ruby repeated softly.

'And don't worry about security for the stone. I've just the thing!' Miss Hart smiled, picturing Twinkle as the new protector of the *Lost Rose*, keeping watch from a throne-shaped dog bed placed directly below the chandelier.

19

Another Adventure Comes to an End

'What a term!' Pippa exclaimed after the twins had finished updating her on what had happened with Miss Hart that morning. 'I just can't believe it! You couldn't make it up if you tried.'

'Tell me about it!' cried Molly. 'I nearly died when Madame Ruby suddenly appeared behind us. Never mind the Warner Brothers audition! I felt as though I was in a film this morning. I wonder what's going on in that meeting and what, if anything, has been decided.'

'Hopefully we'll find out soon. I reckon we should still keep this whole thing to ourselves for the time being though. It's not really our secret to share any more, is it?' said Maria, secretly desperate to let *Yours, L'Etoilette* blow the whole thing wide open in her blog.

'I reckon you're right. It'll all depend on what Miss Hart wants to do with the *Lost Rose*. She might just want to sell it – maybe Dad would buy it!' Molly wondered. 'Although I don't think that's very Miss Hart, to be honest. I just can't imagine her wanting to part with it – not for any sum of money.'

'You're absolutely right. She's far more likely to recommend loaning it to a museum or something so the world can see it. It does deserve to be seen by as many people as possible. It's so beautiful. I can't wait to see it again properly in daylight,' Pippa answered.

'It would be such a shame for it to leave L'Etoile. I almost wish we hadn't discovered it. If it did get taken away, I'd feel as though we'd let Frank and Lola down somehow. It belongs here,' Molly sighed.

'What will be, will be, girls. We just have to hope the Grand Madame and Miss Hart make the right decision . . . if they can agree!' she giggled. 'They might have killed each other by now over this! Come on, let's go down to supper. Having missed breakfast and lunch, I can't remember the last time I had more than a handful of cola bottles as opposed to a proper hot meal . . . even if it is a Mackle the Jackal special!'

'I wonder when this arrived?' Molly asked, spotting an envelope on the floor by the door to their room.

Molly turned it over and read 'Strictly Private: Maria & Molly Fitzfoster'. Then she noticed the small D'Arcy family crest in the top right-hand corner, with the words 'From the Headmistress's Office' in a neat font below.

'This could go one of two ways, girls,' Maria gulped, fearing the worst.

'If I'm really honest, I'm feeling pretty pleased my name isn't on that envelope,' Pippa said, a relieved look on her face. 'I ended the first term in a bit of hot water – just imagine how much trouble I'd be in two terms in a row.'

'Oh girls, have a little faith. How bad can it be?' the ever-optimistic Molly answered, tearing open the envelope.

'You just had to ask and tempt fate, didn't you!' Maria cried in alarm. 'I can't bear it. Go on, Moll. What does it say?'

Dear Maria & Molly,

Firstly I would like to start by thanking you both for your honesty earlier today.

HOWEVER, as you are only too aware, the events of last night were highly irregular and rules were broken which cannot go unpunished.

'Oh here we go,' Maria groaned, but Molly continued, unfazed.

HOWEVER . . . given the wonderful nature of your discovery, I have decided to overlook the bad behaviour on this occasion in favour of channelling both my, and your, energies into a far more worthwhile activity.

Miss Hart, as the undeniable heir to the Lost Rose, has kindly insisted that the stone should remain at L'Etoile in its rightful resting place, and that visitors should be able to come during the summer holidays and partake in their own historical treasure-hunt of sorts. As both punishment and thanks, we would very much like for you both – and for the third party who was present on the evening in question – Miss Burrows, I suspect – to join us in making plans for this suggested summer 'Lost Rose of L'Etoile Mystery Tour', which we hope will become a legendary experience in itself. We would like to start the ball rolling by granting an interview to Luscious Tangerella from the London Gazette, who, I am told, was instrumental in your journey to discover the truth. Miss Tangerella will be in my office at 10 a.m. tomorrow morning and we would like the three of you to be there.

I trust you have no objections and will see you in the morning.

Madame Ruby Rose D'Arcy

Ps. Please do keep this whole affair to yourselves until I make an official announcement.

'Errrr . . . did she really just say all that?' Molly cried.

'Errrr . . . did I really just get busted again?' Pippa asked in disbelief.

'Errrr . . . would you two get a grip. This is brilliant!' Maria squealed, throwing a pillow in each direction. 'I can't believe I'm actually going to meet Luscious Tangerella. Moll, can you believe it?'

'I'm just so pleased for you, Mimi,' Molly answered. 'You sooo deserve it too. Finally, something has come along that's right up your street, rather than you always taking the path that's best for me, so we can be together.'

Maria looked amazed at her sister and then hugged her hard. Sometimes she really did misjudge her. Not in a bad way, but times like this reminded her not to underestimate how clever Molly was, underneath all the curlers and lipgloss.

'I just can't believe we're not in a world of trouble! What a result – and what a great idea about getting visitors in over the summer. I'd so pay to come and relive our adventure, wouldn't you?'

'Absolutely,' said Maria. 'I might write up some notes about the order in which everything happened – so we get our story straight tomorrow. I'll die if we mess up in front of Miss Tangerella. I would love this little introduction to actually lead to something concrete for me when I leave school. Wouldn't it just be amazing if she gave me a job eventually?'

'Mmmm, L'Etoile, the place where dreams really do seem to come true,' Molly muttered, thinking how much they'd all achieved since they'd met in September.

'You can say that again!' Pippa agreed.

20

From One Journalist to Another

Maria's overnight notes were so detailed, Molly and Pippa couldn't help but be prepared for every kind of question and angle Miss Tangerella might throw at them. As the three girls stood outside Madame Ruby's office waiting to go in and meet Maria's heroine, she was a nervous wreck and in danger of totally losing the plot.

'Will you pull yourself together, Mimi,' Molly said, adjusting her sister's ponytail. 'Anyone would think she's royalty, the way you've gone to jelly.'

'I know! How embarrassing is this? In fact I don't ever remember feeling this bothered about anything in my life. I can't believe I actually pleaded with you to do my hair this morning!'

Pippa giggled, watching the sisterly banter unfold. So that's two weak spots she'd discovered about Maria Fitzfoster now – puppies and journalists! She was sure both pieces of information would come in very useful some day!

'Enter!' came Madame Ruby's voice as Miss Hart's smiling face appeared at the door to welcome the girls.

'L'Etoilettes, may I present Miss Luscious Tangerella of the *London Gazette*.'

Molly took the lead, terrified Maria might be too in awe to introduce herself. 'Molly Fitzfoster, delighted to meet you, Miss Tangerella,' she said, calmly stepping forward to shake Luscious's hand.

'Likewise, Molly. But, please, call me Luscious,' the journalist replied. 'And you must be Maria Fitzfoster,' she said, turning to the brunette version of the first twin. 'I understand you were the instigator and investigator behind this fabulous reveal.'

Maria thought she might faint, but somehow gathered herself. 'It was a team effort, Miss Tangerella . . . erm, Miss Luscious. But I have to say that your article was pivotal to our search and subsequent discovery. It's an honour to meet such a wonderful, insightful writer.' Maria could see she'd said the right thing from the sudden twinkle in Luscious's eyes.

'And that leaves Miss Burrows. It's lovely to meet you too, Pippa.' And she motioned to the empty sofa in front of them. 'Please girls, have a seat, relax, and tell me the whole story from start to finish. Maria, perhaps you'd be good enough to kick the whole thing off?'

Maria blushed and then went into her very best reporter mode, leaving no detail undisclosed. Molly and Pippa were relieved not to have to do any of the talking. It was Maria's moment to shine and, boy, was she dazzling!

'Let's see now . . . no . . . in all honesty, I don't think there's anything left for me to ask. That truly was one of the most comprehensive accounts I have ever been given of any story, Maria. You've practically done my job for me! Have you ever thought of a career in journalism? You have quite a gift for investigation and reporting.'

'Oh my goodness, it would be my dream job!' Maria gushed. 'I'm so pleased you think I might have promise.'

'You have talent, Maria, in abundance. Here's my card,' said Luscious, as she plucked a smart black and white *London Gazette* business card out of her briefcase. 'Should you ever need any advice on your writing, or wish to come up to London for some work experience with me when the time is right, it would be my absolute pleasure. Be sure to drop me an email whenever you are ready.'

'How wonderful! Thank you so much,' Maria exclaimed. This was more of a result than she would ever have hoped for.

'And the announcement about L'Etoile opening its doors to treasure-hunters over the summer,' Madame Ruby said, coming out from behind her desk. 'Should I just email you the details as soon as we've finalised them? We'd very much like the girls' input and ideas for how the "mystery tour" will work best. As you know, we've not really had enough time to talk it through, but we hope to remedy that in the next twenty-four hours.'

'No problem at all, Madame Ruby. I'll get cracking on writing up the girls' story over the weekend and then you can email me bullet points for the announcement as and when you are ready. The only thing I would say is that the *Gazette* always does a special Easter edition and this would be a great cover story for the accompanying magazine, *Gazelle*. In fact, could I get a quick photo of you all so there's an image for them to attach to the story? I think that would work well. Any objections, ladies?'

Miss Hart and Madame Ruby looked at each other and then at the girls. None of them could hide their glee at the thought of having their picture in the paper in connection with such a marvellous story.

'Let's take the photo, but I will have to call the girls' parents to check that they're happy with the publicity before you use it. Is that all right with you, girls?' Miss Hart enquired.

The trio nodded. 'Mum and Dad haven't got a clue about any of this yet. We weren't sure what we were allowed to say, to be honest, so haven't said a word to anyone. I'm sure it'll be fine though,' Maria answered for all three of them.

'That's settled then. If you could gather together on the other sofa then, please – girls in the centre with the two ladies on either end . . . lovely . . . now, say "Rubies".'

'Rubies!' the group chorused, smiling from ear to ear.

'Perfect!' Luscious said, grabbing her things. 'I'll be in touch.'

And, with that, Maria's heroine walked out of the

door, taking with her the biggest secret L'Etoile had ever known.

'Wow!' said Maria. 'I know I keep saying it but what else can you say? This whole thing just keeps getting better and better.'

'I'm very proud of you, girls,' Miss Hart said, as she accompanied them back to class. 'Particularly you, Maria. You spoke beautifully today and earned some well-deserved praise.'

'Thank you, Miss,' Maria answered as they hovered outside their classroom door.

'Now, I still think we keep this quiet from the rest of the girls for the moment. If you can work together and put your ideas in an email to me over the weekend, I'll draft an announcement with Madame Ruby and get it to Miss Tangerella ready to hit the newspapers next week. I'll also write to your parents and explain everything.'

'Thank you, Miss Hart,' Pippa said gratefully. 'Thanks for thinking of us in all of this. I can't help thinking Madame Ruby's reaction might have been different if you hadn't stuck up for us!'

'The less said about that, the better. And if I were

you, I wouldn't keep reminding me about all the rules you've broken, girls – I might change my mind about that punishment,' she grinned. 'Now, off to class, and try to behave as normally as possible. I know it has been an extraordinary term for you all!'

'That's the understatement of the decade!' Molly giggled, and the girls joined their class.

21

Let the Games Begin!

With only one more week of term left, it wasn't too much of a chore keeping quiet and getting back to normal school life. The girls mainly spent their time looking for Twinkle so they could give her a cuddle every spare second they had during the day, and at night they sat up excitedly gossiping about what the world would think of their amazing discovery.

The email had been sent to Luscious Tangerella regarding the plans for L'Etoile's Mystery Tour and the girls' parents had, a little hesitantly at first, agreed to whatever the school needed the girls to do, publicity-wise – thanks to Miss Hart's astonishing powers of persuasion. The first the rest of the school would know about it would be when they opened the weekend's papers when they were home for Easter and read the headlines. Apparently every major newspaper in the country was keen to pick up on the story, once the *Gazette* had run it. It was beyond exciting!

On the final Friday morning of term, Sally Sudbury burst into the Fitzfoster/Burrows room panting and waving a piece of paper in the air. She was so over-emotional, the girls couldn't tell whether it was good news or not.

'Sally, sit down and calm down!' Maria ordered, ever so slightly concerned that Sally had somehow found out about the *Lost Rose*.

'What is it?' Molly asked, immediately sharing her sister's concern. The girls had all felt a bit deceitful at not being able to share their news with their closest friends – particularly Sally. Pippa was worried about how offended Sally might feel when she read it in the papers with the rest of the world.

'It's Lucinda!' Sally announced.

'Oh no! What's happening? I knew this lovely peace was too good to be true!' Molly said.

'You won't believe it. She's written to me to gloat about the following: A) She's definitely coming back next term . . . boo! B) It gets worse . . . she's not coming back to L'Etoile alone. Since she's been in LA, she's become the best of friends with a horror-hog called Lavinia Wright. She's the hideous daughter of a frightful American chat-show host, Tallulah Wright.' Sally almost choked as she said her name. 'Believe me, girls, when I say she's hideous – she makes Lucifette look like an angel!'

'Oh dear. Well, don't worry, Sal – we'll all stick together. You're with us now. I tell you what, why don't we see if we can put in a request to move into a room with four beds next term? That way there'll be no chance you'll end up stuck with those two hideous girls,' Molly offered, and Maria and Pippa nodded in agreement.

'Would you? That would be a total load off my mind. Yes please, can we?' Sally said, relieved.

'I've got to go and speak to Miss Coates before I go home anyway, to see if anyone's handed my iPod in. Can't find it anywhere. I'll try my best to talk her into it then,' Pippa promised.

Sally loved these girls!!

'But wait, I haven't finished. The worst is yet to come! Lucifette's also emailed me saying how she's managed to wangle this amazing audition for the new

Warner Brothers film at the start of next term. Can you believe it?! Molly, that means she'll be up against *you*! You can bet your life she already knows you're up for it and has begun bad-mouthing wherever she can, to try and sabotage your chances.'

Molly looked thoughtful for a moment, and then grinned. 'Yes, but has the little faker had an up close and personal audience with His Royal Highness, Prince Henry? I think not! I can't wait to ram that little golden nugget down her scrawny throat!'

'Oh Molly, good attitude!' Sally exclaimed with a smile. 'I was so worried about telling you that. I thought you'd go mad.'

'I would be worried if I was up against someone who might actually get the part – but, let's face it girls, Lucifette might be the daughter of a world-famous film director and a Hollywood actress, but that's where her plus points end. I'm confident I've got more acting ability in my big toe than she has in her whole body!'

'Well said, Moll!' Pippa cheered. 'Look what happened when she tried to play dirty and ruin me last term. She's the one who ended up with egg on her face.'

'I hear what you're saying, girls, but you just don't know her like I do. She's ruthless if she wants something badly enough and she'll tread on anyone or anything to get her way,' Sally answered, her brow furrowing in concern. 'And don't forget, she's got that evil little witch, Lavinia, on her side now. Talk about double trouble!'

'Sally, I love you for feeling so protective, but you've seen how we Fitzfosters and Burrows operate. Anyway, we've got you on side now so that makes us quadruple trouble. Look, don't worry. I vowed the morning we met Miss Marciano—'

'What, when she nearly ran us over?' Molly blurted out, remembering having to dive into the lavender to save her own skin.

'Yes!' Maria cried. 'I promised myself then that I'd never let that little upstart get the better of us, or anyone else for that matter. I for one am ready for a battle. Let the games begin! Anyway, apart from the obvious, it's been quite a tame term all in all. We'll be ready for a bit of drama after Easter.'

'A tame term!' Pippa squealed. 'It's been pretty scary at times, TTD for one. My stomach was in knots every time I took Twinkle out. And then there are all the good things that have happened, like winning my award and most of all hearing you all perform my song so amazingly. With everything we've got up to, I can't believe I've made it to the end of term – by the skin of my teeth!'

'Are you kidding Pippa? What are you talking about? You are the L'Etoile singer-songwriting talent of the millennium! They'd never expel you. Even Prince Henry was on his feet after hearing "Friends Forever",' Sally said.

You have to remember, Story-seeker, that Sally didn't yet know about Agents Fitzfoster and Burrows and their quest for the Lost Rose of L'Etoile.

'I agree with you, Pips. I don't think it's been tame at all,' Molly said. 'Literally ALL my dreams have come true this term; I've met a real live Prince Charming, who even saved me from my clumsy self; I've landed the audition of my life; I've fallen in love with my little Twinkle and successfully found her the loveliest new daddy . . . and, to top it all, I've finally worked out how to create the perfect curl with hair straighteners!'

Maria rolled her eyes. Giggling, Molly added, 'Only joking about the last bit.'

'I suppose you're right, girls,' said Maria. 'And,

Sally, just think . . . who would have guessed we'd be standing here asking you to be our new room-mate for the summer term? We thought you were public enemy number two not so long ago!'

'Oh, girls! Who'd have thought any of us would be as close as we are? It's like suddenly finding you have two more sisters! Bring on next term. Who knows what we'll get up to?' Molly said, grabbing the other three for a group hug.

'One thing I do know is that I'm going to have to re-write "Friends Forever",' said Pippa, a serious look on her face.

'What? Why?' Molly, Maria and Sally said in alarm, worrying they'd said something wrong.

But Pippa just winked and started to sing:

Ooooh . . . just little old me,
Ooooh . . . then we were three . . . I MEAN FOUR!

And the others joined in:

I can't explain the feeling,
The one that leaves me reeling.

I never thought that friends could be
A second kind of family,

Ooooh . . . this ain't no short-term endeavour
Oooooh . . . you know we're friends forever . . .

Would you like to go to L'Etoile too?

Turn the page for a reminder of who's who . . .

Alpha 1

Maria Fitzfoster	Pianist
Molly Fitzfoster	Singer/Actress
Pippa Burrows	Singer
Lydia Ambrose	Cellist/Double Bassist
Belle Brown	Ballet Dancer
Amanda Lloyd	Dancer
Daisy Mansfield	Bassoonist
Alice Parry	Singer/Actress
Sofia Vincenzi	Opera Singer/Actress
Lara Walters	Drummer/Percussionist

Beta 1

Nancy Althorpe	Actress
Elizabeth Jinks	Dancer
Charlotte Kissimee	Singer
Corine Sequoia	Singer/Actress
Heavenly Smith	Dancer
Faye Summers	Fashion Expert
Autumn Costello	Pianist
Betsy Harris	Pianist
Lucinda Marciano	Singer / Daughter of Blue & Serafina Marciano
Sally Sudbury	Actress / the Marcianos' Housekeeper's Daughter

♥ Friends and Family ♥

Fitzfosters
The ever-obliging Eddie   The Fitzfoster Family Driver

Albie Good   The Fitzfoster Online Fashion Delivery Boy

Marcianos
Maggie Sudbury

Elodie Wyatt   Marciano Family Housekeeper

Mr Blue Marciano's Secretary

Burrows
Mrs Olivia Burrows
Uncle Harry Burrows   Pippa Burrows' Mother
Pippa Burrows' Uncle

♥ Talent Spotters and Staff ♥

Blue Marciano   Famous Hollywood Film Director

Serafina Marciano   Famous Hollywood Actress

Emmett Fuller   President, Universal Music Publishing

Calamity Mossback   Top Hollywood Talent Manager

L'Etoile Staff

Ruby Rose D'Arcy	Headmistress of L'Etoile
Miss Helen Hart	Deputy Headmistress of L'Etoile
Miss Sophie Bell	Housemistress of Monroe (Yellow)
Miss Mary Coates	Housemistress of Garland (Blue)
Lola Rose D'Arcy	Founder of L'Etoile
Mrs Rene Spittleforth	1 Alpha Form Tutor and Maths Teacher
Mr Victor McDoody	1 Beta Form Tutor and Science Master
Mrs Irene Mackle	Head Dinner Lady
Miss Natalia Seminova	Dance Teacher
Sister Patricia Payne	School Nurse
Mr Howard Potts	Music Maestro
Miss Emma Fleming	Drama Teacher
Mrs Audrey Butter	History Teacher

Find out what's next for the L'Etoilettes in . . .

Our favourite friends forever are back
for another exciting term. A television show comes
to school and plans are afoot for a glittering end of
term charity fundraiser. But as you know, Story-seeker,
there's never an adventure without a drama at L'Etoile,
and with Molly's Hollywood audition, the dreaded
summer exams & the return of Lucifette Marciano
with her truly hideous friend, we're just not sure
how the girls are going to survive.

978 1 4440 0815 9

£4.99

the

orion star

Sign up for **the orion star**
newsletter to get inside information
about your favourite children's authors
as well as exclusive competitions and
early reading copy giveaways.

www.orionbooks.co.uk/newsletters

Follow 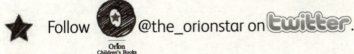 @the_orionstar on .

Orion
Children's Books